THE NEIGHBOR

GEMMA ROGERS

Boldwood

First published in Great Britain in 2023 by Boldwood Books Ltd.

Copyright © Gemma Rogers, 2023

Cover Design: Judge By My Covers

Cover Photography: Deposit Photos

A CIP catalogue record for this book is available from the British Library.

Paperback ISBN 978-1-83603-000-3

Ebook ISBN 978-1-80549-745-5

Kindle ISBN 978-1-80549-746-2

Boldwood Books Ltd
23 Bowerdean Street
London SW6 3TN
www.boldwoodbooks.com

ACKNOWLEDGMENTS

Firstly, top of the list as always is the wonderful Boldwood Team. I'm having the best time writing and will forever be grateful to you for taking a chance on me and my debut novel back in 2019. Seven books later and I think I'm getting the hang of it.

Caroline Ridding, you will always be my dream editor. I think we make a fantastic team and I hope we will work together for many years to come. Thank you for believing in me.

Jade Craddock, thank you as always for your meticulousness when it comes to my books, and helping to polish each one to such a high standard. I can always rely on your keen eyes. Also thank you to Shirley Khan who has proofread a few of my books now and always finds things I've missed!

Again, thank you to my lovely first readers, Mum and Denise Miller. It's immensely important to know I'm going in the right direction and I appreciate your encouragement from the very first pages.

Lastly, thanks to my wonderful husband Dean and two beautiful daughters, Bethany, and Lucy. Your unwavering support means everything to me.

ABOUT THE AUTHOR

Gemma Rogers was inspired to write gritty thrillers by a traumatic event in her own life nearly twenty years ago. Her debut novel *Stalker* was published in September 2019 and marked the beginning of a new writing career. Gemma lives in West Sussex with her husband and two daughters.

Sign up to Gemma Rogers' mailing list for news, competitions and updates on future books.

Visit Gemma's website: www.gemmarogersauthor.co.uk

Follow Gemma on social media:

f facebook.com/GemmaRogersAuthor

X x.com/GemmaRogers79

instagram.com/gemmarogersauthor

BB bookbub.com/authors/gemma-rogers

For Bethany

1

Arthur Chappel pulled down the shutter at the rear of his removal van and wiped his palm on his khaki trousers before offering it to shake.

'All done now, miss, the beds have been put back together and all the boxes are in the right rooms.' His forehead glimmered, beads of sweat nestling in deep crevices caused by years of hard graft.

It was an unusually warm April day, with Easter less than a week away, and I was thrilled I hadn't had to move house in the rain.

I shook Arthur's clammy calloused hand and smiled at him. 'Please, call me Shelly – and thanks, you've both been great.' I watched as his young helper climbed into the passenger seat, rolling down the window, ready to get going. 'I appreciate you fitting me in at such short notice.'

'Ah, you didn't have a lot to move, only needed the one van, and me and Bobby knew we could do it in a couple of hours. We'll invoice you for payment later on this week.'

I'd only brought a few pieces of furniture with me – a TV, a sofa, and two beds plus Lauren's chair, desk and bookcase from her bedroom. Enough to manage until I could replace them for new. Most of Mum's stuff had gone to charity. I knew bringing it with me would mean bringing the memories too and those I was happy to leave behind. There was never any question that I would stay in that cottage.

I rummaged in the pocket of my dungarees and Arthur raised one eyebrow when I slipped a twenty-pound note into his hand.

'Thanks again and please have a drink on me,' I said, turning back to the house before he could protest, and gazing at what was now mine. For the next six months at least. Behind me, I heard the van door slam and the engine rumble to life before fading into the distance as Arthur and Bobby drove out of the close.

The house had been a real gem of a find, a three-bedroom rental property in the catchment area for a place at Briarwood High School where I wanted to send my ten-year-old daughter, Lauren, next year. It was the best school in the vicinity of Crawley in West Sussex, but rental properties were hard to come by, being so close to the airport, and I couldn't buy anything until money from the sale of Mum's house came through. Even so, I doubted I'd be able to afford the half-a-million price tag the last one sold for. Thankfully, there had been enough in Mum's account to pay six months' rent up front and I was positive it had been what swayed the owner to pick me out of a dozen other applicants.

We'd deserved a bit of good fortune after what had been a couple of years from hell. Lauren and I had been Mum's carers until she'd passed away a month ago. Officially, it was a head injury incurred from a fall that had killed her, but she was in the later stages of dementia. It hadn't been easy, juggling work, parenting, and looking after Mum. My dad had left when I was a baby, and there had been little in the way of help, it had all been down to me, so today felt like a new chapter. I wanted somewhere

I could finally relax, somewhere I wouldn't hear the summoning tinkle of Mum's bell every five minutes. A sound so deeply ingrained, I heard it still.

I sighed, slowly turning in a circle to admire the view of the close, sure I saw a curtain twitch from across the green. The sun was in my eyes, and I couldn't be certain I hadn't imagined it, although it wouldn't be out of the ordinary for the other residents to want to find out who their new neighbors were, especially with so few houses in the close.

'Right, what's next,' I said to myself, turning back to the house. The driveway looked like it needed a sweep, but I'd get to it later. I only had two hours before I'd have to pick up Lauren from school and I wanted to get as much of her room unpacked as I could. It was the last day of the spring term and we'd have two weeks' holiday to get ourselves settled in before she had to go back to school.

I made to move, but the warmth of the sun on my back was so good. I soaked up the freedom for a moment, admiring the property, which was a million miles away from the dark 1890s cottage we'd been living in, despite it only being a short drive away. Our new home was a modern red-brick-built detached property with no leaking sash windows or icy slate tiles to be seen. The close, Beech Close – so called, I assumed, because of the single beautiful beech tree which stood proudly in the middle of a circular patch of green – was small, with only six houses dotted around the luscious grass centrepiece. It had the feel of a gated community, a private road for the privileged.

Each house was identical in size and design, even down to the pillar-box red uPVC doors and garages. All had white double-glazed windows and small driveways with a snippet of a lawn. When I had first viewed the property, I was concerned it was a little too perfect, and my old VW Golf sitting on the driveway would devalue the street. The estate agent had laughed off my comment and by the end of the tour I was smitten and offered a deposit, only to be told there were other interested parties, and the owner was going to make the final selection. I offered six months' rent up front and luckily we were chosen.

Lauren hadn't been inside yet, although we'd driven around the close a couple of times. It had all moved so quickly, we hadn't had time for a second viewing. She'd been excited before school this morning at the idea of coming home to a new house. Mum's cottage, where we'd spent the last couple of years, was full of cobwebs and dark corners, and Lauren said she was looking forward to not being cold all the time. She had a point. The cottage was old and needed lots of work, but it was a listed building and sold within days for a higher price than I expected. There was a bidding war between two couples, the estate agent had informed us.

Lauren couldn't wait to leave, and I didn't blame her. It had been tough, her childhood marred and put on hold while Mum was ill. I'd discovered she was planning a housewarming party for all her friends as soon as she could get me to agree. Warranted for all of the times she'd missed out having anyone come to play over the past two years she'd watched her nan deteriorate. I was looking forward to seeing her be a kid again, she'd had too much on her young shoulders recently.

The dog barking nudged me from my thoughts.

'Coming, Teddy,' I called out, striding towards the house to let him out of the kitchen. I'd shut our four-year-old border terrier out of the way of the removal men and the poor thing was likely desperate to go to the toilet.

Rushing inside, I forgot to close the front door so when I opened the kitchen door, Teddy bolted straight for freedom. The pull of new sounds and smells too much for him to resist.

'Teddy!' I shouted, dashing after him. The close was a quiet cul-de-sac, with barely any traffic, but the thought of him being squashed by a neighbor reversing off their driveway made my legs pump faster.

He was quick for a dog with little legs, and I caught sight of him turning left out of the driveway.

'Teddy!' I scowled, hurrying after him.

As I rounded the hedge, I saw him squatting on the neighbor's lawn to release his bowels.

'Oh God, Teddy,' I hissed, looking up at the house and cringing. It was a great way to introduce myself to the neighbors, by my dog crapping on their perfectly mown lawn. I didn't have a bag on me either, although I reached into my pockets to try to find one, despite knowing they'd be empty. 'Come on, let's go get a bag and clear this up,' I said loudly, reaching down to hold Teddy by the collar and walk him back towards the house.

'What the hell do you think you're doing?' came a shrill voice behind me once we were almost at the door. Still clutching Teddy's collar, hunched over, I twisted around to see who was there.

Taking the opportunity to escape from my grasp, Teddy sprinted at the woman standing at the end of my driveway, whose eyes widened in horror as if a monster was hurtling towards her and not a border terrier. He was hoping for a cuddle, but by the look on her face it was more likely she'd kick him to the kerb. Lurching after the dog in an attempt to get to him before he reached her, I stumbled, unable to catch up, her shrieks echoing around Beech Close like a siren announcing my arrival.

2

Teddy launched at her, scrambling on his hind legs, mouth gaping and tongue out. His bronze tail wagged at the prospect of a stroke from a stranger as the woman tried to bat him away, palms outstretched.

'Get off, get off, you vicious creature,' she squawked, and I ran forward to pick Teddy up, who wriggled in protest.

'Don't worry, he won't hurt you,' I said, mildly amused at the image of our soppy Teddy being some rabid beast. *Cujo* he was not.

The woman brushed herself down, the tassels of her violet pashmina catching in the breeze. She looked immaculate in a knee-length skirt and block heels, her strikingly silver hair pulled into a tight chignon. Her face was flawlessly made-up, cranberry nails perfectly matched her shade of lipstick and she oozed glamour despite easily being in her mid-sixties. In comparison, I felt dowdy in my scruffy dungarees and long-sleeved T-shirt, speckled with dog hair and dust from moving boxes.

'I'm so sorry. Teddy escaped before I could close the front

door,' I explained, blowing my fringe out of my eyes, and lifting my face as Teddy tried to lick my cheek.

'I saw you. You let that mutt desecrate my lawn and walked away.' The woman's jaw tightened, her stare slicing through me. She was incandescent and I let out a nervous giggle at her exaggerated performance. Clearly, she wasn't a dog lover.

'I needed to get a poo bag, I didn't have one on me,' I replied with a smile, trying to pacify her.

She wrinkled her nose, shaking her head dismissively. 'Do you think I was born yesterday?'

Teddy continued to struggle, and I put him inside, taking the keys out of the lock and closing the front door. Perhaps I'd try a different tack.

'I sorry, we seem to have got off on the wrong foot. I'm Shelly, I'm your new neighbor. Here, let me get a bag out of my car and I'll clear the mess up.'

'Please do. It's disgusting,' she berated before stomping away, not bothering with an introduction.

I rolled my eyes as I ducked inside my car, pulling a tiny bag out from the passenger footwell.

'Welcome to the neighborhood,' I muttered to myself, trying to shake off the confrontation. I wasn't one of those people who didn't clear up after their dog, but at the same time I didn't keep a poo bag in the pocket of every single item of clothing I owned. She'd overreacted, to say the least. However, the last thing I wanted was to make an enemy of my new neighbor the day I moved in.

I walked back around to the front of her house, glad of the tall hedges which separated her property from mine. Teddy's stomach had been a bit dodgy all day, anxiety due to the move no doubt, and the present he'd left on my neighbor's lawn was difficult to pick up. I did the best I could, dismayed at how much had been smudged into the grass. Oh well, it would serve the miserable old bat right.

'Hi,' called a plummy voice from some distance behind me as I stood and tied a knot in the bag. I turned to see an attractive blonde woman in a Breton T-shirt crossing the green and waving at me. Her hair bounced upon her shoulders in soft waves as she jogged, looking like she'd stepped out of a catalogue shoot. Dark denim straight-legged jeans teamed with bright white Converse trainers, she swung her arms as she slowed to a walk, a broad smile displaying perfect pink apple cheeks.

'Hello,' I replied, trying to muster up the same level of enthusiasm.

'I'm Niamh, we live at number six.' She pointed over towards the last house, the one I was sure I'd seen the curtains twitching earlier. Niamh held out a perfectly French manicured hand, quickly retracting it when she saw what I was holding. 'Oh,' she said, with a girlish giggle.

'Sorry, my dog, Teddy...' I began before thinking better of it. 'I'm Shelly, I've just moved in,' I said, taking a couple of steps towards my house and away from my angry neighbor's lawn.

Niamh followed, clapping her hands together. 'So, I see. Welcome to Beech Close. It's lovely to meet you. We could do with some fresh blood around here.'

'I'm not sure everyone would agree with that,' I replied, looking back over my shoulder.

'Oh, don't worry about Valerie, she's the same with everyone, ignore her.' Niamh waved her hand dismissively and I instantly lifted. 'Is it just you and the dog?' she continued, gesturing to the poo bag I was still holding.

'My daughter too, she's ten. Do you have any children?' I asked hopefully, Lauren would love to have a playmate living in the same street.

'God no, plenty of time for that, I'm only thirty,' she laughed. 'My husband, Finn, wants to travel before we're drowning in nappies and breast milk.' Her expression was one of distaste and I tried not to laugh.

'Are there any other children in the close?'

'Afraid not. Listen I've got to dash, I'm late for Pilates, but perhaps I'll have a little soirée this week so you can meet some of the other neighbors.' Niamh raised a heavily plucked eyebrow, a twinkle in her eyes.

'Sure, thanks,' I replied, a little bewildered. Perhaps the close was a tight-knit community and they all socialised together? At least she was more friendly than the other woman, Valerie.

Back at Mum's we were one of three cottages at the end of a quiet lane and the neighbors barely acknowledged us. Despite making an effort when we'd first arrived. Since then, I'd got used to being left alone. Maybe they were much more social in Beech Close, although I wasn't sure how I felt about that. I valued my privacy.

Niamh waved as she marched back across the green towards her house.

I checked my watch, time was running out if I was going to get Lauren's room sorted before collecting her. I had to get a wriggle on.

Teddy was pawing and barking at the front door when I opened it, excited to see me, and I ruffled his head. 'You are a pain in the proverbial,' I said with a chuckle.

He followed me upstairs, laying in the hallway as I unpacked sheets into the large airing cupboard before making Lauren's bed. I tackled the boxes with her name written in black marker on the top, which had been stacked neatly in the corner opposite the door.

The walls were a pale yellow, which matched her Hufflepuff

bedding. My daughter was mad on Harry Potter and currently working her way through *The Prisoner of Azkaban*, the third book in the series. I'd left the dog-eared copy on her bedside table, along with her radio, notepad and pen. Lauren loved to record her dreams, which were so vivid she had to write them down. I was jealous, I only seemed to have nightmares since Mum passed, which the doctor had told me was common under the circumstances. He'd kindly given me a prescription of sleeping pills, but I was rubbish at remembering to take them. They sat dormant in the bathroom cabinet for emergencies.

Balancing on Lauren's bed in front of the window, I put up the grey curtains we'd brought with us from Mum's, grateful the windows were of a similar size. Fairy lights were wrapped around the white framework of Lauren's bed, and I laid the fluffy rug on the carpet beside it, imagining her little feet enjoying the comfort as she climbed out in the mornings.

Both bedrooms had fitted wardrobes, which meant I had got rid of the old rails on wheels we'd used before. It wasn't long before all Lauren's clothes had been unpacked and were neatly hung up. I left a box of toys for her to do herself but managed to get through everything else. By the time I'd finished, her desk and chair were back together and the bookcase had been rebuilt, her Harry Potter collection stacked neatly on the top shelf.

Before I left to pick Lauren up, I admired my handiwork, a warm glow in my chest picturing her face when she came home. If nothing else, she had a safe space to call her own. No longer would I have to lock her in at night because of Mum's tendency to wander. There would be no more occurrences of Lauren screaming after waking to discover a solitary figure standing at the end of her bed.

Waiting outside the school gates with Teddy, I managed to find some shade for us to stand in. Despite the breeze, I was always paranoid Teddy would overheat after one disastrous afternoon at the beach when he was a puppy. Too much sun and consumption of sea water had left him dehydrated and he'd spent a night at the vets. Lauren was beside herself we were going to lose him. It was a traumatic time for both of us and ever since then I've been on high alert.

My best friend, Josh, ribbed me all the time that I was as paranoid about Teddy's safety as I was about Lauren's. Last Christmas, he'd bought me one of those funny dog portraits with Teddy in a *Peaky Blinders* hat and waistcoat. It was going to take pride of place over the mantelpiece where I could giggle at it every day. Whilst I waited for the bell to ring and the influx of children into the playground, I dropped him a text to let him know we'd all moved in fine, and did he want to come over tomorrow?

Lauren loved Josh, but tonight I wanted it to just be the two of us. We were going to order pizza and try to watch a movie, if I could get the television set up. Perhaps Josh could stay Saturday

night and we could have a few drinks to celebrate. I couldn't wait
to hear his reaction when I told him about the battleaxe next
door. I knew he'd tell me to 'kill 'em with kindness', as was his
favourite phrase.

The school bell rang and when I looked up from my phone,
the parents at the gates had multiplied. A curly-haired toddler
was sat on the grass, surrounded by bluebells, stroking Teddy as
her mother looked on.

'He's so good with kids, isn't he,' she remarked, and I nodded.

'He is, not got a bad bone in his body,' I replied with a smile.

I stood on tiptoes to watch for Lauren coming in the throes of
children. She knew where I'd be. Dogs weren't allowed in the
school grounds, so I always waited outside, on a footpath which
ran parallel with the length of the playground. From Mum's
house, we used to be able to walk to school, but now we'd have to
drive and park nearby, until Lauren went to Briarswood High
School anyway.

Admissions for the following school year opened in
September, as Lauren would be starting her last year of junior
school. With the six-month lease, I'd taken out we'd still be at
Beech Close so inside the catchment area. I intended to buy somewhere nearby to the school and liked the quieter part of Crawley,
somewhere calmer for Lauren to grow up rather than the town
centre, with its sometimes raucous nightlife. Although I wasn't
looking yet, renting gave me the freedom to find the right place
and not rush into anything.

All the years I'd struggled financially, living in a bedsit, and
raising Lauren alone, from a few months old, at least money
wouldn't be an issue now. In fact, being a cash buyer with nothing
to sell meant I was in the best possible position when it came
to buy.

'Mummy!' Lauren came skipping out of the gate, her ponytail

swinging, waving goodbye to her best friend, Holly. She'd inherited my heart-shaped face and thick dark hair. Her eyes were the colour of molten honey in sunlight. Mine were more treacle in colour and slightly larger. Her narrow chin and nose came from her father, and I was grateful it was all he'd given her.

'Hello, popsicle, did you have a good day?' I asked, bending down to give her a kiss before she fussed over Teddy. The toddler had been dragged away moments before, leaving the poor dog bereft.

'It was great, Harrison brought in his pet iguana! And I've got no homework. Mrs Burt said not to eat too many chocolate eggs, but I'm going to eat at least ten.' Her words came out in a rush as though she'd been saving them for me all day. She beamed, holding out a wonky Easter basket she'd woven and decorated with fluffy chicks.

'Ooh that's lovely, perfect for collecting chocolate eggs,' I said, taking the basket. She squeezed my hand as we walked, and I felt a rush of love for her. Lauren had me wrapped around her little finger. When people talked about unconditional love for your child, how as a parent you'd throw yourself in front of a bus to save them, I got it. 'Although I'm not sure about ten, you might be sick,' I laughed. 'Shall we go check out the new house?'

Lauren jumped on the spot, squealing she couldn't wait, and Teddy's ears stood to attention, his tail wagging.

I'd parked a few roads away so Teddy could stretch his legs. I hadn't had a chance to take him out for long that morning because I was packing the last bits when the removal men came. I still had the keys to Mum's place, which was now empty bar a couple of larger pieces of furniture which hadn't been collected yet. The exchange of contracts was a week away, but as soon as the death certificate came through, I'd closed Mum's accounts and transferred the funds into mine.

William, my financial advisor, was going to collate everything and deal with the inheritance tax once the sale of the house had gone through. Then I could see if I had enough to buy a house outright and live mortgage-free, which would be a dream.

'Mum, will you buy a new car soon, because this one is *really* old!' Lauren moaned as she climbed into the back seat and fastened Teddy's harness to the seat belt before doing her own.

'Of course, m'lady, and what sort of car would madam like me to buy?' I asked in a posh lilt, watching as she considered, her tongue sticking out.

'Ummm, how about a BMW.'

'I'll see what I can do, kiddo.' I started the car, soaking up Lauren's excitement as we got closer to Beech Close and our new home.

When we pulled into the close, she bounced in her seat as the detached house came into view.

'Just remember, I've only done your room, okay. There are boxes everywhere, but we're going to use the Easter holidays to get ourselves straightened out.'

'While eating lots of chocolate though, right? Please can we have an Easter egg hunt?'

'Of course we can,' I replied.

I'd told my clients I wouldn't be around for two weeks while Lauren was off. I was a freelance virtual assistant on the books of two agencies who specialised in helping companies outsource their day-to-day administrative tasks. I took on duties like inbox and diary management, expenses, website updates or social media posting. Whatever they needed at the time. The money wasn't bad, and the work was varied so it was never boring. It meant I could work from home, which was fantastic while I was caring for Mum and navigating the school runs.

'Come on!' Lauren said impatiently, already out of the car and at the red front door, tugging on the silver handle.

'Okay, okay,' I said, coming up behind her with Teddy in tow, and sliding my key into the lock.

As soon as I pushed the handle down, Lauren bounded in ahead, Teddy chasing her. Lauren's eyes darted all over the place, hesitating for a second before sprinting up the stairs to find her room.

On the floor in the hall was a plain white sealed envelope with no addressee. I picked it up and followed Lauren.

'I love it!' Lauren said, spread out on her bed clutching Jules, her favourite Build-a-Bear.

'I thought you might. Want to go and have a look at the rest of the house... Guess what, we have a shower now.' I pointed towards the bathroom. There'd only been a bath at Mum's, and we'd dreamt of the day we could have a hot shower instead of those incessant tepid baths we'd have to share.

I watched Lauren run from room to room, taking it all in, following behind as I opened the white envelope. Perhaps it was a New Home card one of the neighbors had put through the door. Although it felt more spongey than hard. I put my hand in to find soft tissue, then the stench of something foul hit my nostrils and I wretched.

_____

4

Teasing open the envelope carefully, my throat closed as I found a scrunched-up tissue inside, the centre of it smeared with dog mess. It stank and I thrust it away from me.

'What's that?' Lauren said, turning to see why I was no longer trailing down the stairs behind her.

'Nothing,' I said, my voice unnaturally high, whipping the envelope behind my back and forcing a smile.

Lauren turned back, unperturbed, and continued her tour, chattering mindlessly.

I took the envelope to the kitchen, intent on finding a plastic bag to dispose of my welcome present.

How dare she? How could that woman put something so repulsive through my door? She'd obviously taken it upon herself to clean the rest of the grass, wipe away what I hadn't been able to pick up, but I couldn't believe she'd post it back to me. Just five hours into taking the keys of Beech Close and I was already at war with my neighbor. Blood pulsed in my ears as I tried to remain calm and ignore the rage bubbling beneath the surface. What if Lauren had opened it? Not only was it disgusting, but dog mess was also dangerous. Couldn't it send you blind if it got into your eyes?

Why would someone do that? It was an accident and I had apologised. I flexed my jaw, grinding my teeth as I debated whether to go round and hammer on her door. Give Valerie a piece of my mind, but I didn't want to give her the satisfaction of a confrontation. I found an empty carrier bag and put the envelope inside, tying the handles together tightly and tossing it out of the back door into the garden to deal with later. Teddy chased it, gave it a sniff and carried on exploring the garden.

'What's wrong, Mummy? Don't you like the house?' Lauren said, noticing my brows knitted together.

'Of course I do. Right, shall we find you a drink and a snack? I'm sure there's a box around here somewhere,' I said, dousing my hands in the antibacterial gel I kept in my handbag. I had no idea where I'd packed the hand soap. I opened each box with my front door key, slicing through the tape. Now was as good a time as any to try to get the essentials unpacked.

Pushing Valerie from my mind, I unloaded the boxes with Lauren's help. Putting everything on the kitchen side and letting Lauren choose what would be the cupboard for the plates, the saucepans and Tupperware. The place had been left clean, everywhere smelt of bleach, and I was grateful, although I still wiped the sides before we got started. Lauren enjoyed being involved and it should have been fun, but I couldn't help but stew on the envelope that had been put through the door.

There was no point entering into a confrontation with my neighbor, especially not on the first day we'd moved in. What she'd done was out of order, even if Teddy had crapped on her lawn before I'd even had a chance to say hello. She'd wrongly assumed I was going to leave it there for her to clean up. It was a misunderstanding, but she'd taken it too far. I'd have to talk to her about it when I next saw her, or perhaps mention it to Niamh, she seemed like she knew Valerie well. Well enough to know how to handle her.

It was almost dinnertime when we'd finished unpacking the kitchen. At least now we had plates and cutlery. I could make a cup of tea too, as I'd had the foresight to buy some long-life carton milk last week. I deliberately hadn't brought anything refrigerated with us.

'Can we share a Hawaiian pizza please?' Lauren asked as we discussed takeaway options. She slurped from her school water bottle. I hadn't even unpacked her bag or emptied her lunch box yet, the afternoon had run away from me.

'Sure, I'll order one now,' I said, looking on my phone for the Domino's website. I knew there was one in town and hoped it wouldn't take too long. It was a Friday, the end of the week, as well as being the end of term, and lots of people had celebratory take-aways. We often did, it was a 'phew, we made it' pat on the back in the form of naughty food and a night off cooking.

After a few clicks, the order was in. I let Teddy back into the house and moved on to the lounge. The dog took position on the blue leather sofa expecting me to sit beside him for a cuddle, but I wanted to unwrap the television and get it set up. Otherwise, Lauren and I would be in for an evening playing Monopoly or Twister and I didn't have the energy for that.

Lauren amused herself popping the discarded bubble wrap and I was amazed to find the television worked, although I couldn't get the Freeview or Netflix going initially. Then I remembered I had to plug the modem in and call BT to ensure the internet was switched on. After twenty minutes on the phone, it was up and running and Lauren watched *A Series of Unfortunate Events* while I worked through the boxes for the front room. There wasn't much – some books, photos in wooden frames and curtains that didn't exactly fit but would suffice for a week or two.

I needed to order a new TV stand and bookcase, but we'd make do for now. The TV was on the floor facing the sofa, next to it piles of books waiting to find a home. I got to my feet and flattened the packing boxes. Teddy, growing restless, jumped down, it was six o'clock and our pizza still hadn't arrived. I fed Teddy and made sure his bed was unpacked, as well as the throws for the sofa, so he had somewhere soft and warm to sleep once I'd taken him out for a quick lap of the close.

'Pizza's here,' Lauren said, jumping off the sofa and rushing to the front door as the heavy knocker thundered through the house.

'Jesus,' I cringed at the loud booming sound. I'd jump out of my skin every time someone came to the door.

We ate the pizza at the table straight out of the box, Teddy sitting patiently at our feet waiting for the occasional piece of ham Lauren slipped him when she thought I wasn't looking. I'd missed lunch and my stomach absorbed the carbohydrates gratefully. Lauren wiped the herb sauce she'd been dipping her crusts in from her mouth with a paper towel and rubbed her belly.

'So nice.'

'Shall we take Teddy for a quick walk around the close?' I asked, as Lauren yawned. 'Then we'll come back, you can have a shower and get into your PJs.'

She nodded and stretched before retrieving Teddy's lead and slipping her shoes on.

'Put your cardigan on, it might be chilly,' I said, passing the navy school cardigan to her before shrugging into my scruffy mohair one I kept over the back of the sofa.

Ensuring I had keys, and poo bags, I stepped out onto the driveway, unable to believe it was so quiet. The only sound was the chattering of birds. No cars, no loud music and no children shouting. I was almost afraid to talk in case I disturbed the peace.

The sun was just starting to set, the sky a pretty rose gold. We made our way quietly around the close, listening to the sound of our shoes slapping the concrete pavement. I'd turned right so as not to pass Valerie's house, I couldn't deal with another altercation today.

'They all look like our house, don't they,' Lauren pointed out as we passed number two and number one, both now showing signs of life. Number two had a polished red MX5 two-seater convertible on the driveway, which was anything but a family car. Their doorstep decorated with spiralled topiary trees in bright white pots. Number one had a modern lamp illuminating their living room, vertical blinds tilted to deny inquisitive eyes. A new silver BMW was parked next to a zesty yellow Mini Cooper which was also barely a year old.

'They do, ours has the number three plate on the wall, but otherwise they're all pretty much identical.' As we slowly passed, I looked up to see the glow of soft lighting through bedroom windows. Every car in the close was new or nearly new, glistening in the sinking sun. Just as I'd feared, I'd lowered the tone with my VW Golf, which was fifteen years old and had its share of dents and scratches.

Teddy stopped to sniff occasionally and as we reached the entrance to Beech Close, I crossed over to let him enjoy the green in the centre. The first thing he did on the extendable lead was trot over to the beech tree and pee against it.

'That's his tree now,' Lauren giggled.

'It certainly is,' I replied, glancing over at Valerie's house to find her staring out of her bedroom window. Straight at us.

5

I shuddered, unsure whether it was standing in the shadow of the beech tree or Valerie's icy glare that sent palpitations through my chest. Either way, I refused to break eye contact with her, despite my knees feeling like they were going to buckle. There was no way I was putting up with any intimidation.

'When we get back, can we play hide-and-seek?' Lauren asked, interrupting my standoff.

'Sure, after your shower,' I replied, my gaze shifting to Teddy as he sniffed, turning in a circle for the perfect place to release.

Once he did, I stared up at the window, Valerie still watching us, and took a poo bag out of my pocket. With Lauren's back turned, I theatrically waved it at her and bent to pick up what Teddy had left. I had good mind to shove the bag through her letter box, see how she liked it, but I wasn't going to stoop to her level.

'Come on then, we can let him out in the garden later and chuck the ball if he gets restless,' I said, as we trotted back towards number three.

Inside, I threw away the pizza box and went to get the shower ready for Lauren. I was sure the novelty would wear off. Could she play with her Barbies in the shower as well as she could in the bath? Once she was in, I made my bed, which was a basic double divan. The removal men only had to clip the two halves back together and throw the mattress on top. The blue velvet headboard could wait until Josh visited as it was heavier and needed two people to fit it.

Lauren was singing away to Ariana Grande and seemed in no rush to get out, so I put up the ill-fitting curtains and began unpacking my clothes into the fitted wardrobe and drawers at the base of the bed. By the time she was finished, standing in the doorway, her hair dripping over the carpet, my clothes had been put away. We'd got further with unpacking than I thought we would have, but I'd had enough for one day.

My stomach was bloated from the pizza, and I changed into my cotton pyjamas Josh always ribbed me about. I didn't care they were a salmon-pink check and unflatteringly baggy. They were comfy and who was I trying to impress anyway? There'd been no one serious on the scene since Lauren's father. I wasn't interested. Lauren and I called ourselves Team Lucas, we didn't need anyone else. I hadn't had a father figure in my life growing up and it hadn't done me any harm. I had no interest in trying to track my dad down, even when Mum got sick. He'd walked out on us and I wasn't going to beg him for help.

'Mum, I can't find my pyjamas,' Lauren yelled from her room.

'They're under your pillow already. Also please don't leave your towel on the floor,' I called back, knowing she did this every time she had a bath.

'It's not on the floor... it's on the bed,' came her sarcastic reply.

'Oi, cheeky, if you want to play hide-and-seek, you need to pack that up,' I said, laughing.

Lauren was pretty well behaved, I couldn't complain, but I had an inkling she was going to be a wild teenager, like I'd been. She liked pushing boundaries, to see how far she could go, although her teachers admitted they loved her cheeky side and found it hard not to laugh. I was the same; she was funny and had a way of getting around me. Perhaps it was because it was just the two of us and had been for so long.

I remembered my mum being so miserable when I was growing up, she was lonely and resented me for it. When Lauren's father, Sebastian, had walked out on us when she was barely a few months old, Mum said history was repeating itself, but I was determined not to end up bitter like her. I wanted to be a fun parent, I needed Lauren to look back and have fond memories of her childhood and the things we did together. Not have to watch a revolving door where men were concerned, coming in and out of her mother's life.

'Go downstairs, Mummy, and count to a hundred,' Lauren instructed, handing me her towel to put back on the rail in the bathroom before rushing back to her room. She had on pug pyjamas and fluffy socks, her wet hair piled on top of her head, secured with a scrunchie.

'Okay,' I relented with a yawn, wishing I could collapse onto the sofa and stare mindlessly at the television.

I trudged downstairs and looked out of the lounge window onto the quiet close. I could see across the green to Niamh's house, a second car now on her driveway, which presumably was her husband's. Did she work or did she spend her days at the gym and brunching with friends? Oh, to be so free. At least I had a couple of weeks off to look forward to. I'd have to get the office up and running before my holiday was over.

Slipping my phone out of my pocket, I checked to see if Josh had replied to my message from earlier inviting him over tomorrow. He had: two words, 'sure thing', which meant he had to have been busy at his call centre job. Josh managed a team of sales staff, selling double glazing and garage doors. His workforce were all so young, it was tough to keep them in line. I sent a message back.

Hope you're feeling pumped. I'll cook if you bring your screwdriver... X

He'd already offered to lend a hand with any heavy lifting or building I needed doing. He'd helped me move from the grotty bedsit into Mum's a couple of years before. However, I'd hardly anything to move then. We hired the smallest van we could and did it between us.

'One hundred,' I shouted loudly, aware Lauren hadn't come downstairs, or I would have seen her. The layout of the house meant the stairs were in the lounge. Two large rooms downstairs, the lounge and kitchen/breakfast room, plus a toilet off the tiny hallway. Upstairs, there were two double bedrooms, one with an en suite, a family bathroom and a box room which would become my office. It was modern with clean lines, a palace compared to the dank cottage.

I pulled the curtains closed and switched on the lamp, the night outside creeping in. It was gone seven and we'd have to put a movie on soon, otherwise Lauren wouldn't stay awake to watch it all, neither would I for that matter.

I clattered around, making noise as though I was trying to hunt for my daughter, calling her name and imagining Lauren giggling from her hiding place.

After a few minutes, I climbed the stairs, noticing the third one creaked when I stepped on it. Upstairs, the landing light had been left on, but the rest of the rooms were in darkness. Lauren wasn't terrified of the dark, but like any child, she didn't love it, so I couldn't imagine she'd be in one of the two wardrobes or under her bed. Perhaps she was hiding in the shower or lying flat in the bathtub?

I checked both bathrooms, certain she wasn't there. There was no lump underneath my duvet or hers, and under her bed were the storage boxes I'd put there earlier.

'Where are you, Lauren Lucas?' I called in a sing-song voice before I stood in the hallway. There was only one place left she could be.

Wrenching open the door to the airing cupboard, Lauren screamed as the light blinded her.

'Found you!' I said, reaching in to grab her. Lauren was sat cross-legged on top of the folded towels and bedding I'd put in there earlier. She'd taken her hair out of the scrunchie and was twisting a thick strand around her finger. She fitted inside easily, it reaffirmed how big the cupboard was, although it did house the boiler. With my meagre collection of towels and bedding, the space was barely used.

'I'm the best at hiding,' Lauren stated, raising her eyebrows.

'You are. Want to pick a movie? I'm pretty tired,' I admitted, and Lauren shrugged. I was surprised she hadn't put up a fight for more rounds of hide-and-seek, but it had been a long day.

Smoothing down the now crumpled bedding in the airing cupboard, I caught sight of a scratch in the wall, right down to the plaster, like someone had been at it with a compass. I frowned and remembered there were likely kids in the house before, and the cupboard was great for a secret den or hidey-hole. Leaning inside, I pushed down Lauren's cloud duvet cover to take a closer look, cold unease creeping into my chest. It wasn't just a scratch, it was two words spelt out in deep jagged scratches.

LEAVE NOW

6

I ran my finger across the crevices of each letter, imagining the author dragging whatever sharp object they'd used, burying deep into the plaster. Why had they written it? Who had written it? I guessed it must have been the owners who had lived here before, but who was the message for? I frowned, staring at the word as though it would give me the answer, but nothing came. Nothing except a lingering sense of dread which wrapped its tendrils around me.

Grabbing some sheets from another pile, I covered the carving, not wanting Lauren to find it later and ask questions. The last thing I needed was for her to get spooked. She'd been through enough. Beech Close was supposed to be a new beginning without anything hanging over us.

'Mum, I found *Encanto*,' Lauren called from the lounge downstairs. Already I could hear the familiar music, we'd seen it so often.

'Coming,' I shouted back, closing the door to the airing cupboard so I could forget I'd seen the message on the wall.

Although I knew it wasn't going to be easy to push it to the back of my mind. The fact it was there gave me the creeps.

Lauren made it through three quarters of the film before her head bobbed. She was snuggled on the three-seater, in between me and Teddy, who rested his chin on his paws. The excitement of the day and end of term had caught up with her and she yawned repeatedly. I suggested going to bed as it was half past eight, but she begged to stay up until the end, only making it another twenty minutes before nodding off.

Lauren had got so big, I could no longer carry her up the stairs and she groaned when I woke her. With a little encouragement, I managed to get her to the bathroom to clean her teeth before tucking her in. She didn't seem at all fazed by her new surroundings and rolled over with her teddy to go to sleep before I'd even said goodnight. I kissed her cheek and headed back downstairs to make a cup of tea.

Teddy was scratching at the back door, and I let him out, shushing him as he barked into the night as he sometimes did. Sounding off, as though to warn others he was there. I was sure Valerie wouldn't appreciate it, but he stopped as soon as I told him off. I left him outside, having a sniff, going back as the kettle finished boiling to make tea. Ten minutes later, he was still exploring, ignoring my call to come in. I let him be, he was getting acquainted with his new surroundings and all the exciting smells that came with it. Eventually when he didn't come in of his own accord, I had to put on a stern voice before he begrudgingly came back inside, going straight to his bed instead of joining me on the sofa.

It was my least favourite time of night. As much as I wanted peace and quiet during the day when the world was manic, the silence at night made me jittery. I kept expecting to hear the chime of Mum's bell which she rang whenever she wanted something: a drink, the toilet, something to eat or just to be difficult. Because of the dementia, she would often eat, then forget she'd eaten, so she'd ring the bell for her dinner I'd given her half an hour before. I'd get called every name under the sun for not giving her more food. She insisted I was cruel, trying to starve her or occasionally trying to poison her, depending on her mood. She'd ring the damn bell for hours until eventually I hid it. It didn't stop her, she howled like a dog or wailed like a banshee until we came running. It was utterly exhausting.

The nurses had warned me how bad she'd get, but towards the end she was intolerable, abusive even. It made it hard to mourn her, all I had was guilt I couldn't stop the disease ravaging her brain. I couldn't make her see I was there to help, to look after her and that despite everything I loved her. She thought I was her enemy.

I hated going to bed because all my nightmares were about her. I used to wake and find her standing over me, watching. It was terrifying and I resorted to locking Lauren and I in so Mum couldn't scare her.

Mum had never been overly maternal, I was considered more of a nuisance, especially as a child, so it wasn't as if I was losing a loving parent, but watching her deteriorate was heart-wrenching. I felt bad for exposing Lauren to it, so I overcompensated with fun activities, trips to the cinema and trampoline park, bike rides and bowling. Whenever one of the nurses would come in to offer respite, I'd take Lauren somewhere for a while, a chance to blow off steam for both of us. We were grateful for the new start Beech Close offered, a life that would be less stressful and allow more time for fun.

I slurped my tea on the sofa, deciding to go to bed once I'd finished it. Pointless staying up by myself when I was tired too. I could wake earlier in the morning and finish the rest of the boxes.

If I cracked on, we could be done by the end of the weekend and use the rest of the Easter holidays for family days out with Teddy, take a drive down to the beach at Shoreham or picnic in Tilgate Park. It would be something to look forward to.

* * *

I slept better than I had in months, just being in a different space, one that didn't smell like Mum, or where I could see her sat in every chair or standing in every corner. It reinforced my decision to sell. Despite my run-in with Valerie yesterday, we'd make a go of it here. If my charm didn't work, I'd keep out of her way. We weren't bad neighbors – there would be no loud music, no shouting or screaming and no house parties. Maybe Valerie was a bit anxious about who she would have to live next door to? Although, when I thought of her clipped tone, anxious wouldn't be a word I'd have used to describe her. Either way, it was no excuse for what she'd put through my door.

As I'd gone to bed around nine, I was up before seven. The house was still quiet, as was Beech Close early on a Saturday morning. I took the opportunity to run through the shower and get dressed before going downstairs, although when I got there, I wished I hadn't bothered. The floor and Teddy's bed was covered in a puddle of vomit. All of Teddy's whiskers around his mouth were matted together with yellow bile, his water bowl almost empty. He'd obviously got sick in the night, perhaps he'd eaten something whilst we were out without my knowledge.

Over the years, there'd been all sorts, but I quickly learned from frequent vet visits, Teddy had iron guts and rarely got ill from eating a dropped kebab or anything found on the pavement he deemed edible.

'Oh, Teddy,' I sighed, giving his face a wipe with a damp floor cloth. I took the bed and Teddy outside. I couldn't wash it as I had no idea how to plumb in the washing machine, a job I'd reserved for Josh today.

Teddy seemed fine, wagging his tail and not remotely lethargic. I gave him some more water and a proper clean with some doggy wipes. He tore off around the garden, taking his time to find the perfect place to relieve himself. As I watched him, something glistened in the morning sun, catching my eye. Like a magpie, I was drawn to it, a silver wrapper by the fence flickered in the breeze.

I moved to pick it up, thinking it was someone's rubbish that had blown into the garden only to find it was a half-eaten bar of chocolate. I snatched it before Teddy came bounding over. Who'd left it here? Whoever it was, didn't they know chocolate was poisonous to animals? I was sure it hadn't been in the garden yesterday, I would have seen it when Lauren and I were outside. Teddy had obviously got hold of it and it had made him sick. The bloody dog would eat anything he could get his paws on. But how had it got here?

I looked again at the spot I'd found the wrapper, wedged half in the soft soil of the flower bed, as though it had been plonked into the earth. Dropped from a height, like someone had reached over the six-foot fence and let it go. If that was the case, it could only be one person, as the fence separated mine and Valerie's garden.

7

That vicious cow was my first thought before I questioned whether it could have been an accident. What if the chocolate bar had been thrown from the other side, from number two's garden on the left? I had no idea who lived there and hadn't seen anyone to introduce myself. Although Niamh had said there were no other children in Beech Close and I couldn't imagine an adult lobbing it. I looked across the width of my garden. It would have had to have been a hell of a throw too. There was no one at the back of us, only woodland, a disused railway line, so overgrown it was impassable.

I didn't want to jump to conclusions, but it looked as though Valerie had deliberately tried to harm Teddy. I couldn't prove it, though, and there was no way I could hammer on her door and demand to know what she was playing at. Hopefully, it would all blow over in a day or two, but I'd have to come into the garden with Teddy or put him on a lead every time, which would be a pain.

There was no point in dwelling on it, I didn't want Valerie's actions to ruin my mood. I'd woken energised and ready for the day. Josh would be over at some point, after lunch as he rarely got out of bed before midday at the weekend. Then I could tell him all about my neighbor from hell, out of earshot of Lauren of course. He'd know how to handle her. What would he make of the scratched message in the airing cupboard? As hard as I tried to forget I'd found it, the words played on my mind. It freaked me out.

Herding Teddy back inside, I threw the chocolate in the bin, before taking it out and putting it high in a cupboard Lauren wouldn't be able to reach. If I confronted Valerie, I wanted to have evidence. If the retaliation for Teddy pooing on her lawn was to poison him, I hated to think what would happen if we really pissed her off. It was one hell of a reaction.

What if she thought we were too noisy? Lauren loved to play in the garden, especially in the nicer weather. We'd played badminton at Mum's, over the washing line, and I wanted to get her a swing for the summer as there was more space here. Over the years she'd begged for one and I wasn't going to be put off using our garden by Valerie. She clearly had a few screws loose.

Teddy seemed fine and happy to eat his breakfast, which I gave him in the lounge while I cleaned the kitchen floor. The acidic smell of vomit was quickly replaced with a pine-fresh aroma and the kitchen looked as good as new. Having powered through the boxes for the kitchen and lounge yesterday, I rearranged a few cupboards before making a cup of tea and waiting for Lauren to wake.

She came downstairs at eight, wayward hair sticking out in all directions.

'How did you sleep?' I asked, still drinking my tea.

She flopped into the seat opposite me at the table. 'Okay,' she replied, rubbing her eyes. Teddy sat at her feet, waiting patiently for a cuddle, wagging his tail when she eventually obliged.

'We need to go food shopping this morning, but I can rustle up some cereal if you like?' I suggested.

'Rice Krispies please,' she replied, and I got up to fill a bowl, delivering it along with a glass of water. I hadn't bought any juice yet.

I sat back down to watch her eat, filling her in on the plans for the day.

'A quick dog walk, a pop to the shops and then Josh will come by to help with the bigger stuff.'

Lauren nodded, her mouth full, she was still half asleep.

I'd just stood to clean my teeth when I heard the snap of the letter box and the telling sound of something hitting the floor. My shoulders tensed as I remembered yesterday's delivery. Without a word, I moved to the front door. Another white envelope lay on the mat, although this one had my name on it in flourishing handwriting. I put my finger under the flap and tore through, opening the envelope to reveal the note inside.

Drinks and Appetisers at No. 6
4 p.m. onwards
Niamh and Finn

Oh God, Niamh *had* arranged a get-together. It didn't say anything about me being the new neighbor, but I had no doubt it was in reference to our conversation yesterday. I hadn't thought she was being literal at the time, but the idea of an intimate get-together with the residents of the five other houses in the street filled me with dread. Especially if one of the guests would be Valerie.

I rubbed my forehead. I couldn't go anyway, Josh would be here, and I needed his help with the washing machine and the headboard, amongst other things. I'd have to go round and give our apologies.

'Leave your bowl in the sink when you're done, I'm going to clean my teeth,' I said, placing the invitation on the table.

* * *

An hour later, we'd been to the supermarket and whizzed around the aisles. Lauren liked to sneak food into the trolley, which I would then remove. She had a sweet tooth and lived for snacks, pretty much like every other kid, but left unchecked she'd graze all day long. We compromised on some treats, and I picked up a six-pack of beer in case Josh wanted one as a reward for his help later.

Teddy was waiting for us by the front door when we returned, mourning the removal of his bed, and Lauren and I took him out as soon as we'd put the refrigerator food away. He pulled on his lead straight for the green, circling and sniffing the beech tree. We loitered until he relieved himself. He hadn't regurgitated his breakfast, so I concluded his stomach was all right again.

'Come on, let's get out of the close,' I suggested to Lauren, who skipped along beside me. I didn't want to stay on the green in case Valerie was watching.

The sun hadn't made an appearance yet, the sky an ominous grey like it was about to rain any minute. We'd put our coats on just in case, having been caught out many times before by April showers. The weather in spring was always unpredictable; one day it was warm enough to just wear a T-shirt, the next day it could rain so hard you needed your wellingtons.

'What's that?' Lauren asked as we emerged into the next road. I was too busy admiring the houses to notice what my daughter was pointing at, already a few steps ahead.

'What's what?' I asked, giving Teddy's lead a tug so we could join her.

Lauren stood by a lamp post, looking at a poster flapping in the breeze. It looked old with torn edges, no longer white but more an insipid beige. The poster had the word MISSING in large red block capitals and beneath was a photograph of a gorgeous fluffy dog with small black eyes and floppy ears.

'Ah,' I said, experiencing a tug on my heart strings.

'His name is Barney,' Lauren said, 'and he's lost.'

Lauren stared at the flapping sheet, tied to the lamp post with string. Barney, who looked like a cockapoo, had gone missing last year, a week before Christmas. I held Teddy's lead a little tighter, the notion of losing him any time was horrific, but right before Christmas was unthinkable. Poor Barney's family, whoever they were. The poster had no address, but there was a mobile number and the name Danielle Stobart listed as a contact.

'Hopefully, he's been found,' I said to Lauren, gently tugging her away.

'Then why is the poster still up?' she asked.

I shrugged. Why indeed?

'Maybe his owners haven't got around to removing it.'

That seemed to appease her and we carried on along the road, Teddy enjoying the new sights and smells he wasn't accustomed to until Lauren asked to return home, eager to play on her iPad. As we walked back towards the house, my phone bleeped. A message from Josh letting me know he was on his way. I kept my head down as we entered Beech Close, worried Niamh would be loitering, hoping to catch me to confirm attendance for her drinks that afternoon. I'd have to let her know I wouldn't be coming but could put it off until a bit later. However, I saw none of the neighbors and managed to slip inside the house without bumping into anyone.

Josh arrived after lunch. I heard his convertible Fiat 500 blaring before I saw it. He had a thing about nineties music and 'Trash' by Suede was playing at full volume. I winced, opening the front door and putting my finger to my lips. I could imagine Valerie would be having a coronary if she was in.

'What?' Josh said, frowning, his hands on his hips as he climbed out of the car.

'Your music is so loud... Quick, come in,' I beckoned as Teddy wriggled through my legs and jumped up to greet Josh.

'Well, at least someone is pleased to see me,' he said drily, tickling Teddy under the chin.

'I am pleased to see you, thank you for coming and bringing your muscles with you,' I teased as Josh came in. He was wearing a tight black T-shirt which clung to his biceps.

'Well, you know, if you've got it, flaunt it,' he winked, and I chuckled darkly, subtlety wasn't one of Josh's virtues.

When we'd first met, during a shift behind the bar of our local pub when we were eighteen, I'd fancied him rotten until I heard him speak. It was clear Josh was gay as soon as he'd opened his mouth and from our first lock-in, knocking back Blue WKDs after hours, we were as thick as thieves. He was Lauren's godfather, much to my mum's disappointment – she'd never liked Josh and made it plainly obvious, but luckily it went over his head.

We did everything together, from our fake tan faux pas and navigating online dating to failing our driving tests the first time. Josh even brought me with him for moral support when he came out to his mum, Joyce, who'd simply laughed and told us she'd known since he was seven. She was the mum I'd wished I'd had, although I felt guilty for thinking it. It was obvious she thought the world of Josh and always had his back. Not once did she voice her disapproval or criticism in his choice of career or partner.

'I brought us some gin and tonic,' Josh said, snapping me back to the present by pulling cans out of his rucksack. 'I hope you've got ice,' he continued.

'I do, of course, but work first, play later,' I laughed, putting the cans in the fridge alongside the beer I'd bought earlier.

'This is lovely,' he said, twirling his finger and gesturing to the modern kitchen.

'Come on, I'll give you a tour.'

I took Josh around the ground floor, listening to his decorative suggestions, but his taste was a lot more out there than mine. I wasn't into feature walls or patterned wallpaper, panelling or bright colours. I wanted a calm space, preferring to inject a bit of personality with cushions, ornaments, and artwork.

'I see Teddy's going up,' Josh said as we passed the canvas resting on the mantelpiece. Teddy in his *Peaky Blinders* cap and waistcoat.

'Of course!' I replied.

'Hi, Josh,' Lauren called from upstairs, and we followed her voice. She met us on the landing and wrapped her arms around Josh's waist.

'Hello, pickle.' Josh squeezed her tight before reaching into his rucksack to retrieve an oblong gift wrapped in yellow tissue paper.

'What is it?' Lauren asked excitedly as she peeled the paper away.

Josh had bought her a hand-painted nameplate for her

bedroom door. *Lauren* in black swirling handwriting on a pastel yellow background, surrounded by pretty bumblebees.

'Thanks, Josh. I love it!' Lauren took him by the hand to show him her room. Josh made all the right comments, and Lauren was beaming when he eventually was allowed to leave.

'It sickens me how much she loves you,' I teased, to which Josh gave me a wink.

'She has good taste. Right, so what's on the list?' he asked.

'Headboard, washing machine, helping me put some bits in the loft if you can. I still need to order some furniture, so there's nothing to build, I don't think.'

'What do you need to buy?'

'Loads. A television unit, bookcase for downstairs, a new desk. I'm thinking about a trip to Ikea.' I watched Josh's eyes light up.

'Oh my God, yes! I could do with a shopping spree.'

* * *

An hour later, the extravagant blue velvet headboard had been fitted, which changed the whole identity of the bedroom, and the loft partly filled with some of Mum's things I wanted to keep. Josh had found a small box of junk left by the water tank which he retrieved, and I put out the front by the bins for the dustmen to take away. He also managed to plumb in the washing machine and heave it into position, which meant I wouldn't have to walk around it any longer. The kitchen looked instantly bigger. I was grateful he was so handy, but he'd had to be growing up without a dad around. It was one of the many things we had in common.

I put Teddy's bed on a wash as soon as the washing machine was in, so the vomit would be a distant memory. Lauren was settled in her room, playing Roblox with a snack of Iced Gems so Josh and I could relax after a full-on afternoon.

'Drink?' I offered, we deserved one.

'Definitely. So, what are your neighbors like?' Josh asked, sliding into a seat at the kitchen table whilst I fetched ice and a glass for the gin and tonic.

'Well, a bit weird, if I'm honest.'

His eyebrows shot up and he stared at me expectantly so I filled him in on my confrontation with Valerie and the saga of Teddy. His eyes widening as I told him about the present through my letter box.

'Christ! I'm sure she'll warm up. If not, you'll just have to kill her with kindness. Send her some flowers, go out of your way to be nice.'

I grimaced, I wasn't sure if Valerie was the type to be swayed with kind gestures.

'Oh, and you've got to see this,' I said, rising from my chair and grabbing Josh's arm.

I led him with his puzzled expression up the stairs.

'Check this out,' I whispered, opening the airing cupboard door and pushing the sheets down to reveal the scratched message.

'Leave now?' Josh read.

'Freaky, isn't it? I mean, it gives me goosebumps,' I replied.

Josh shuddered and squinted at the markings, running his finger over the plaster as I had done. 'It's like something out of a horror movie. You haven't moved into a cannibalistic cul-de-sac, have you?' He laughed and we went back downstairs.

'I hope not.' I giggled, masking my unease.

As we resumed our seats at the kitchen table, Teddy at our feet, I took a long swig of the refreshing gin and tonic, wishing I'd bought lemons at the supermarket. The ice clinked in our glasses and Josh looked deep in thought, a million miles away, but just as

I was about to ask him what was on his mind, someone knocked at the door.

'Bloody hell,' Josh jumped.

'I know, it's like someone is ram-raiding the door, isn't it,' I said, referring to the overly loud knocker.

'Ooh, I hope it's one of the neighbors, let me answer it.' Josh raced towards the door, with me hot on his heels.

9

'Hi!' Josh said, pulling open the door before I could get there.

I watched as Niamh's smile froze on her face.

'Hello,' she said, face bewildered.

I pushed Josh, who was deliberately trying to fill the door frame, to the side.

'Hi, Niamh, sorry, this is my friend, Josh.'

'Oh, hello, pleased to meet you,' she beamed at him before turning to me. 'Shelly, I wanted to pop by and see if you received my note about drinks this afternoon? Starts in an hour and we'd love to have you. Everyone is coming.'

I hesitated, wishing I'd popped round to give my apologies earlier but with how busy Josh and I had been it had completely slipped my mind.

She carried on, filling the silence before I could answer. 'Finn and I sometimes throw an impromptu bash, always well received with the neighbors.' Niamh grinned at me, her straight white teeth dazzling.

'Ummm,' I managed before Josh interrupted.

'Of course she'll be there. Shelly invited me round to look

after Lauren especially.' He squeezed my shoulders, towering above me, as though I was his child, and he was letting me out to play. I gritted my teeth, I was going to kill him.

'Wonderful, see you in a bit. Number six, remember, straight across the green.' Niamh practically skipped down the driveway and round to Valerie's house at number four. She must have been knocking on all the doors in the close.

'What did you do that for?' I hissed, shoving Josh out of the way and closing the door.

'Getting to know your neighbors is important.' Josh's voice dripped with sarcasm.

'It's going to be painful!' I whined, knowing I wasn't great at socialising at the best of times. I had one friend, some varied acquaintances and I didn't need any more.

'You've got to put yourself out there. For all you know, there might be a cute divorcee who lives on the street.'

'I've told you, I'm not interested,' I sniped. Josh was forever trying to get me to date, just because his flat had a revolving-door policy, courtesy of the Grindr app.

I necked the rest of my drink and opened another can of G&T. Sloshing the lot into my glass and scowling at my best friend.

'I wanted to stay in with you,' I grumbled.

'It won't go on for long and it's probably been thrown in your honour, as the new neighbor. It's rude not to go. I can rustle up something for dinner in the meantime and have it ready for you when you get back.' My shoulders slumped, there was no way I could get out of it now and I resolved to come up with an excuse to leave early so the torture wouldn't be prolonged.

* * *

An hour later, Josh pushed me out of the door, clutching a lukewarm bottle of Chardonnay I hadn't had any space for in the fridge. It was the best I could do at short notice. Josh had forced me to change my pink sweatshirt for a more grown-up blouse and take my hair out of the ponytail it usually lived in, so it fell in dark waves across my shoulders. I shook my head, fringe permanently in my eyes.

'Oh, for God's sake, Josh. I'm not meeting the bloody queen,' I sighed when he looked me over.

'First impressions are everything, and, like I said, who knows who you'll meet over there. Just think, your future husband could be a mere hundred yards away.'

I rolled my eyes but did as I was told.

I walked around the green, staying on the pavement so my journey took longer, heart sinking with each step. I hated social occasions, especially ones where I didn't know anyone. Lifting my chin, I rolled my shoulders back, telling myself it would be okay. I'd slap on a smile and be polite, but afternoon drinks and canapés weren't really me. I was more of a gin and tonic out of a can kind of girl, maybe a packet of Doritos to soak up the alcohol. I wanted to turn around, run back to the haven of number three Beech Close. Back to Josh and Lauren, who wouldn't judge me on what I was wearing, the age of my car, or the fact I was a single parent.

Checking my watch, I reached number six at quarter past four, hoping I wouldn't be the first to arrive. Niamh's house was identical to mine, although she had hanging baskets filled with a colourful arrangement of petunias in white, purple, and pink. Hung in the windows were cream vertical blinds and even though they were slightly angled, I could see movement inside.

Steeling myself, I knocked on the door. Within ten seconds, it opened, and Niamh smiled manically. The woman was intense, it put me on edge.

'Hi, welcome,' she said before calling over her shoulder to a crowd gathered in the kitchen, 'it's the guest of honour.'

I cringed as everyone turned to stare, like I was the new animal at the zoo.

'Come in, Shelly.'

I stepped inside, wiping my feet on the large doormat. From the entrance, I could see straight into the lounge and through to a large open-plan kitchen/diner at the back. It was the same layout as mine, but Niamh had extended into her garden, with bifold doors opening onto a decked area. The floor was a cool grey tile which looked expensive, but I'd bet was slippery when wet, inappropriate for children.

'This is for you,' I said, handing her the bottle of Chardonnay. 'Shall I take my shoes off?' I was stalling for time before being thrust into introductions. Deliberately avoiding looking at the mingling guests, already aware of my pulse accelerating at the notion of small talk. Why had Josh made me come? Why hadn't I refused, said I was busy, like I did with most other things.

'No, it's fine, come through and meet everyone,' she said, holding her arm out for me to walk in front of her.

I took slow steps, my cheeks burning.

'Everyone, this is Shelly, our new neighbor at number three. Just moved in yesterday.'

Around the large marble top kitchen island stood five people, three men and two women. I smiled, raising my hand in a limp wave, face on fire.

'Welcome to Beech Close,' the oldest of the men said. He had a grey beard and receding hair, brushed to the side, with bright blue eyes which matched his smart checked shirt. He had to be in

his late fifties, early sixties maybe, although it didn't appear he
had a wife with him.

'This is Derek Plaistow, he lives next door at number five,'
Niamh said, pushing a flute of what looked like champagne into
my hand. Salmon canapés and asparagus wrapped in Parma ham
filled the worktop, the second man shovelling them in at an
alarming rate.

'Pleased to meet you,' I said to Derek, whose kind eyes twin-
kled. I took a sip from my glass, the bubbles fizzing up my nose,
almost making me sneeze.

'And this is Becky and Maxwell Sumner, they are your neighbors at number two.' Niamh gestured to the man whose mouth
was chewing rhythmically. He didn't even look up, still perusing
the trays of canapés before making his next selection. Maxwell's
olive-green grandad shirt was straining at the seams and his skin
had a sheen to it, as though the air temperature was a few degrees
too warm for his liking.

His wife, Becky, looked on, her cheeks flushing. In contrast,
she, like Niamh, looked effortlessly stylish. She wore navy culottes
with a cream slouch fine-knit jumper which hung off one bony
shoulder, her auburn hair tied in a purposefully messy bun.

The pairing of the couple seemed odd. Had she married for
money? Immediately, I felt guilty for even thinking it. Whatever
the reason, it was none of my business.

'Lovely to meet you,' Becky said, her words spilling out like an
avalanche. 'Niamh tells us you have a dog, but we haven't heard
him bark at all. Not like the last one, God it never stopped
yapping. Yours we don't hear a peep out of.'

Before I could answer, a voice came from behind me.

'Oh, you mean the mutt that defecated on my lawn?'

10

I turned to see Valerie standing behind me, wearing dark sunglasses and a cape like she was Audrey Hepburn. It felt like she was glaring at me. I moved aside so she could enter the kitchen, shrinking back against the wall.

'It won't happen again,' I said, a little exasperated. It was petty to raise it now, especially as Niamh had gone to so much trouble.

'That's what dogs do, I'm afraid, Val.' The third man, who had a cultivated goatee spoke from across the kitchen island, winking at me conspiratorially. 'I'm Leo, and this is my wife, Amber, we're at number one.'

His wife was tall yet curvy, with olive skin and beautiful black hair which reached her lower back. She smiled tightly but didn't speak. They had to be around my age but looked overly glamorous. Other than Maxwell, the guests around the island could have been models, there for a photo shoot. I couldn't help feeling like the poor relation.

'Tell us a bit about yourself,' Niamh piped up, and I cringed inwardly. I didn't know anyone who enjoyed talking about themselves.

I took a large swig of champagne, sure I saw Amber grimace.

'Okay, well I'm Shelly Lucas, I'm thirty-three and I've moved into number three, oh funny that.' I giggled awkwardly. 'Ummm, I have a ten-year-old daughter, Lauren, and a dog called Teddy. I work from home a lot, freelance, admin mostly, and, ummm, that's about it.' I swallowed the lump in my throat, mouth dry, and gulped down the last of my champagne. Perspiration dampened my underarms, and I blew my fringe out of my eyes, wishing the ground would swallow me up. It was every bit as hellish as I'd imagined.

'Is there a Mr Lucas?' Leo asked.

'No. Just me,' I said, a little too quickly, sure I'd heard Valerie tutting.

After a short pause, the group continued talking amongst themselves and Niamh turned to me.

'They're a good bunch mostly. We try to look after each other if we can. We've all lived here for five years now. It's a real community with only six houses in the close.'

'Is number three the only rented house?'

'Yes, I believe so. All of us bought ours from new.' Niamh's comment, although without judgement, confirmed I was very much the outsider.

'I love what you've done with the place,' I said, looking above my head to the large skylight flooding the kitchen with glorious sunshine. The cabinets were a white gloss, the worktops grey marble. Everything styled to perfection. A red SMEG fridge and expensive-looking coffee machine were the only colour in the room.

'Oh the extension, we built it over New Year. My husband, Finn, has a good job; he works and I decorate. It's an obsession of mine, I should have gone into interior design.' She giggled and I smiled tightly, a wave of jealousy hitting me. If only I'd had it so easy, met a man who worked so I could play. It didn't matter. Lauren and I were a team and she was the only other half I needed. Niamh continued, 'He's still at work, unfortunately, some last-minute problem, otherwise I'd introduce you.'

Over the next few hours, Niamh moved me around the room strategically, so I could talk to every neighbor. She must have heard about my altercation with Valerie as thankfully she avoided her. Derek was a pleasant, retired headmaster of a local primary school, widowed five years ago. Becky worked in public relations for a high-end holiday company, so I dropped in the services I offered, if she ever needed additional administrative support on an ad-hoc basis. She was the most friendly, other than Niamh. Her husband, Maxwell, who'd finally finished scoffing canapés, told me he was an IT consultant and worked mostly from home.

Despite itching to make my excuses and leave Niamh kept refilling my glass as soon as it emptied, and my bottom lip was going numb by the time I got to speak to Leo and Amber. She gripped hold of her attractive husband with his gelled blond hair, as though I was thinking of stealing him. Leo was friendly, if not a little flirty, so I understood his wife's demeanour. He was the finance director for an international shipping company. Like Niamh, Amber didn't work as such, she was an artist specialising in abstract expressionism. She warmed up a little when she spoke about her paintings until her husband cut her off.

'Ahhh, here he is. This is Remy.' Niamh had opened the bifold doors, but the air temperature wasn't overly warm despite the afternoon sun. I'd positioned myself into a square of sunlight in the corner, wishing I'd brought a cardigan with me. Following Leo's raised glass, I saw a tall man I'd yet to be introduced to, standing behind Valerie, his large hands covering her shoulders. He had long dark eyelashes and a chiselled jawline, which made my mouth flood with saliva. Instantly, my face reddened, aware I was likely already tomato coloured with the added alcohol injection. I smiled awkwardly as he came over holding out his hand.

'I'm Remy,' he said, giving my hand a firm shake. His breath smelt of minty chewing gum and I inhaled him, flustered at the proximity.

'Shelly,' I managed.

'Lovely to meet you, I'm just popping in to pick up Mum, she's had far too much fun and no doubt needs a rest,' he quipped, turning to grin at Valerie, whose face had morphed from her usual stony expression to one of pure adoration.

'My handsome boy,' she preened to Niamh, whose expression seemed to darken for a second. She passed Valerie her handbag, who snatched it from her grip.

Remy turned to make his way back to her, and I panicked, wanting to prolong our exchange.

'I think I upset your mum the other day, my dog, Teddy, he—'

'Don't worry. Mum's got early-onset dementia, it can make her a bit agitated. I'm sure she's forgotten all about it already,' he said, dismissively, as though he'd heard all about it.

I doubted she'd forgotten, not when she'd tried to poison my dog. Not to mention the dog mess through the letter box.

I watched Remy leave, stopping to shake hands with Maxwell and Leo as he passed.

'He's gorgeous, isn't he,' Becky said wistfully. I hadn't realised she'd sidled over to me, obviously feeling the effects of the champagne as well.

'I guess,' I said, trying to keep my cool. The last thing I wanted was all the neighbors to see me drooling, although Becky wasn't exactly hiding it. Maxwell was oblivious, pulling out a cigar and stepping onto the decking to light it.

'He practically lives here now, so we see him quite a bit. She relies on him being around.'

'Oh,' I said.

'Val's been found dancing around the beech tree in her nightie more than once,' Becky whispered.

I shuddered, glad Lauren's bedroom was at the back of the house, and she'd never get up in the night to witness something that would be terrifying to a ten-year-old girl. Although she'd seen quite a lot already over the past two years with Mum.

Perhaps I should reach out to Remy, offer some advice or at least a sounding board. Dementia was tough to cope with, especially alone. It explained why Valerie was quick to anger that day. Mum's personality had changed the worse she got, the illness morphing her into a different person in the end. Now I knew what Valerie was going through, I should cut her some slack. Be a good neighbor and look out for her. I could even extend an olive branch, perhaps drop round some flowers or a plant as a peace offering.

I watched Valerie go, Remy's arm around her shoulders almost like he was holding her up. But Valerie didn't look like a little old lady as she threw back her head and laughed at something Remy whispered in her ear. In fact, she didn't look like a woman with dementia, she looked like she knew exactly what was going on. To an outsider, she appeared a force to be reckoned with, a matriarchal type, one who no doubt kept a tight leash on her son. Tight enough to lie about her condition to keep him close?

11

The thought played on my mind as I made my way gingerly across the green towards the sanctuary of number three. It was gone seven and my stomach growled instinctively. Maxwell had eaten most of the canapés and, with all the talking, I hadn't even had a chance to use the bathroom, let alone pause to eat. I'd thanked Niamh before I left, the party still going strong, using Lauren as an excuse to get back. After my nerves had worn off, the get-together hadn't been as bad as I'd thought it would be. Everyone had been more than pleasant.

I was more than a little merry, desperate for the toilet and pondering whether my neighbor was faking a diagnosis to keep people close to her. You forgave a lot of behaviour with dementia. I had no evidence to back it up, only the stark contrast between the impeccable Valerie and my mother who'd fallen apart at the seams.

Casting my mind back to when Mum was first diagnosed, it had started with the usual things, forgetting where she'd put her keys or finding the milk in the cupboard instead of the fridge. It wasn't long before she was getting the days of the week mixed up and calling me by her mother's name, Susan. From there, the mood swings had escalated, sometimes fits of aggression, mainly borne out of frustration, but she hadn't been easy to manage when her mind was failing her.

My shoulders were bunched around my ears, and I forced them down. It was all a little too close to home for my liking. I'd moved to get away from the memories, not to relive them.

'You're home!' Lauren yelled when I came through the door, running towards me and flinging herself into my open arms, Teddy bounding behind her, his tail wagging.

'I am, and it smells delicious. What have you been cooking?' I asked, seeing Lauren's red splattered apron.

'Bolo...' She frowned, trying to summon the rest of the word but unable to remember it.

'Naise?' I suggested and she nodded proudly. I dreaded to think what the kitchen would look like. However, I was surprised to find Josh at the sink washing up, a large pan simmering on the stove.

'How was it?' Josh asked, his face expectant.

Lauren pulled bowls out of the cupboard ready to serve and proceeded to lay the table with cutlery.

'It was okay, there's certainly an array of characters in Beech Close, that's for sure.'

Over dinner, I told Josh and Lauren all about the drinks, explaining who was married to whom, what number house they lived at and what they did for work. They listened intently, drinking in every word as I described Amber and Leo, Becky and Maxwell, amongst others. When Lauren asked to leave the table I told Josh about Valerie's appearance.

'Do you think Valerie could be faking it?' Josh's eyes were wide, disbelief apparent when I told him what her son had said about his mother's condition.

'I don't know, but it's a possibility. She was a bit snippy, then Remy turned up to take her home,' I said, deliberately leaving out how much my stomach had flipped when Remy shook my hand. Josh would have a field day that I was finally attracted to someone, teasing me it had been so long I was becoming asexual.

* * *

A couple of hours later, after ice cream and a game of Monopoly, Lauren was soaking in the bath with the door open and Josh and I were on the sofa, our feet up. As she splashed, playing with a mermaid doll, we worked our way through the remaining gin and tonics.

'I've got a headache, I shouldn't have stopped drinking when I got back from Niamh's,' I complained.

'Schoolboy error, should have pushed through,' Josh chuckled.

I twisted around, laying my feet across Josh's lap, a wave of tiredness washing over me. Teddy was spread out on the floor, his head resting on his paws.

'Thanks for helping out today, I appreciate it,' I said.

'Don't get all mushy on me. You know I've got your back, girl,' he said in an awful American accent.

I sniggered.

'So, are you ready to become one of the Desperate Housewives of Beech Close?' Josh said, referring to Amber and Niamh.

'If only, no rich husband for me. Anyway, Amber's an artist and Niamh, well, she decorates, she said. I think she thinks herself a bit of an interior designer.'

He rolled his eyes. 'Well, this place could do with an injection of colour, you should get her round,' Josh said, waving his glass around at the bare magnolia walls, nose wrinkling.

'It's a rental, remember. I'll get some cushions and a rug, tie the colours in, it'll be great,' I replied defensively.

'Mum!' A shrill scream came from upstairs, the sound of water sloshing over the bath and hitting the floor. Within seconds, I was on my feet, Josh behind me, tearing up the stairs at lightning speed.

I reached the bathroom to find Lauren cowering naked in the corner, goosebumps covered her pale flesh. The bath water rolled from side to side, dripping over the edge onto the floor. Lauren shivered as she sobbed, her legs pulled tight to her, ghostly skin against black tile.

'Lauren, what is it?' I said, dropping to my knees and clutching her to me, the dampness of her body seeping through my blouse.

'Nanny! She's here. I heard her bell. She's found us.'

I reached up and pulled a towel from the silver rail, wrapping it around her as Josh loitered on the stairs, giving Lauren her privacy.

'Lauren, that's impossible, Nanny's dead, you know she is.'

'She was here,' Lauren said, her voice unwavering.

Josh came into the bathroom once I announced Lauren was decent and let the plug out for me, the water gargling. He looked out of the window, onto the circular green illuminated by street lamps as dusk edged in. Turning back to us, he shook his head to indicate nothing was out there, before mopping the puddles of water with a spare towel.

Lauren's body was heaving with sobs, her shoulders shuddering.

'Come on, let's get you dry and into pyjamas,' I said gently, easing her up. I couldn't understand what had happened. I didn't believe in ghosts, although we were both haunted by what had happened in the cottage. Whatever Lauren was experiencing had to be some kind of post-traumatic stress, the reality of what we'd endured, the prolonged strain of what my mother had suffered finally hitting her.

Lauren refused to sleep alone and drifted off on my lap as Josh and I sat on the sofa, a comedy played on the television neither of us were in the mood for. We'd sobered up quickly, the buoyant atmosphere of earlier dissipated. We talked in hushed tones, and watched as she twitched, eyelids fluttering, sleep fitful.

'It's finally caught up with her, all what happened with Mum. I should never have exposed her to it,' I admitted, eyes stinging with oncoming tears.

'Hey, you did the best you could, Shel, you managed the situation. You looked after your mum and raised one hell of a little girl at the same time.'

'I didn't have a choice,' I whispered, letting the tears fall.

Josh wrapped his arm around me, pulling me into his chest as Lauren shifted. I ran a palm across my face, brushing the tears away.

'I'm just glad it's over,' I sighed, stroking Lauren's thick hair. After what we'd been through with Mum, I'd never let anyone hurt us again.

12

On Sunday morning, the mystery of the bell was solved as Lauren and I took Teddy for his early walk. Josh was still snoozing on the sofa, his mouth hanging open, and I had to refrain from taking a photo. We'd got up early. Lauren had slept in my bed and fidgeted all night. At seven, I'd thrown some clothes on, to get Teddy out before breakfast, when Lauren had asked to come with me. She'd never been clingy before, but she still seemed anxious after last night, so I agreed, figuring the exercise would do us both good.

As soon as we stepped outside, I heard the tinkle of a bell. Lauren froze, her body rigid as though she'd seen a ghost. The chime continued, a gentle but erratic tune, and I let Teddy pull me down the driveway to follow the sound. As I peered around the hedge into Valerie's front garden, I saw a wind chime swaying in the breeze, dangling from a bracket intended for a flowered basket by the front door.

'Lauren, come see,' I called, smiling as she shuffled down the drive towards me. 'Look, that's what you heard last night. Nothing to be scared of,' I reassured her. Our bathroom window was at the front of the house and the noise must have floated up.

Lauren didn't look convinced, and she didn't say much during our walk despite my coaxing. We walked out of Beech Close and down towards the park. The sky was a cloudy grey, but the breeze gentle. The weather had promised sun later, but I wasn't convinced it would appear.

'There's another one of those posters,' Lauren said as we reached the large playing field and I let Teddy off the lead to stretch his legs.

Another missing poster for Barney had been taped to the bin at the entrance. I nodded, walking on, but Lauren lingered.

'This one looks newer,' she called, commenting on how little the paper had weathered before running to catch up.

'It's sheltered a little by the fence,' I explained.

We'd brought a tennis ball with us and threw it so Teddy could have a good run around. The field was empty, bar one other dog owner who stayed at the opposite end, and Lauren took the opportunity to go on the swing in the playpark. I circled the fence with Teddy. There was nothing like a good walk in the morning to blow out the cobwebs, although I was looking forward to the warmer weather.

'We better get back for Josh,' I said eventually, my stomach calling for breakfast.

Lauren hopped off the swing and we walked back the way we came.

'Do you think Nanny is at peace now?' Lauren rarely talked about Mum, so I was taken aback by her raising the subject. I knew I'd been right about it being on my daughter's mind.

'Definitely,' I replied, watching relief spread across Lauren's features.

Despite my answer, she remained quiet on the way back, deep in thought.

As we entered the close, Teddy headed straight for the green and the beech tree, pulling me along.

Derek was drying his freshly washed car with a cloth, buffing it to a perfect shine. I smiled and waved, surprised when he walked over to join us.

'Hello, Shelly, and who might this be?' He beamed down at Lauren, and I remembered him telling me he used to be the head-master of a primary school. You could tell he had a way with kids as Lauren introduced herself and Teddy, answering all Derek's questions about the dog as he lowered himself onto one knee to pet him. I looked on, smiling, and Derek winked as he got to his feet.

'Do you miss it? Being at school?' I asked Derek.

'Of course he does, silly,' Lauren said knowingly before chasing Teddy around the tree.

Derek raised his wayward eyebrows. 'Out the mouths of babes, eh?' he chuckled.

'Did the person who lived at number three before me have children?' I asked, thinking about the message in the airing cupboard and who the author could be.

'No, she wasn't here long.' Derek paused before continuing, 'She had a dog though,' he volunteered.

Had Valerie driven her out because she'd had a dog? The idea was absurd; the woman, whoever she was, could have left for any number of reasons and I didn't believe it was because of victimisation from her elderly neighbor.

'Well, it's lovely to see you again, Derek. I better get these two inside for breakfast.'

Derek gave me a nod and waved as he headed back to his car. His friendliness lifted my spirits; if only he lived next door, he'd be the perfect neighbor.

'There was me thinking you'd have a cooked breakfast ready,' I chided Josh when we came through the front door. He was still on the sofa, rubbing the sleep from his eyes.

'I cooked dinner last night, you cheeky minx, what more do you want.'

'Some wife you turned out to be,' I retorted, winking at Lauren, who giggled, used to mine and Josh's banter.

I put the kettle on and told Josh about the wind chime as Lauren fed Teddy his kibble. He rubbed at the crick in his neck from sleeping on a sofa too small for his heavy frame. Trying to fold his enormous body onto a small three-seater that was not made for sleeping on.

'What are you doing today?' I asked Josh as we sipped steaming hot coffee.

'Like I don't do the same thing every Sunday?' Josh pulled a face.

'Mum's roast, of course. I forgot it was Sunday for a second there.'

'Not all of us have two weeks off work, you lucky thing. You could always come with me, you know. Mum would love to see you, and Lauren of course.' Josh eyed me expectantly, but before I could speak, Lauren cut in.

'I want to go around the green later on my scooter.'

'I'm probably going to spend the day finishing unpacking, getting things straight, you know,' I said, apologetically.

'Oh sure, of course.' He waved me away.

'I'll text you about Ikea though,' I said, reminding him of our plan for one day next week.

'Definitely, let me know.'

I toasted crumpets for breakfast and made sure Josh ate before he left, thanking him for all of his help yesterday. Once he'd gone, I unpacked anything we hadn't already got to. There wasn't too much, and after a couple of hours I had a neat stack of packing boxes on the driveway to return to the movers. My office had piles of files and software on the carpet. The laptop left in the corner, where the desk was going to go. Having my own office was going to be a luxury and I had visions of the shelves I'd put up, the pretty pinboards and storage boxes. Somewhere I wouldn't be embarrassed to switch on my camera for a meeting over Zoom. Hopefully it would be somewhere to inspire.

The office overlooked the back garden, a pleasant view of tall sycamore trees shot up from the abandoned railway line. I could also see into Valerie's garden. She was on her knees turning over the soil of a flower bed. Teddy and I had barely been in the garden since I'd found the chocolate. I was waiting for her to cool off before risking antagonising her again.

Lauren made me hang some photos in her room, mostly of us, two of Teddy. I displayed her most recent school photo downstairs on the fireplace and hung the canvas over the mantelpiece with tough sticky pads so I wouldn't have to mark the freshly painted walls. I'd brought a couple of cushions and a throw with us, draping it on the sofa. With some of our trinkets on show, the place was more homely than yesterday. I had a list as long as my arm of what I needed to buy, but Mum's money remained untouched in her bank account, other than what I'd used to pay the rent up front on number three Beech Close. It was more money than I'd ever had access to before, Mum had been squirrelling it away for years, spending only what she had to. We'd lived on a shoestring budget, with her counting every penny. However, it didn't feel like mine to spend. I was the only family she had, but it felt wrong to take something I hadn't earned, something Mum wouldn't have given willingly.

13

'Can I go outside on my scooter now?' Lauren asked.

'Put on a cardigan first,' I replied, knowing it wasn't warm enough for the T-shirt and leggings Lauren had chosen to wear. The sun had come out as promised, but the air was still cool.

Outside, I grabbed the flattened boxes I'd leant against the house and tucked them neatly between the bin and the hedge, hoping it wouldn't rain before they could be collected.

Lauren whizzed around the pavement, the wheels of her yellow scooter rattling on the concrete. Beech Close was quiet, the Sunday early-afternoon lull perfect for a long walk or curling up on the sofa with a book. I swept the driveway to keep myself occupied whilst keeping an eye on Lauren, then emptied out the rubbish which had accumulated in my car.

When I'd finished, Lauren showed no signs of wanting to come in. Round and round she went, slowing when she got to Derek's house as if hoping he'd come outside and entertain her again. It was times like that I felt guilty she was an only child. It was sad Sebastian hadn't stuck around long enough to give me another child, or even be a father. Although being a single parent was hard enough with one, let alone two, and I knew now that Sebastian never intended to make an honest woman of me.

He'd made no effort to contact Lauren and build a relationship, sending money through every six months or so until she was around six and then it stopped altogether. I assumed he'd had another family to feed, conveniently forgetting about his first child. He had changed his number and moved out of the area. To be honest, I was glad not to bump into him. Despite the lack of maintenance, I believed we'd got off lightly. He would have been the type to promise Lauren the world and not deliver. This way, her heart wouldn't get repeatedly broken when he didn't show up to collect her or if he forgot her birthday.

Pushing Sebastian from my mind, I loitered on the driveway, not wanting to leave Lauren outside by herself. Visions of her being thrown into a white van and on the motorway in minutes plagued me. I always had to keep her in sight, keep her safe. As I repositioned the bin, I noticed the small box of junk Josh had brought down from the loft. I hadn't paid much attention to the contents, but as I had nothing better to do while Lauren circled the close, I sat on the doorstep and rooted through.

Inside was a folded local newspaper from the first week of November last year, the front page showing pictures taken from the local Shocktober Fest at Tulley's Farm, where residents paid for an evening of Halloween scares. It wasn't obvious as to why it had been kept and I scanned the photos on the front and names beneath, although nothing jumped out at me.

I reached inside the box to see what else there was, pulling out a battered copy of *The Wasp Factory* by Iain Banks, which looked like it had been a favourite read. I ran my thumb over the pages, skimming the edge, when a slip of paper fell out of the middle into my lap. I turned it over in my hands, a receipt from the local pet shop. A 2.5kg bag of Canagan adult dog food had been purchased on the tenth of December. I slipped the receipt back inside the book and returned it to the box, this time retrieving a hand-knitted bright orange scarf coiled at the bottom. Wrapped inside was a small blank envelope which contained a photo of a couple. A woman had her head resting on the shoulder of a man outside a fountain. Both of them smiling into the camera, squinting in the sun. She was pretty, blonde hair in tight corkscrew curls, her smile was wide and infectious. The man's grin wasn't as sincere, and it looked like he was about to roll his eyes when the photo was taken. He had his arm loosely around the woman's waist, black sunglasses rested on top of his shaven head. At the bottom of the envelope was a necklace, a silver infinity symbol on a delicate chain, the clasp broken. I put them both to the side.

The last item in the box was a man's watch, dark spots stained the tan leather strap, which looked suspiciously like blood or maybe oil. It was a strange array of items to keep hold of. Had they been left behind by the last occupant? Had the owner of number three Beech Close boxed them up with the intention of forwarding them on and perhaps not got around to it? Puzzled, I turned my attention back to Lauren, who I could no longer see nor hear from the doorstep.

Jumping up, I jogged to the end of the driveway, relief flooding through me when I spotted her the other side of the beech tree. She was talking to a man I assumed was Derek, but as I got closer, off the driveway and across the road, I didn't recognise him at all. The hair on the back of my neck stood to attention and I quickened my pace, trying to catch what my daughter was saying to this stranger.

'Excuse me, can I help you,' I said, rounding the tree to find my daughter handing the man a daisy chain she'd made.

'This is Finn,' she smiled at me, her face a picture of innocence.

The man, a sandy-haired stocky unit who was easily twice the size of me smiled sheepishly. 'Sorry, yes, I'm Finn. Lauren was telling me you've moved into number three.'

I continued to frown at him, folding my arms across my chest.

'I'm Niamh's husband,' he explained, his voice throaty. My cheeks coloured – of course, we hadn't met at the drinks she'd organised.

'Sorry, yes, you were working when Niamh invited me over. I'm Shelly,' I said, softening my voice.

'Welcome to Beech Close,' he said, as if it was a prepared statement for whoever entered the cul-de-sac. It amused me, as though I was being ordained into a cult.

'Shelly, hi!' Niamh strode over, a shawl over her shoulders, silver earrings swinging from her ears. I almost did a double take. She'd tried to cover it with make-up, but it was obvious Niamh had a black eye. The whites around her sky-blue eyes looked bloodshot, especially the bruised one.

'We're off to Tenerife for a few days, getting away before Easter, you know.' She saw me staring and looked away, fussing with her hair.

I opened my mouth to speak, but closed it again. What would I say? I hardly knew her well enough to pry.

'Are you going on a plane?' Lauren asked, twiddling the daisy chain Finn had given back to her.

'We are,' Finn replied.

'I haven't been on one,' Lauren said, grimacing, and my face flushed again.

'We will, poppet. Now we don't have to look after Nanny, we can go wherever you like,' I said, trying to convey it was circumstances as opposed to money as to why Lauren hadn't yet been abroad.

It was a lie. We hadn't had enough for a weekend in Worthing, let alone a trip to the Canary Islands. I hadn't paid rent living with Mum but contributed to the bills and the food, and I'd managed to save a little, even with the reduced hours I was working. Mum had taken up almost all of my time when I wasn't with Lauren. It was cheap living but had come at the cost of our sanity at times. Now we did have the money for a holiday. Perhaps we'd go Whitsun half-term for a week ahead of the summer rush. I could book something as a surprise and whisk Lauren away. The idea already formulating in my mind.

'Oh I'm sorry, that must have been hard,' Niamh said, linking her arm through Finn's, her expression one of genuine sympathy, which made my throat tighten.

Before I could speak, Lauren piped up.

'She had a bell, and she would ring and ring and ring and ring...' she explained, shaking her head for dramatic effect, so Finn laughed despite himself.

'That's enough, Lauren. Niamh and Finn have got a plane to catch. We don't want to keep them.' I pulled Lauren into me, squeezing her tight to distract her from volunteering too much information. I still found it difficult to talk about Mum.

'Yes we better be off. Lovely to meet you finally,' Finn said, already turning away, his arm around Niamh's shoulders, maybe a little too tightly.

'You too. Oh and thanks again for the drinks, Niamh, really lovely of you to invite me to meet everyone,' I called to their retreating backs.

'Any time. You're one of us now,' she called over her shoulder, her voice as cold as a winter's morning.

14

Niamh's words played on my mind all afternoon, not to mention her black eye. I didn't want to be *one of them*. Whatever that was? Her phrase seemed innocent enough, but her tone had an edge to it. One I couldn't put my finger on. The residents of Beech Close had been welcoming. I'd met all of them within two days of moving in, most of them friendly with the exception of Valerie, but perhaps it was to be expected since Becky had enlightened me on her condition and Teddy had crapped on her lawn before we'd even been introduced.

According to Derek, the woman before me hadn't lived in the house for long. I guessed it was her belongings in the loft. The receipt for dog food supporting my theory. Derek said she had no children but did have a dog. Was she the one who had scratched *LEAVE NOW* into the wall of the airing cupboard? But why?

Curiosity plagued me – why had the previous resident moved on? Had she been hounded out by Valerie? If she had, why would she leave her scarf and necklace behind? The contents of the box, which I'd brought back inside on returning to the house didn't feel like lost items. They felt like keepsakes, and the idea, however ridiculous, made my stomach churn.

Once Lauren was in bed, much more settled since discovering the wind chime was the source of the noise she'd heard, I dug through the rental agreement I'd signed to see if I could get a name for the owner of 3 Beech Close.

Unfortunately, the contract I'd signed was with the estate agent who managed the rental agreement. If I had any problems with the plumbing or electrics, I contacted them directly, not the landlord. It wasn't unusual to pay for a company to manage the letting. It saved you from being bothered with calls about leaking roof tiles or damp patches in the ceiling. Perhaps the estate agents would be able to give me the name of the owner if I called and asked tomorrow. They wouldn't be answering their phones on a Sunday night.

Lauren had laid out our plans for the next day already, she wanted to go to the cinema to see the sequel to *Sonic the Hedgehog*, but I was sure it was really a ruse for an extortionately priced bag of pick and mix. Seeing as I'd given her free rein for the Easter holidays, I was happy to chill in the comfy seats and shovel in popcorn for a couple of hours if it kept her entertained. It was going to be the first day of her break, and with the unpacking finished, I wanted us to have fun while I was off work.

I curled into the sofa, giving in to the temptation to check my emails on my phone, whilst a cup of camomile tea grew cold beside me. I had two administrative contracts I was managing side by side, and despite being on holiday, I liked to keep my eye on things. I knew one of the other contractors from the agency was covering my leave, but I'd been burnt from previous experiences. The last thing I wanted was to come back to everything in a mess. I'd built a good relationship with my clients, which is why they repeatedly asked for me when they needed someone on a short-term basis.

Halfway through checking a spreadsheet requested by a market research company I supported, a loud thud hit the window behind me. I leapt off the sofa, knocking over the mug of lukewarm tea, and turned around to see a pair of eyes staring through the darkness back at me. Cupped hands pressed against the glass, white skin practically iridescent in contrast to the backdrop. Shrieking, I staggered back, trying to place the person peering into my front room. Then they were gone, a silver streak whisking past the window.

I raced to the front door, heart pounding, and threw it open, yelping when Valerie almost fell inside. Her mouth was twisted into a snarl, she looked wild, hair loose and flailing in the wind. She wore a white floor-length nightgown which billowed around her legs, feet bare on the driveway.

'Get out, get out, get out,' she hissed as I froze, open-mouthed, unable to utter a response. Valerie flung out a wrinkly hand to grab me and I tensed, waiting for her touch, but it never came.

'Mum!' Remy stormed down the driveway, grabbing her by the shoulders and dragging her away as if she was a rag doll. 'I'm so sorry,' he called over his shoulder as my muscles slackened and I melted onto the floor.

I couldn't speak, unable to formulate the words, staring after them until they disappeared around the hedge and out of sight. Beneath the sound of the wind chime going crazy, I could hear Remy's reprimanding and the slamming of Valerie's front door.

Eventually, I pushed the door closed with my foot and went and drew the curtains. The imprint of Valerie's face squashed against the glass remained until I blocked it out. Adrenaline rocketed around my system as I tried to process what had just happened. Had Valerie come to attack me? Threaten me and my daughter? She'd looked like a ghost at the window, frightening me half to death. My heart was still racing, refusing to slow.

When Becky said Valerie had danced around the beech tree in her nightgown, I'd imagined this ethereal creature, gown flowing as she pranced, but what had arrived at my door had been almost otherworldly. Valerie couldn't have looked more different from the woman I'd met two days ago, the perfectly poised ice queen had been a witch from a fairy tale tonight.

I got a cloth to wipe the spillage and left my mug in the sink. Goosebumps covered my arms, and I couldn't shake off the chill which sank into my bones. Had it been a mistake to move here? Had I made a rash decision in haste to get out of the cottage? So desperate to rid myself of the memories I'd leapt out of the frying pan and into the fire?

Listening at the bottom of the stairs for any movement and hearing nothing, I was grateful Lauren had slept through my shrieking. I put the kettle on to make another cup of tea, this one to calm my nerves, when I heard a subdued tap at the door. Not the door knocker, but the rapping of knuckles instead. I stiffened, straining my ears in case I'd imagined the sound, but another tap came, and I knew someone was outside. Was Valerie back? My scalp prickled as I tried to calm my racing pulse. She couldn't be back again, could she?

I pulled the curtain aside tentatively and peered out, only to see Remy at the front door, inspecting his shoes as he waited for his knocking to be answered. Instantly relieved, I ran my fingers through my fringe, glad I hadn't yet resorted to changing into my pyjamas. He didn't notice me looking through the window and seemed resigned to the fact I wouldn't open the door. When I did, his eyes widened, mouth turned down in a grimace.

'Shelly, I'm so sorry about that. I had to come and apologise.' He clasped his hands together beneath his chin, as though he was praying for my forgiveness. The same hands that had roughly grabbed his mother less than ten minutes before.

'Is Valerie okay?' I said, my voice sounding hollow as it left my throat, whisked away by the wind.

'Can I come in, I'll explain everything?'

15

Remy's knees cracked when he lowered himself into the chair at the kitchen table and I loitered by the kettle, waiting for it to boil.

'Do you have anything stronger?' he asked and for a second I assumed he was joking until I saw his weary expression.

'Jack Daniel's?' I replied, reaching for the bottle I kept in one of the high cupboards, out of Lauren's way, and setting it on the table, returning to the fridge to get ice from the freezer drawer.

I flicked off the kettle which had already begun to whistle and joined Remy, pushing a glass tumbler towards him. He did the honours while I studied his face, the crow's feet around his eyes and the greying sideburns which only served to make him look more distinguished. I aged him at around early forties, sure he had maybe ten years on me. His skin looked weathered, as though he worked outside in all elements. Nails bitten to the quick, but clean hands wrapped around his glass.

'My mother,' he sighed, as if he didn't know where to begin, 'she's got worse over the past few months. Sometimes she fine, she's lucid and knows who everyone is, but then other times...' he

trailed off, shaking his head, and taking a mouthful of the bourbon, wincing. I did the same, gullet burning as it slid down.

'My mother had it too, so I understand. It's tough to watch
someone you love slowly deteriorate.'

'The nights are the worse, I've had to practically move back in.
It's not the first time she's been out,' he paused, giving his head a
tiny shake. 'Wait, I'm sorry, did you say your mother had it too?'

'She did, she passed away last month, but I cared for her for
two years and it's no picnic,' I said.

His shoulders visibly sagged, and I cursed my honesty.

'Don't worry about tonight, she gave me a scare, that's all.'

'I don't know what's got into her,' he sighed, rubbing his forehead with his left hand, and I noticed the absence of a wedding
ring.

'They call it sundowning.'

'What's sundowning?' he asked, a fork appearing between his
eyes.

'When dementia sufferers get agitated in the afternoon or
evening. They can get confused about the time, the light fading,
it's weird, but it affects them. My mother used to wander around,
down to the shop or randomly knock at the neighbors. Eventually,
we locked her in, so she couldn't get out, but she used to scratch at
the door or wail continually. It frightened my daughter, Lauren.
Mum was easier once I locked the front and back door, but she
roamed the house at night, ringing a bloody bell until I hid it.' I
stared off into the distance, the memory of those nights flooding
back until Remy reached across and softly touched my arm.

'You okay? You went somewhere then.' He moved his hand
away as our eyes met, and I blushed, taking another drink, the
warmth from his fingers evaporating.

'Memories,' I explained, twirling a strand of hair between my
fingertips.

'Mum didn't wake your daughter, did she?' Remy asked, turning around to look towards the hallway as if Lauren might suddenly appear. It was half past nine, early for some kids, I guessed, especially in the holidays, but like me, Lauren loved her sleep.

'No, she's a heavy sleeper that one,' I replied.

A few awkward seconds passed between us. Remy drained his glass, and I noticed the sleeve of his T-shirt was stretched, like it had been gripped or pulled in a tussle. Was Valerie getting heavy-handed with her son?

'Well, it's good to know I'm not alone in this. It's... isolating. My mother can be,' he paused again, 'difficult sometimes.'

I appreciated he was choosing his words carefully. I didn't want to chip in and say, despite the dementia, his mother was an evil old bag who'd tried to poison my dog. That was something I wouldn't be able to get past, but Remy had enough on his plate.

'Is your dad around?' I asked.

Remy shook his head. 'No, he passed away eight years ago, prostate cancer.'

'I'm sorry,' I said, looking down into my glass.

'I apologise if you feel she's harassing you. I heard about the dog mess incident,' Remy said.

'It's fine, perhaps Teddy and I will give Valerie a wide berth. Seriously though, if you need anything, practical advice or to offload, feel free to visit.' My voice rose and I knew my neck was mottled, partly from the bourbon and partly because Remy was looking directly into my eyes. Teddy's head lifted from his basket, his ears cocked after hearing his name.

I swallowed, my mouth dry, taking the opportunity to break eye contact and finish my bourbon too. I hated it neat but didn't want to be seen as weak for having mine with Coke.

'Thanks, Shelly, it's good of you, considering. I'm sorry about tonight. I need to get better security measures in place. She's sneaky, you know, getting out when my back is turned.' Remy stood to leave, and I showed him to the door.

As I pulled it open, the heel of my slipper caught the box of stuff I'd found in the loft. I nudged it to one side out of the way.

The wind howled, and I shuddered involuntarily as Remy stepped onto the driveway.

'Some spring, eh?' I joked.

'Hopefully it should warm up soon,' Remy said, rocking back on his heels.

'Hopefully,' I agreed, leaning against the door frame and crossing my arms.

He was taking a long time to leave, as though he didn't want to go back home at all. He looked drained and I noticed the dark circles beneath his eyes in the unflattering glow of the security light.

'Sorry again, for my mother.'

'No problem. Let me know if you need anything. We're neighbors after all,' I said, watching his mouth twitch, a smile almost forming. He gave a quick nod and left.

Back inside, I poured another Jack Daniel's, swirling the liquid around in my glass. Why was I so awkward around Remy, he put me on edge, although I wasn't sure why? He was attractive, sure, but I had so many questions I wanted to ask him. Was he married, or had he been? Did he have any children? What did he do for a living? I knew nothing about him and despite myself I wanted to know more.

Clearly Remy had a lot on his plate with Valerie. Was he like me and had no siblings to share the load? It was isolating, he was right. Being a carer was a lonely place to be, but I'd offered help, even if it was only having somewhere to come and vent, to someone who knew what he was going through. Dementia had the ability to change a person until they were a shadow of who they were previously. Had Valerie been a loving mother, one he was already grieving for? Or was she like mine, bitter her life hadn't been different? Taking out her resentment on those closest to her.

Dementia hadn't turned my mother into a monster. She'd already been that before the disease took what was left.

Lauren was awake early, excited it wasn't a school day. She'd been playing Roblox online with her friends since around seven o'clock and wasn't overly impressed when I dragged her out to take a turn around the green with Teddy. He needed to do his business and stretch his legs and I wasn't at a point where I was happy to let him go in the back garden unattended. Who knew what Valerie would do next? I wouldn't put it past her to chuck some razor blades hidden in cocktail sausages over the fence for him to feast on.

'I don't see why I had to come, we're only on the green. You could have left me at home. I could have watched you from your bedroom window,' Lauren said, flinging her arm towards the house.

'Because I like the company,' I lied, not wanting to admit it was so I could ensure she was safe. The last thing I wanted was for her to feel uneasy in her new home, and I didn't want to leave her inside alone. She hadn't mentioned seeing Nanny since I'd shown her the wind chime, and I was sure it had been her imagination and nothing more, but I didn't want to tempt fate. In a matter of days, the exchange of contracts on my mother's house would go through and we could put those difficult years behind us. Although, if Valerie was going to keep causing problems and scaring the living daylights out of us, our time at Beech Close would be short-lived. All I wanted for Lauren, and I, was an easy life. Having said that, I wasn't going to bullied out by an old lady, dementia or not. Perhaps I should have more sympathy, but there was something about Valerie that didn't sit right with me.

Keeping her house in view, we did two laps of Beech Close and two further circuits of the green in the centre. All was quiet at number four. However, we saw Leo leave for work in his shiny silver BMW, waving as he passed. Derek came out too, dragging his bins to the end of the driveway, gesturing to me it was bin day. I nodded and stuck my thumb up gratefully. My recycling bin was full to the brim with brown paper after unpacking, so I was pleased I wouldn't have to wait long for it to be emptied.

On our way back, our neighbor on the other side, Maxwell, climbed into the MX5, which looked too small for his large frame. His stomach was practically touching the steering wheel. He awarded us a begrudging smile as he pulled away. I waved before turning to Lauren and rolling my eyes.

'That looks like a mid-life crisis car if I've ever seen one,' I said.

'Shelly,' Becky called, and I turned back to see her standing in the open doorway, clutching a mug of something hot. She'd come out to see off her husband in fluffy slippers and dressing gown, her hair piled on top of her head and secured with a scrunchie.

'Oh hi, Becky,' I called back, hoping she hadn't heard my slight on Maxwell.

She beckoned me over and I pulled Teddy towards the house. He'd become distracted sniffing something underneath our hedge and I could tell he wanted to go back inside.

'How are you?' I asked, knowing she was well on her way to

getting smashed on Saturday over at Niamh's when I left. I bet she had the mother of all hangovers yesterday.

'Good, thank you. I need to get ready, I've got a meeting at nine, online thankfully, but I can't get motivated this morning.' She chuckled.

'We can't all be morning people,' I offered, although Becky looked fresh-faced and glowing without make-up on. I could hardly pretend I looked that good just out of bed.

'Quite!' she agreed.

'This is Lauren, and Teddy,' I said as Becky bent to give Teddy a pat on the head. He'd wandered right up to the doorstep in case there were any treats on offer.

'Hi, Lauren.' Becky waved and Lauren waved back, her cheeks pink as she loitered at the edge of the driveway before venturing forward to join us. 'I'm glad I've seen you, I wondered if you'd stop by later and give me a run through what you offer admin wise. I'm out and about so much now, I've been campaigning for a PA, but perhaps they'll agree to me having support on an ad-hoc basis if the price is right.'

'Of course, I have a presentation I can fly through, show you what I've done for some clients.' Immediately, my voice morphed into posh work mode, and I cringed at the change. I didn't want Becky to think I was mimicking her.

'Fab, around three, is that okay?'

Lauren tugged at my arm, her face like thunder. I hesitated, remembering we had plans.

'Actually, we're going to the cinema after lunch, but I can come when we get back, if that's any good?'

'Of course, no problem. I'll see you then.'

We said our goodbyes and Lauren's scowl turned into a smile as we rounded the bordering hedge and back home.

'I wasn't going to ditch our date at the cinema,' I teased, but Lauren raised one eyebrow, she knew better.

* * *

A few hours later, we were in a dark and slightly chilly cinema watching Sonic, a bright blue hedgehog on a quest for an emerald. That was the most I'd got out of the plot before my mind wandered back to Niamh's black eye. I hoped the injury had an innocent explanation and Niamh wasn't suffering at the hands of a violent husband. You never knew what went on behind closed doors and often victims refused to talk.

Lauren was oblivious to my worries, she was wrist-deep in her pick and mix bag, chewing a strawberry bon-bon furiously. Despite it costing me seven quid and the bag only being half full, I was pleased she was happy. I didn't have a lot of time for the cinema; whenever I went to see anything, I'd always fall asleep.

Knowing it was either freezing or boiling inside the screen, depending on which one you got, I always wore layers. I shuffled down and lifted the hood of my sweatshirt over my head, burying into it for warmth. Lauren was oblivious as I closed my eyes for a second to doze. Trying to ignore the loud whizzing noise the hedgehog made every time it moved. What seemed like a minute later, Lauren was nudging my elbow, embarrassed as the lights had come on and people were starting to leave.

'Has it finished already?' I said, wiping the corner of my mouth.

'Yes! Really, Mum, can't you stay awake for one movie?' Lauren said, admonishing me.

'Was it good?' I asked and Lauren give me a rundown of the plot as the screen began to empty. I stretched, waiting for my legs to come back to life.

On the way back to the car, I checked my phone for messages. I had a photo through of a torso from Josh, another proposed Grindr date, asking me for my opinion. I shook my head in mock despair as I replied.

What do you want me to say…? I can't see his face!

There was also a voicemail from Ebony, my solicitor, who had called to let me know everything was lined up for exchange of contracts on Saturday, the buyers had pressed for a weekend. They had the funds ready, and it was just a case of pushing the button. I called Ebony back as we climbed into the car, listening to the phone ring repeatedly.

As I'd already moved out, there wasn't much left to do, only the larger furniture items I hadn't dealt with yet. There was a huge bookcase, and a pine dresser I hadn't dismantled, as well as an antique chest which had to be solid oak. It was ridiculously heavy, with ornate carvings, an heirloom Mum had received when her parents died. It lived at the end of her bed and was used to store blankets and bedding. Whenever I was naughty, she would lock me in it, leaving me there for hours while she went about her business downstairs. I'd stare through the crack, waiting to be released, my limbs folded in tight, muscles cramping so I'd be in agony.

It wasn't until I was older, and had Lauren, that I understood how barbaric the punishment was. I couldn't bear to look at the chest and didn't want it in my house. It was another memory I'd be happy to leave behind. The sooner contracts were exchanged, and the cottage belonged to someone else, the better.

17

When Ebony finally answered, a little out of breath, I asked her to offer the remaining items of furniture to the buyers should they want them. It was a little late in the day, but if not, I'd give them to the Alzheimer's Society. It would be easier for me if I didn't have to organise the removal, so I'd happily let them stay even though they weren't on the initial fixtures and fittings list. If I'd thought about it properly, I could have got Arthur, the delivery man, to take them away but I was so desperate to get out of there and into Beech Close I'd overlooked the opportunity. Ebony said she'd relay the message and get back to me. I'd keep my fingers crossed I wouldn't have to go back to the cottage.

I let Lauren out in the garden with Teddy to run around in the sunshine. It had warmed up and was one of those days where inside was colder than outside. I did a quick circuit of the garden to check nothing had been thrown onto the lawn or into the flower beds, but it was all clear.

Lauren used the opportunity to list the things she wanted me to buy for the garden and where she intended on putting them.

She reeled off various pieces of play equipment: a climbing frame, and a slide, despite us only having agreed on a swing.

'We'll see,' I laughed. 'Chuck the ball for Teddy, would you?'

I went back inside and stuck the kettle on to make a cup of tea. The small bag of popcorn I'd had at the cinema had left me thirsty. Opening the window to let in the spring air, I watched Lauren chase Teddy, giggling as he jumped and scrambled over her when she fell.

'I presume you don't want a snack. Still stuffed with sweets?' I called, and Lauren patted her stomach. She'd eaten the entire bag of pick and mix, so I wasn't surprised. Once in a while it wouldn't do any harm. We could have a late dinner, roasted vegetable pasta or something easy to throw together where I could attempt to get a couple of her five-a-day into her.

While Lauren was out of earshot, I called the letting agent who managed number 3 Beech Close and was put through to a nasally woman who sounded like she had a cold.

'Hi, I'm Shelly Lucas, I live at number 3 Beech Close. I believe you manage the property?' I didn't know why I was asking the question. I knew they did. I'd signed the contract with them.

'We do, how may we help you today?'

'I wondered if you could tell me who owns the property?' I might as well get straight to the point.

'I'm afraid we're unable to give out that information due to GDPR rules. Are there any problems with the property you wish to report?'

'No. Although, I don't suppose you can give me the name of the previous tenant, could you?' I asked, chancing my arm.

'Afraid not,' she replied brusquely.

'If you could let the owner know I've found a box of things in the loft, I believe from the previous tenant. I could drop them in to your office perhaps, for you to forward on?'

'Of course, that would be fine,' the nasally woman replied, seeming in a hurry to end the call.

'Okay, thanks for your help,' I said, hanging up. I wasn't overly surprised they wouldn't give me a name, I guessed it was standard practice. The whole point of a letting service was to keep your tenant at arm's length. For now, I'd hold on to the box Josh had discovered in the loft and see if I could find out who the contents belonged to. If I couldn't, then I'd take it to the letting agent so it could be passed on.

I booted up my laptop as I drank my tea, to familiarise myself with the presentation I was going to show Becky. I hadn't needed to present to any clients in a while. Most of the work came through the agency I subscribed to, but if Becky was interested, I could invoice her directly and it would cut out the middleman. The contract I had for the market research company was coming up for renewal, which meant I could wind it down and take on more work. It all depended on how I gelled with Becky, if I believed she was someone I could work with. The fact we were neighbors could be both a positive and a negative.

'Lauren, I'm going to pop round and see Becky, can you put your shoes on and come with me?' They were still in the garden, messing around with a rope toy, playing tug of war. Teddy always refused to let go, but Lauren was stronger and determined to win.

'Okay,' she panted.

'Lauren, make sure Teddy comes in with you, okay? Don't leave him alone out there.' I hesitated, fiddling with the strap on my laptop bag.

She rolled her eyes and came back inside, Teddy at her heels. I knew my overprotectiveness annoyed her – if it wasn't her, it was the dog – but she was only ten years old. Ten going on twenty-one sometimes.

As I stepped out of the front door, I spotted Valerie at the end of the driveway. She wore a wide-brimmed sun hat and gardening gloves with an oversized white shirt which reminded me of the nightdress she'd had on yesterday. I watched her for a second, listening to her humming as she clipped the hedge dividing our properties. Steeling myself, I walked towards her, hoping it wouldn't be awkward, but I had to remember she wasn't a well woman.

'Hello, Valerie, how are you today?'

She turned and looked at me, raising a solitary eyebrow, but her mouth morphed into a tight smile regardless. It was the most agreeable I'd seen her, and I tried to hide my surprise. Did she have no memory of looking through my window last night?

'Quite well, thank you. How are you?'

Taken aback by her friendliness, I practically stuttered. 'Good, thank you. I will get around to doing my side of the hedge, once we're settled. I have some shears somewhere.' Everyone's hedges were perfectly manicured as though there was a gardener brought in once a month to tend to Beech Close – mine was currently the exception.

'Remy normally does it for me, but it's such a lovely day, some vitamin D will do me good.' Valerie smiled at the sky, her hand holding on to her hat. Her face was relaxed, a stark contrast to the twisted menace of her features last night. It was hard to reconcile they were the same person.

Lauren hung back, pulling the leaves from the hedge and crunching them up in her palm.

'It's good Remy looks after you,' I said, at a loss of what else to say but eager not to seem rude and negate the progress I'd made.

Valerie awarded me a withering look. 'Children are generally disappointing,' she said flatly and resumed trimming the hedge, turning her head so the large brim of her hat concealed her face.

I stood open-mouthed before taking it as my cue to leave, glad

Lauren hadn't seemed to absorb her words, still playing with the leaves. What an odd thing to say. At Niamh's soirée, she'd looked adoringly at her son. Perhaps all wasn't as amicable between them as I'd first thought?

We rounded the corner to Becky's, relieved at least one of my neighbors were normal. She opened the door looking a lot more glamorous than she had this morning, now out of her dressing gown and wearing wide-legged red trousers and a white satin blouse. I hadn't realised her auburn hair was so long. She'd straightened it and the shine made me green with envy. It was beautiful. I shook my heavy fringe, desperate for a cut, out of my eyes and tried to stand tall, rolling my shoulders back.

'Come in. Would you like a cappuccino? I've just switched the machine on.'

'Sure, that would be lovely,' I said, following her into the kitchen, which was the same size as mine. Unlike Niamh's glossy white cabinets, Becky had gone for a classic navy with wooden countertops. It was lovely. She directed me to a round stripped-back wooden table which displayed a large navy jug filled with daffodils as its centrepiece. It was homely and was much more my style than Niamh's clinical taste.

'You have a lovely home,' I said, looking back towards the lounge at the L-shaped cream leather sofa and plump colourful geometric cushions. Lauren nodded her head enthusiastically. It was great to see other people's houses, especially when they were a carbon copy of your own in layout. It allowed you to see the potential, although there wasn't much you could do when renting. The rules could be specific, even down to what colour the walls were painted.

'Thank you, we like it. The kitchen was only done last year. We had a horrible beech finish before which the house had been built with. I hated it as soon as I saw it, so bland and unoriginal and finally Maxwell got a bonus, and it was either the kitchen or a cruise. He wanted a cruise, but I put my foot down.'

I smiled, listening to the coffee machine hiss and chug as the filter coffee dripped into two mugs side by side. I wouldn't tell Becky my house still had the beech finish kitchen she despised.

'There's things I'd love to change, but I'd have to enquire with the estate agent, they can get funny when you're only renting.'

'Oh yes, I know what you mean. It's a managed letting, is it? I don't suppose you know who the landlord is?' Becky enquired, delivering a cappuccino to me, before offering Lauren a can of Diet Pepsi and sliding into the seat opposite.

'No idea,' I admitted, blowing the steam rising from the cup. I usually had sugar, but Becky hadn't offered, and I was too polite to ask.

She pulled her hair across one shoulder, raking her fingers through it before speaking. 'We've wondered, you know, it's the only house on the street that is rented, but none of us knows who owns it. It as though it's some big secret.'

I frowned, wrapping my hands around the cup. 'Oh really?' I said, my interest piquing.

'Yes, and no offence, but the tenants never stay too long – six months here, a year there. It would be nice for someone to stay, you know.'

I gave a noncommittal shrug, reaching over to slide my laptop out of my bag. Lauren fidgeted in her seat, already bored.

'Because we have no idea who is going to move in until they arrive,' Becky sighed, and I sensed that was the real issue.

Aside from Valerie, everyone had seemed so welcoming; Niamh had practically thrown me a party. But it occurred to me now, maybe it wasn't a welcome party, maybe it had been an interview?

18

I shivered, as though someone had walked over my grave. To minimise the chill, I took a sip of my cappuccino to warm me up.

'Clearly we lucked out with you of course,' Becky said with a chuckle.

I smiled, trying to ascertain if she was being sarcastic or not. She obviously hadn't relished living next to the previous tenant, with their yappy dog.

It was time to get back on track, Lauren was already glaring at me to get on with it.

'This won't take long, Becky, but I'll show you what services I offer and how I'm managing the two other clients I have at the moment.'

She leaned forward and I swivelled the laptop around as it came to life.

Less than fifteen minutes later, I'd showed her my presentation and displayed some of the work I'd done for the market research company and the hospitality suppliers I'd been contracted to help.

'Here you can see I organised their database of customers and using this programme they were available to bill them directly, ensuring the process was smoother and faster,' I said, watching as Becky nodded at the screen.

'I think you'd be a great asset. I'm looking for someone who can be a bit of a PA, look after my diary, someone to organise me. I'm out and about visiting stakeholders now.'

'What is it that you do?' I enquired.

'I'm the PR Manager and I have a small team who specialise in communications, producing web content, that kind of thing.'

'Sounds interesting,' I replied.

'Well, I can manage a team, but I'm terrible at admin, any kind of paperwork really. Maxwell has to do all the house stuff, I don't have the patience for it.' Becky giggled.

'I'm sure I'd be able to help. Shall I put together a proposal for you? How does a four-week rolling contract sound, you can show it to your boss and see if they'll agree.'

'That would be fabulous,' Becky said, draining her coffee as I closed the lid of my laptop and slipped it back into my bag, already rising from my seat and watching Lauren follow suit.

'Excellent, I'll have it to you tomorrow. Thanks for the coffee and the Pepsi. I better get back, I left Teddy on his own.' Using the dog as an excuse.

'No problem, I suppose I should start thinking about what I'm going to feed the man of the house when he gets home.' Becky rolled her eyes and pulled at the collar of her blouse as though she was desperate to change into something more comfortable. Perhaps we weren't so different after all.

'Did you like your neighbor before?' I asked Becky as she walked us to the front door, the question niggling at me.

'Danielle? Yes, she seemed nice, although she kept herself to herself, if I'm honest. The bloody dog barked all the time though. However, one minute she was here the next she was gone, but time goes so fast these days, doesn't it? We're all rushing about one hundred miles an hour.' She laughed, brushing a finger over a perfectly drawn eyebrow. 'I think Derek knew her best, he was always talking to her...' Becky's words tailed off. Derek hadn't mentioned he'd known her well. 'Shelly, are you okay?' Becky's voice jolted me from my thoughts.

'I'm fine, probably low blood sugar,' I lied. 'I haven't eaten much today. Thanks again for your time, Becky, and I'll have a proposal to you tomorrow.'

'Oh, I forgot, here's my card,' Becky said, handing me her business card. Her name, Rebecca Sumner printed in a bold italic. Her job title of PR Manager sat beneath with the blue swirly logo of Luxor Travel on the right-hand side.

'Thank you,' I said, slipping it into the laptop bag.

'Have a lovely evening,' she said before closing the door.

I squinted in the low afternoon sun as I rounded the driveway back to my house. Where had I heard Danielle's name before? It was vaguely familiar, but I couldn't place it. It seemed Becky didn't know her well, perhaps none of them had got the chance to before she moved out again. When I spoke to Derek before, he hadn't been forthcoming with information on Danielle, yet Becky said they'd talked a lot. Maybe he was miffed she'd gone so soon?

Had Valerie been behind Danielle leaving? The woman wasn't all there, and I could see how her behaviour could be scary for someone who hadn't had any dealings with dementia at all. Had she shown up at Danielle's house in the middle of the night? Shouting at her to get out? I'd ask Derek next time I saw him.

Back home, Lauren resumed playing with Teddy in the garden until he was panting, tongue hanging out.

'Can I go upstairs and play on my iPad?' Lauren got to her knees, brushing grass off her leggings when Teddy decide to take some refuge in the shade beside the fence.

'Of course, I'll do dinner for around half six.'

Lauren grimaced, obviously still not hungry after devouring sweets at the cinema. Teddy trotted inside after her and I fed him, knowing he would curl up afterwards for a nap after, having charged around the garden with Lauren.

I found my phone to call Josh, hoping he would have finished work. When he answered, I could tell I was on loudspeaker and he was in the car, traffic noise in the background.

'What did you think?' he said, instead of hello.

'Of what?'

'The bloody six-pack I sent you. He looks fitter than a butcher's dog and guess who's having drinks with him in just over an hour's time.' Josh used a sing-song voice and I giggled down the phone, having forgotten all about the semi-naked photo he'd sent me earlier.

'You're insatiable!' I laughed.

'I know, can't help myself. Anyway, how's your day been?'

'Oh, you know, *Sonic 2* at the cinema, not overly exciting.'

'Parenting win though.' I guessed it was. When Lauren was happy, so was I.

'I saw my nutty neighbor again. I think she drove out the girl who lived here before me.' The words were out before I could stop them, although I had no evidence to support the theory I'd conjured up in my head.

'I'm not surprised, she sounds like a right witch. I hope you were nice to her,' Josh said.

'Of course, killing with kindness,' I replied sarcastically.

'That stuff from the loft must be the previous tenant's. Have you been through it yet?'

'Had a quick nose. Weird, the stuff she left behind though – a necklace, a photo and a newspaper from last November.'

'Hmmm, the mystery continues. Right, I better be off, I've just got home, and I need to run through the shower.'

'Have a great time tonight and be careful,' I instructed, my mothering instinct kicking in.

'Will do, love you,' Josh said before hanging up.

Retrieving the box from the hallway, I brought it to the kitchen table and unpacked the contents, unsure why I was looking again. Something about the way Danielle had moved out so quickly unsettled me. Maybe I could find her and ask her what happened and if it had anything to do with Valerie. I didn't want history to repeat itself and forewarned was forearmed after all.

19

I cast my eyes over the items. What did I know about the previous resident of 3 Beech Close? I knew her name was Danielle, and she had a dog, which I'd found out from Derek and from the receipt from the pet shop found inside her copy of *The Wasp Factory*. I knew what she looked like – pretty, blonde curly hair and she wore an infinity necklace. The watch that may or may not have spots of blood on it likely belonged to the man in the photo, who could have been her boyfriend. Neither Derek nor Becky mentioned a man living with her, so as far as I was aware it was only her and the dog. There was always the possibility these things might not have been Danielle's at all. Although I believed she was living here at the date of the paper, Thursday 4 November.

I opened the crinkled pages of the local rag, some stuck together, and tried to absorb each news story. Why would it have been kept? I found the answer on page twenty-eight when I recognised a curly-haired blonde dressed as a witch posing beside a barrel as children bobbed for apples. The article had been written about a Halloween fayre at a nearby junior school called Green

Fields, put on to raise money to purchase shade sails for the playground. It wasn't the same school Lauren attended; this one was in walking distance of Beech Close.

Ms Danielle Stobart was named as the teacher of class 4DS who had organised the event. I had another flash of recognition, aware I'd seen the name elsewhere. The missing dog poster. I chewed at my nail, swiping my fringe away from my forehead as Teddy snored quietly from his bed. I had a burning desire to see the poster again, but it would be mean to wrench him from his slumber and drag Lauren out so soon after letting her go upstairs to play.

Instead, I busied myself cooking pasta, throwing on a roasted vegetable sauce and steaming some sweetcorn and broccoli. Even with a mound of grated cheese on top, Lauren picked at her food, but my mind was so preoccupied with Danielle, I barely noticed. If the missing dog poster was hers, it made little sense to move whilst her pet was lost. Surely you'd want to stick around in case it wandered home.

'Come on, let's take the dog out,' I said, abandoning my dinner, the bowl still half full. The dishes could wait.

'Do we have to?' Lauren groaned.

'Yes, come on. We won't be long,' I said with forced enthusiasm.

'But I've got a tummy ache.'

'A walk will help with that,' I replied, ushering Lauren out of the room to put her shoes on.

I practically marched out of Beech Close, heading for the lamp post where we'd seen the poster, although now it was nowhere to be seen. Had I got the right one?

'This was where the poster was, wasn't it?' I asked and Lauren nodded.

'There's another at the park, remember. I've got Teddy's ball,'

Lauren offered. The fresh air seemed to have perked her up, although it was likely the pull of the swings.

We headed for the park and on entering I saw the poster still flapping in the breeze. A tiny buzz fluttered in my chest. Sending Lauren into the playground, I discreetly removed the poster and stared at it. I had remembered correctly, underneath the picture of Barney the cockerpoo, the name Danielle Stobart and a phone number.

I tossed the ball for Teddy, watching him sprint away. Lauren was swinging high, singing to herself, a solitary figure inside the playground. Pulling my mobile out of my pocket, I dialled the number on the poster with no real idea what I would say to Danielle if she answered. It sounded mad, the new occupant of her old home itching to know why she'd left. How would I feel faced with the same call if I'd been the one to leave abruptly?

Teddy returned with his ball as the phone took a while to connect. I tossed it again, seeing another dog walker the other side of the field, a large dog off lead. The phone didn't even ring, jumping straight to voicemail, a cheery voice in my ear.

'It's Danielle, you know what to do.' There was a small giggle at the end, and I smiled, picturing her saying it, before hanging up in a panic as I hadn't prepared to leave a message.

Teddy brought back the ball and I rounded the fence to the playground, the opposite end to Lauren, who was swinging so high it made my heart race. I waved at her to slow down and lobbed the ball for Teddy, who was waiting patiently at my feet.

Dialling again, I cleared my throat and waited for the pre-recorded message.

'Hello, my name is Shelly and I'm living at number three Beech Close. I was hoping to speak to you. Can you call me back on this number when you get a chance? Thanks.'

The light was starting to fade, and another dog walker

appeared on the field, a fluffy shih-tzu wearing an illuminous jacket trotting beside its owner. I did one last lap outside the playground before signalling to Lauren it was time to go home. The poster was folded and tucked inside the pocket of my jeans. I didn't want Lauren asking questions as to why I had taken it.

'Who were you on the phone to?' Lauren said, bounding over, wild hair flailing behind her. She stopped and stroked Teddy, trying to retrieve the ball from his mouth.

'Just leaving a message for Josh,' I lied, pulling my phone out again and texting him with an update. I now had a phone number for Danielle, although the mystery of why she left still eluded me.

Beech Close was quiet when we returned. Valerie stood at her bedroom window, brushing her silvery hair which was almost down to her waist. I smiled and waved, but her blank expression didn't change, she stared straight through me. There was no sign of Remy, or the white Mercedes I'd come to recognise as his on the driveway.

'Sundowning,' I muttered to myself as Lauren skipped around the tree in the centre of the green. Somewhere Teddy had to mark his territory daily, either on the way in or out of the house. Beech Close was ours now and whatever had happened with Danielle, we had to grab hold of the fresh start we'd been offered and run with it. 'Come on, let's go inside,' I said, turning to Lauren, glancing up at Valerie's window, a loud noise interrupting the peace. Air rushed from my lungs. She was no longer peacefully brushing her hair but banging her head against the glass so hard I could see it shake in its frame.

20

'Lauren, take Teddy inside quickly, here's the keys.' I chucked them at Lauren but didn't wait to see her catch them, I was already racing towards Valerie's front door. I banged on it, then knelt down, opening the letter box, and calling Valerie's name through the gap. I had to stop her before she damaged herself or put her head through the window.

'Valerie, Valerie, it's Shelly, can you let me in?' I shouted, but all I heard was the rhythmic thud of her head against the glass.

Out of desperation, I tried the handle, intending to shake the door to draw her attention, but to my surprise it opened. The handle hadn't been pulled up hard enough for the lock to catch.

Thud, thud, thud, the sounds kept coming as I raced for the stairs. Reaching Valerie's bedroom and pulling her back from the window by her shoulders, my fingers caught in her silver hair. We stumbled backwards onto the bed, and I inhaled the scent of floral perfume, like Parma Violets, as I pulled away, righting myself. Her eyes were vacant, and she seemed to have no idea I was there, a large red welt in the centre of her forehead had blossomed.

'Valerie, can you hear me?' I said, reaching out to her shoulder and giving her a small shake, trying to bring her out of her catatonic state. Her skin was papery to touch, punctuated with age spots and she seemed so like Mum, it hurt to look at her.

Valerie blinked, slowly turning her head as though she was a puppet, eventually focusing on me. I watched as her pupils shrank to pin pricks, lip trembling before she spoke.

'You're not safe,' Valerie whispered, her bony fingers locking onto my wrist in a vice-like grip.

I opened my mouth to speak, but no words came out.

'Mum!' A shout carried from downstairs, before thundering footsteps followed.

Valerie released her hold on my arm, hand dropping to her side.

'Mum, the door was open...' Remy said, rounding the stairs, before he entered the bedroom to find us there.

I spoke before he had a chance. 'I think you should call an ambulance, your mum has been bashing her head against the window,' I said, my words rushing out in quick succession. I brushed a tendril of hair out of Valerie's face, but she shook me off, recoiling from my touch.

'I most certainly have not,' came the familiar tone. Whether she remembered it or not, a large egg-shaped bump was already forming, and fingerprint smudges littered the window, illuminated by the glowing street lamp.

'I'll call them now.' Remy's face paled and he reached for his phone inside his blazer pocket, standing to put the light on and chasing the shadows away. Dusk had settled on Beech Close and all I could see in the window was mine and Valerie's reflections, the sharp edges of her shoulders protruding the silk of her dressing gown.

I experienced a pang in my chest as I thought of Mum and instinctually reached for Valerie's hand.

'Get off me,' she hissed, back to full form now. They were more alike than I'd realised.

'It's okay. As soon as Remy is back, I'll leave.'

Her lip curled upwards in a snarl. 'You're not good enough for him, you know,' her words venomous.

'Mum! That's enough,' Remy snapped, standing in the doorway and catching our conversation.

'It's fine,' I said to him. I'd had much, much worse from my own flesh and blood.

'An ambulance is on its way. Thank you, Shelly.' Remy rubbed at his stubble, and I stood to leave, slipping down the stairs as hushed angry whispers came from above. Remy berating Valerie, no doubt. Was she so bad she could no longer be left alone without harming herself? How much pressure must Remy be under?

I was numb as I opened the front door to number three, Teddy already at my feet, jumping and wagging his tale. Dealing with Valerie brought back so many memories. It was like Mum was still here, haunting me, unable to let me move on. Perhaps Valerie had driven Danielle to the point where she couldn't bear to live next door to her any more. Home was supposed to be a sanctuary, somewhere you could relax, not a place where you had to be on your guard all the time. It was enough to wear anyone down.

'Everything okay, Mum?' Lauren asked as I came into the kitchen. Bless her heart, she'd started the washing up I'd left behind when we went out to walk the dog, kneeling on a chair so she could get her arms fully in the sink. I grabbed a tea towel to help her dry.

'Thanks for washing up.' I laughed as foam spilled out from the sink and onto the worktop. 'Go easy on the bubbles next time.'

Lauren flicked some at me and before I knew it we were

engaged in a bubble fight. By the time we'd finished, the tea towel was sodden from mopping the mess we'd created.

Lauren's grin stretched wide on her face and inside I beamed, pulling her into a hug and kissing the top of her head. I was so lucky to have her, I'd never take her for granted.

She hadn't mentioned Valerie or why I'd rushed off, leaving her to look after Teddy. I didn't bring it up either and she took herself off for a long shower, singing at the top of her voice to a Korean boyband who were 'massive' apparently, although I'd never heard of them.

As I was about to remove my jeans and slip on pyjama bottoms, I saw the ambulance outside Valerie's house, surprised it had arrived so quickly considering it wasn't a life-threatening emergency. I watched as, ten minutes later, Valerie was wheeled out, strapped to a chair and onto the back of the vehicle, Remy at her side. They must have been taking her to get checked out, most likely for concussion, if nothing else. My scalp prickled, watching Valerie bang her head against the glass was like something out of a horror film and it wasn't something I wanted to witness again.

Perhaps Remy could get some carers in place, someone to be there when he had to work. It was none of my business, but I'd mention it to him when we next crossed paths, gently of course. I used to hate getting unsolicited advice when I was looking after Mum. Carers and acquaintances offering their opinion felt like a slight when I was doing the best I could. Looking back, I could see I took it personally when I shouldn't have. They were just trying to help, but I had assumed they were poking their noses in, judging me and my capabilities.

Would Remy come back tonight, check to see if I was okay? The blood rushed to my head as I remembered his touch on my arm the last time he'd visited. It was like a switch had been flicked. I pushed the pyjamas back under my pillow, checking my reflection in the mirror. I looked okay, brown waves and the unruly fringe which gave me character, Josh said. I sprayed some perfume and went back downstairs to check my phone. There were no calls from Danielle or messages from Josh, but he was on his date, so I didn't expect to hear from him.

Putting the television on in the background I worked on the proposal for Becky. A four-week rolling contract wasn't as good as six months but who knew where it would lead. Plus, I'd earn more if the travel agency Becky worked for paid me directly. It was too early to count my chickens yet, but I tapped away, glad for a distraction from Remy and Valerie.

Lauren came back downstairs and changed the channel, her hair wrapped in a towel. I made us a hot chocolate and went back to work. By the time Lauren had watched an episode of *Sam and Cat*, I'd sent the quote over to Becky. I hated sitting in my jeans, much preferring to lounge in my pyjamas, and shifted uncomfortably, aware something was poking into my side. The missing poster had worked its way out of my pocket and the corner of the folded paper dug into my skin.

Reviving the laptop, I typed Danielle Stobart into Google, not sure why I hadn't thought of it before. The first hit was from a Facebook post. Anxiety swirled in the pit of my stomach as my eyes scanned the page. One word leapt out at me from the screen.

MISSING

21

Danielle Stobart was missing. I stared at the word, jaw slack, before coming to my senses and clicking the link. It took me to Facebook, and I logged in, ignoring the notifications of things Josh had tagged me in. It seemed to have lost the original link, so I clicked back to Google and opened it again. This time the post came up. Twenty-seven-year-old Danielle Stobart was missing, last seen on the twenty-first of December.

The poster taken from the park was wedged down the side of the sofa and I checked Lauren was fully engrossed in the television before pulling it out to check the date. Danielle's dog, Barney, had disappeared three days before, on the eighteenth of December. It made no sense, first Danielle's dog disappears, then she does too. There were seventy or so comments and I clicked each one.

Most were well-wishers, sending their prayers or gestures of good wishes. The most prolific commenter was a man called Mark Fearn; he seemed to be trying to keep the search for Danielle alive. Clicking on his name, I saw in his profile he was a schoolteacher at Green Fields, the same school the newspaper mentioned in the Halloween fayre article. Perhaps Mark was her boyfriend, although he wasn't the man standing next to her in the photo from the loft.

I sank back into the sofa, still reeling from the discovery. Derek and Becky said Danielle hadn't been at number three long. She must have moved out prior to her disappearance, though, otherwise where were all her belongings? I frowned at the screen, clicking back to the missing post and the comments, the last one posted by Mark a few weeks ago. I sent him a friend request, then an instant message to explain who I was and that I was living in the house Danielle was last in. Hoping it would be enough to pique his interest. I wanted to know if she was still missing.

Despite Lauren sitting barely three feet in front of me on the floor, the house suddenly became eerie, the atmosphere shifting. Valerie's wind chime tinkled outside and the hairs on the back of my neck stood to attention.

'Time for bed,' I said abruptly to Lauren, shutting the lid of the laptop and ushering her upstairs despite her protests. Whilst she cleaned her teeth, I put my pyjamas on and washed my face. I had no intention of letting Remy in tonight even if he did stop by. I wanted to close all the curtains and lock the doors.

Could my neighbors have known Danielle was missing and neglected to tell me? Perhaps they didn't know. Although the police must have been around doing door-to-door enquiries. They would have spoken to Becky and Valerie at least, but no one had mentioned it. It disturbed me that I may have been deliberately kept in the dark. And to what end?

I put Lauren to bed and went downstairs to check everything was locked and secure. I imagined Danielle roaming the same rooms, performing the same actions. It chilled me to my core, and I tried to shake the image from my mind. Tiny pulses ran up and down my arms and legs, like ants scurrying across my skin. I couldn't ignore the unsettled feeling which sat like a lead weight in my stomach. The last time I'd felt that way was when Mum had tried to get into our rooms at night while we slept.

I tossed and turned into the early hours, the wind chime seemed especially loud, or perhaps it was just windier than usual. It jangled violently and I wanted to plug my ears so I wouldn't have to listen, but at the same time, if anyone was breaking in, I had to be able to hear it. My imagination always ran away with itself at night; something about the dark and how easy it was to hide in the shadows made my anxiety rocket. In the end, I stood and walked to Lauren's room to check she was safely asleep still in her bed.

Carefully opening her door, I found her on her back, mouth open a slip, snoring lightly. Tension in my shoulders fading away, I returned to my bedroom and debated going downstairs for a camomile tea. They always knocked me out.

Absent-mindedly, I peeked through the crack in the curtains out onto a slumbering Beech Close, surprised to see the security light on at number six. Part of their property was blocked by the large beech tree on the green, but I just made out a figure emerging from the front door, moving quickly.

I gasped and took an involuntary step back. Was I witnessing a burglary? Looking out again, the figure was striding straight towards the house. He'd seen me. Tongue glued to the roof of my mouth, I froze, unable to move as he came closer. Slowly, he came into focus, and I saw it was Remy, his quick pace and long strides, as well as his build, gave him away. It wasn't me he was walking towards, it was Valerie's house. He disappeared behind the hedge and was gone from view.

I sighed, my chest heaving. What a fool. I was becoming paranoid. Discovering Danielle was missing had spooked me more than I cared to admit. Dragging the curtain until it overlapped the other, I checked the clock on the bedside table. It was one in the morning. What was Remy doing at Niamh's house so late? Weren't they on holiday? Tenerife, Finn had said, for a few days at least. That was Sunday so they had to still be away.

Perhaps Remy was keeping an eye on the place for them while they were gone? They could be good friends, for all I knew. Or maybe Valerie had wandered over there in the middle of the night, having come back from the hospital, dazed and confused. If she was back. Remy's car had returned, although I hadn't heard it, I must have been asleep at the time. My head throbbed, something strange was going on and I didn't know what.

* * *

I dragged myself out of bed at eight to feed Teddy and Lauren, despite not feeling like I'd had enough sleep. The sun was out, shadows chased away, and in the safety of daylight I was irritated rather than afraid. I'd moved for a fresh start, an easy life after the rough time Lauren and I had, but I was getting drawn into another drama. *You could just drop it*, the voice in my head protested. I knew I couldn't. It would niggle at me until I found out what had happened to Danielle. I needed to hear back from Mark.

22

'Can we go to the park again?' Lauren asked, bright as a button after her early night.

'Sure,' I said, pulling open the cupboards. 'Let's eat first, then we can throw some clothes on and take Teddy out.'

After toasted crumpets, we hit the park. Lauren sang to herself on the swing as I walked the perimeter, deciding I needed to find another place to walk Teddy. If I didn't, the park was going to become boring. I needed to mix it up a bit. He loved me throwing the ball though and on the plus side a quick half an hour was enough. By the time we left, Teddy was spent, panting and glad to be returning home.

'What are we doing today then, kiddo?' I said to Lauren, already dreading the answer. I'd taken time off work to spend time with her, and I knew I'd love it, but entertaining an only child was sometimes exhausting.

'Swimming!' Lauren exclaimed and inwardly I scowled. I'd have to get the razor out when I got home if I was going to be wearing a costume in public. 'Holly FaceTimed me yesterday, she wants me to come for a sleepover tonight and I think her mum is taking her to Chessington World of Adventures tomorrow.' Holly was Lauren's best friend. Her mum, Anna, was another single parent and we often got together for playdates, helping each other out with childcare when we could. I'd been meaning to text her, but what with the move, I hadn't been sure I'd have much time to hang out over the Easter holidays. I'd visualised still being knee-deep in boxes four days after moving in, but unpacking had been relatively smooth. I did need to get some furniture soon, the place was looking sparse and the television on the floor made for uncomfortable viewing.

'Mum, did you hear me?' Lauren asked, tugging at my hand.

It was always awkward when the kids had arranged something between themselves. As they both had iPads, they could call each other via their email addresses without having a mobile phone.

'Ask Holly to get her mum to text me,' I replied as we loitered on the green, waiting for Teddy to finish sniffing.

I looked over at number six, but Niamh and Finn's house had no signs of life. Finn's Range Rover was still missing from the driveway, I assumed he'd left it at the airport. Maybe I was mistaken about Remy being inside the house last night, perhaps he'd been looking through the windows and I hadn't seen him come out of the front door at all? It was all the way across the green after all, and the tree was obscuring part of the view.

'They've gone away,' came a disembodied voice behind me and I whipped around to find Valerie in her dressing gown and slippers. She'd crept up behind me and my hand flew to my chest instinctively. Lauren backed away, disappearing behind the tree. I nearly followed suit.

'Valerie, you scared me. Are you feeling better?' I asked, although her forehead still had an egg-shaped lump, the skin surrounding it turning from an angry purple to red.

'I'm fine,' she said stiffly, as if I'd insulted her.

'Mum, come inside,' Remy called from Valerie's driveway, the car door wide open as if she'd already given him the slip. He gave me a wave and a shrug as he gestured for his mother to return. I smiled back. Remy looked dishevelled, clothes crumpled like he'd slept in them. I imagined his tall frame squashed into one of those uncomfortable hospital chairs. Although I knew he hadn't been in one of those all night, not when I'd seen him cross the green in the early hours.

'Remy's calling you,' I said, pointing over Valerie's shoulder towards him as though I was communicating with a child.

'You're not welcome here,' she spat, looking me up and down. Her mouth forming a sneer.

I bristled. 'There's no need to be rude, Valerie,' I shot back, my shoulders clenching. If Lauren hadn't been in earshot, I would have given her a piece of my mind. I didn't believe her demeanour was wholly down to dementia.

Her narrow eyes bored into me, a stare which could turn milk sour, before she tutted and turned away, muttering, 'They never leave.'

'What is with her?' Lauren said, coming out from behind the tree once Valerie had shuffled back to Remy, who was still waiting patiently beside the car. A maroon overnight bag at his feet.

'I don't know, but stay away from her, Lauren, she's not well.'

'She's a mean old bird,' Lauren said, and I bent over laughing. Where had she heard that expression from?

* * *

I forgot about Valerie as my morning morphed into a whirlwind. Lauren had got her way and after breakfast, and a shower, we went to the local pool. It was heaving, as was expected during the holidays, with children everywhere. I shivered, trying to swim as much as I could in the shallow water to keep warm as Lauren zoomed down the slide again and again. She'd bumped into some friends from school who were there with their dads. I wasn't comfortable going over to chat in my swimming costume, so loitered in the corner, swimming widths of the pool and scraping my knees on the bottom.

Finally, after an hour, Lauren had had enough and was willing to get out. We came back home with freshly washed wet hair, cheeks glowing, exhausted and starving. When I had a second to check my phone over a hot cup of tea and a slice of cheese on toast, there was both good and bad news waiting for me. Ebony, the solicitor, had left a voicemail explaining the new vendors of Mum's house wanted all of the furniture I'd offered, except the chest. I sighed, the chest was heavy and would take two people to lift it, which posed a problem, not to mention the utter sensation of dread I felt at having to go back to the cottage. I penned a quick email back to Ebony, thanking her and assuring I would remove it before the exchange of contracts on Saturday.

Anna, Holly's mum, had text asking if Lauren could come for a sleepover. I called Anna back rather than text.

'Hi, Shelly, how are you? Are you surviving the Easter holidays so far?'

'Just about. We've moved, and I've managed to fit in swimming and *Sonic 2*. What about you?'

'Oh yes, I remember you said you were moving! No, we've not done much, but we went to the zoo yesterday. You know Holly is animal mad.' Anna gave a hearty laugh and I imagined her throwing her hair back, a mass of honeyed blonde ringlets. She was wonderfully curvaceous with a bust I envied. Everyone would turn to look when she entered the playground. It was hard not to, she was loud, funny and everyone wanted to be her friend.

'Of course she is, I'm assuming you got conned out of another stuffed animal?'

'You know her so well,' she chuckled.

'I got your text and tonight is fine for a sleepover if you want. Shall I drop Lauren over to you later?'

'That would be great. Around four okay? Also, I have a some two-for-one tickets for Chessington. I'm taking Oliver, so Lauren can join us to make four. What do you think?' Oliver was Anna's first born, two years older than Holly and Lauren.

'I think she'd love to. Are you sure?'

'Of course. I'm sure you could do with a bit of time to unpack.'

I didn't admit it was mostly done and was already thinking about an impromptu trip to Ikea with Josh if I could get him to take the day off work.

* * *

I dropped a super excited Lauren off later with her overnight bag, Jules the teddy bear and the iPad. At the door, I gave Lauren a hug and a kiss before pushing a twenty-pound note into Anna's hand and bounding down the path before she could return it, knowing she would protest.

'Buy them all an ice cream at Chessington tomorrow. It's the least I can do,' I called as I unlocked the car, waving as Anna gesticulated wildly from the front door.

'We should be back by 7 p.m., I'll drop her to you tomorrow night. Text me your new address,' Anna called back.

'Will do. Any problems, call me,' I replied, waving goodbye.

Driving away, I had a niggle of guilt at the pleasurable mood of freedom a night without Lauren gave me. I hardly ever had time away from her and my mind raced with the endless possibili-ties of all the adult activities I could partake in.

23

I called Josh on loudspeaker as I made my way back to Beech Close. I had so much to tell him, all about Valerie's manic behaviour, as well as finding out Danielle was missing. I was sure he'd want to tell me about his date too. When he answered, I knew the call wouldn't take long, he was whispering and therefore still at work.

'Are you free tonight?' I asked, jumping straight in.

'No, we've got a bloody awards ceremony. It's going to be horrendous,' he whined, and I deflated, my partner in crime wouldn't be around for my intended night of debauchery.

'Bummer! I've got the night off. Lauren is staying over at a friend's. What about tomorrow, do you think you could get a day's holiday? We could hit Ikea?' I suggested and heard a sharp intake of breath at the other end.

'I'm in, even if I have to pull a sickie. Ah, love, I'm gutted about tonight, we could have hit Bar Med, it's two-for-one cocktails on a Tuesday.'

'Another time. Okay, text me later and we can sort out plans for tomorrow. We've got loads to catch up on!' I said, grinning.

'Later, babes.' He ended the call and I let out a loud sigh. I hoped we'd be staggering out of somewhere in the early hours of the morning back to mine via the kebab shop, but it wasn't to be. The endless possibilities now consisted of organising my sock drawer. I hated being at a loose end.

I pulled onto the driveway, grabbing my phone out of the cradle when I noticed Remy waiting for me.

'Hi,' I greeted him, climbing out. He'd changed clothes, now wearing jeans and a green polo shirt.

'No Lauren?' he asked.

'She's got a sleepover,' I said, leaning against my car, my gaze travelling the length of Remy. He was easy on the eye, and I preferred him in casual clothes. He looked more relaxed and potentially more fun. He arched his dark eyebrows, a sloping smile forming. I'd been caught gawping.

'How about I take you out for dinner, to say thank you for helping me out with Mum the other day?'

I licked my lips which were suddenly dry, a knot forming in my stomach. 'Umm, sure.'

Remy didn't seem at all put off by my hesitancy, his smile spreading. Was he someone who preferred the chase? 'Great, six o'clock?'

'Sounds good,' I replied, my voice a little hoarse.

When I got inside, I gave the house a quick tidy and fed Teddy before jumping in the shower for the third time. Still trying to wash off the chlorine smell which stubbornly refused to go before figuring out what to wear. I surveyed my choices, wrapped in my towel. I wanted to look nice, obviously, but also not like I was trying too hard. Remy was wearing jeans, so I'd wear the same, choosing a flattering dark denim with a red top which looked great against my dark hair, which I curled into surfer-girl waves.

Remy arrived at six on the dot, his eyes widening for a second when I pulled open the door. It gave me the boost I needed as I was jittery with nerves, my hands shaking as I climbed into the passenger seat of his white Mercedes.

'How about an Indian?' he suggested.

'I'm easy.' I shrugged, wincing as he laughed but thankfully didn't comment on my choice of words.

On the drive, we chatted about Beech Close, if I was settling in. I refrained from mentioning Valerie so early into the evening as I didn't want to dampen the mood. I could hardly admit everyone had been welcoming, except for her. I got the impression we both needed to cut loose.

Jai Ho was a restaurant I'd been to before, the food was excellent and staff always polite and accommodating. Remy wasn't shy about asking for a table in the corner, out of the way, and they happily obliged. It was reasonably busy, a few families and couples spread out in the restaurant, and I loved that about the place. The waiting staff never bunched customers together if they could help it.

The aroma of spices made me salivate and I was eyeing up the food on other guest's tables, distracted from what Remy was saying to me as we sat.

'I'm sorry, what?' I said, hearing my stomach growl.

'I said, how often do you get a night off?'

'Barely ever, the joys of single parenting, though, right?' I admitted.

The waiter came to take our drinks order, Remy requesting a bottle of red wine, and we took the opportunity to order our mains too. I always had the same thing: chicken tikka masala, pilau rice and a peshwari naan.

Once alone, Remy admitted he'd never wanted children, he was too selfish. I was taken aback by his frankness and couldn't help but experience a twinge of disappointment as the words spilled out of his mouth. We were obviously not going to be anything more than friends. At least I knew where I stood from the outset. Although Josh was right, it was so rare for me to fancy anyone, it was a shame the dinner wasn't going to lead anywhere.

Remy's honesty allowed me the opportunity to talk freely, there was no need to be guarded or reserved. I told him about Sebastian walking out and how I'd had to learn to be a single parent. I told him I had a good friend in Josh and some of the other school mums, but ultimately Lauren was my responsibility. The buck stopped with me.

'I'm sure your time will come again when Lauren's a bit older. In five years, she'll be what?'

'Fifteen, almost sixteen.'

'Exactly, you'll have more freedom. She'll be out with her friends and not so reliant on you.'

I'd be thirty-eight then, a couple of years shy of forty. Who knew where we'd be? Perhaps I was destined to be on my own, always.

As the alcohol flowed, Remy kept refilling my wine glass from the bottle whenever it ran low and my lips loosened further. He'd stopped at one glass because he was driving, moving onto tonic water, and I felt obliged to drink the rest. He asked me about Mum, and I gave him the highlights. How she had swung from neglect to Victorian punishments depending on her mood. It appeared he didn't have it easy growing up either. High expectations when not met had swift repercussions. It seemed Valerie had ruled with an iron fist and, like my upbringing, not all reprimands were verbal.

'Does she lash out with the dementia? Has it made her worse?' I asked.

'Definitely, she's like a woman possessed sometimes. It's hard not to hate her, you know.' Remy stared into his empty wine glass.

I sensed he always spoke his mind and it was refreshing albeit intimidating.

'Did you know Danielle Stobart? The girl at number three before me?' I blurted out, bolstered by the alcohol.

His brow furrowed as he considered the name. 'Not well, it's only recently I've been at Mum's more. I don't know many of the neighbors, except for Finn and Niamh.' He pushed away his empty plate and leaned back in his chair.

'Is that why you were over there in the early hours of this morning?'

Great, now I'd made out I was a curtain twitcher. A sad, single mum who had nothing better to do than keep tabs on her neighbors.

He chuckled, his lip curling upwards as he eyed me curiously. 'Well, you don't miss a thing, do you?'

24

'I assumed they'd asked you to keep an eye on the place, with them in Tenerife,' I stumbled over my words, trying to dig myself out of the hole, Remy's stare making my lip twitch.

'Always good to help out a friend.' He drained his glass of tonic water and nodded towards the waiter for a refill.

'Are they... happy?' I asked, remembering Niamh's black eye.

'As far as I've seen, they are. Why do you ask?' Remy seemed intrigued, but I waved him away. I grasped at something else to fill the gap.

'Did you know the girl I mentioned, Danielle, is missing? Her dog is too,' I revealed, a hot flush creeping up my chest, turning my skin a shade away from the top I was wearing.

He arched his eyebrows and scratched at his chin. 'I did not. That's concerning.'

'I would have thought the police might have spoken to your mother.'

'Why, do you think she could be involved?' He let out a mirthless laugh, ridiculing the idea I didn't believe was so preposterous.

Valerie had violent tendencies, I'd seen it with my own eyes, even to the extent of hurting herself.

The atmosphere shifted and I sensed Remy was annoyed. Our evening wasn't going as I'd originally hoped. I shifted in my seat, the tikka masala curdling with the wine.

'I think I better head back soon, I've got an early start tomorrow,' I hinted. Remy remained expressionless and gestured for the bill.

Another waiter arrived to take our plates and I stood to go to the bathroom, desperate to get away.

In the toilets, I leant against the sink, my head spinning as I grimaced at my blotchy reflection. Was Remy being weird or was I just annoyed he had no interest in me? Had I mistakenly assumed him taking me out for dinner was a date when it was him thanking me for helping out Valerie, as he'd said? The more I questioned myself, the more churned up I became.

When I got back to the table, Remy was waiting, holding out my jacket for me to slide into. He was gentlemanly, I had to give him that, helping me on with my jacket, opening the door to the restaurant and then to his car for me to get in.

He turned the radio on, and we didn't speak for the majority of the journey. I looked out of the window at the bright lights whizzing by wishing the ground would swallow me. The atmosphere in the car was palpable, as though a frost had materialised. I checked my phone and found a message from Anna, letting me know the girls were having a great time. I quickly replied, thanking her and adding our new address at Beech Close.

'I'm sorry if I seem defensive about my mother. I know she's difficult. She's a lot of things, but I don't think she's capable—'

'I should be the one saying sorry,' I said, cutting him off. 'I wasn't implying...'

Our eyes met as we pulled into his driveway, both laughing at the awkwardness of the situation. He turned off the ignition but remained where he was, hands resting on the steering wheel, looking straight ahead. My pulse quickened and I waited for him to speak.

'What do you have to get up early for tomorrow if Lauren is away?'

'I've got to move one last bit of furniture from my mum's. It's too heavy to lift alone, so I need to see if my friend, Josh, can help me.'

Remy turned to face me. 'I can help you, I'm free for a few hours in the afternoon if that's any good.'

I rubbed my suddenly damp palms on my jeans, unable to contain the grin spreading across my face. 'That would be amazing actually,' I admitted. Perhaps not all had been lost.

We got out of the car, and he walked with me to my front door, the security light bathing us as I fumbled for my keys.

'Thanks again for helping with my mother. It's great to have someone to talk to, who's been on this roller coaster ride before.'

Without considering the implications, I reached up and planted my lips on his, the urge to have his warm body against mine too strong to ignore. He responded, an arm around my waist, pulling me closer. His hand stroked my neck, fingers enclosing, squeezing gently. It was dangerous, forbidden, and my legs liquefied as he pushed me against the door, his weight pinning me upright.

The desperate ache in my groin was all I could focus on. It had been so long since I'd been touched I gave in to it without question. It didn't matter about tomorrow, or whether anything would develop between us. I didn't care if the whole street could see. Instant gratification was all-consuming and everything else seemed to melt away. Until a loud ear-piercing shriek sounded from the shadows behind us, and I came to my senses, sobering up immediately.

Remy took a step back, his hands still on me, our eyes locked as we caught our breath. The skin on his chin was rubbed red from kissing and he scowled at the interruption, expression contorting in a way that turned my blood to ice.

I knew who it would be before he moved out of my field of vision. Inside, Teddy began to bark, scratching at the door, the need to protect me prevalent.

Seconds passed until Remy could bear the howling no longer. He turned to look over his shoulder at the figure at the end of the driveway, shrouded in darkness. Valerie wore her long white nightgown, two spindly legs silhouetted against the fabric looking more ghostly than ever. Her mouth was open. Dragging her nails down her face again and again, she wailed like a banshee.

'No, no, no, no, no.'

Our moment had gone, evaporated. Frustration boiled in the pit of my stomach. Remy gritted his teeth, his hand dropping from my neck, the skin tingling in its absence. He stormed down the driveway, gripping Valerie roughly around the shoulders and practically lifting her bare feet from the asphalt before dragging her back home.

My scalp prickled. He was so angry, the forked vein in his forehead had been pulsing. He wouldn't hurt his own mother, would he? I stood for a second, my body caressed by the wind until the feeling came back in my legs and I forced myself to go inside.

I let Teddy out to urinate, waiting for him to calm down and fussing him to let him know I was okay. Then I crawled upstairs to bed with him at my heels. I got in fully clothed and pulled the covers over my head, curling my knees to my chest. Teddy took his place at the end, keeping my feet warm as I tried to process what had happened. I breathed deeply, closing my eyes, remembering

Remy's hand on my throat and how the intensity of his kiss had turned me inside out. It had been years since a man had that effect on me. I believed I was as hard as stone, but Remy had me yearning for him like a schoolgirl.

What was he doing next door? If we weren't detached, I'd be at the wall listening, my ear pressed against a glass. Was Remy tearing strips off Valerie for ruining his chances at getting laid, or was he gently bathing her face where she'd torn at her own skin?

Deep down, I knew whatever might have happened with Remy tonight, it wouldn't amount to any more than a fling. We were so different: I had baggage, a child, responsibilities and although he had Valerie to look after, I knew he didn't see it the same way. When Mum was alive, when she became ill, she'd taken over our lives, every waking moment was about her. Perhaps it was different for sons, or maybe Remy hid it well, but he seemed to be able to detach himself. Perhaps if I'd done the same, if I'd put Mum in a home, she would never have died.

25

I fell into a fitful sleep, jerking awake in the early hours disorientated. Confused as to why I was still clothed, and why my badly fitted curtains hung open. The street lamp bathed my room in a soft yellow glow, although it left me anything but warm. Events of the previous evening came crashing back into my mind, creating an air of dread as Valerie's wailing played on loop. The night had been a mixture of emotions, from pleasure and excitement to disappointment. Removing the uncomfortable denim, I slipped my pyjamas on before drawing the curtains and flopping back onto the bed.

It was always strange to be without Lauren, the two of us normally joined at the hip, but she'd had a few sleepovers over the past couple of years, when I'd eventually relented, realising she wasn't a baby any more. Usually if she did stay away, it meant a night out with Josh where I'd come home hammered and wouldn't wake until gone nine the following morning. Valerie's arrival had sobered me up pretty quickly last night. Remy was going to need to get her on some stronger medication. Guilt washed over me for ever believing she was faking. If she was, someone had to give her an Oscar.

If Valerie's doctor didn't intervene soon, she was going to hurt herself or someone else. Rolling onto my side and pulling the duvet to my ears, I accepted sleep wouldn't be forthcoming and reached for my phone, discarded on the pillow. Blinking to acclimatise to the bright light, I scrolled through Instagram, Twitter and Facebook, before noticing I had a little red dot on the Messenger icon. Mark Fearn had accepted my friend request and responded to my message. I hurriedly clicked through to it.

Hi Shelly, thanks for your message. I'm afraid to say Danielle is still missing. Perhaps if you're free we could meet?

I responded, agreeing we should, and asked Mark to let me know where and when was convenient.

Still missing. The words bounced around my brain. People don't disappear into thin air. I was eager to find out more and hoped Mark would be able to fill in the gaps. I'd wait to see where he suggested meeting, and ensure it was during the day and somewhere public. I wasn't in the habit of meeting strange men through the internet for any reason, especially after some of the true crime shows I'd seen. But Mark seemed to care about Danielle, and I wanted to find out what had happened to her.

I scrolled through my phone until my eyes stung, eventually drifting off around three and being rudely awakened by the handset vibrating against my forehead.

'Hello,' I grunted, peeling my eyes open to see it was daylight, and almost nine o'clock.

'Morning! I'll be with you in about half an hour,' Josh trilled down the phone as I threw the covers off and leapt out of bed.

Teddy raised his head to find out if he was getting fed today, I ruffled his fur apologetically.

'Okay, see you soon,' I replied, hanging up and dashing downstairs to fill Teddy's food bowl and open the back door to let him out into the garden.

Getting dressed ahead of Josh's arrival, Lauren FaceTimed me on Holly's phone from the back of the car as I hastily applied some make-up. She looked thrilled at the prospect of a day trip with her best friend, and I hoped it wouldn't evaporate when she realised how long they'd spend queuing for the rides.

Once ready, Teddy and I managed a quick couple of laps of the green, one of which Derek joined us for. He was going to London to visit an exhibition on the *Titanic*.

'Did you know Danielle was missing?' I asked as we strolled.

'No.' Derek appeared aghast, his face paled and he stopped abruptly.

'Apparently she is, although I don't know exactly when it happened. I'm guessing it couldn't have been while she was living here,' I said.

'I didn't see her before she left, which is a shame because she always had time for a chat. I saw the transit being loaded with furniture, but when I went over, they told me she was at work.'

'Who told you?' I asked.

'The removal men,' Derek said.

'Did she leave in a hurry then?'

'I don't know, perhaps. She didn't tell anyone she was going, and of course, one doesn't like to pry.' Derek carried on walking the remainder of our lap, his hands clasped behind him, looking every bit the headmaster.

I'd warmed to Derek, he had a friendly nature and was always keen to talk. Perhaps he was lonely? It made me keen to make an effort with him. I wanted to be a good neighbor, one he could rely on if he needed to. Someone who would always make time for a chat. I'd have to invite him over for a cup of tea on a day when I wasn't rushing around.

Derek bid me goodbye as Josh drove into the road fifteen minutes late, his radio blaring. He'd borrowed his mum's enormous Volvo, knowing I'd be buying furniture and we could put the seats down at the back. I waved and walked back to the house, where Teddy got a better reception than I did.

'Looking a bit peaky, love,' Josh said, eyeing me suspiciously.

I wasn't about to tell him what I'd got up to last night, not on the driveway, when anyone could be listening.

'How was your awards thing?' I asked, diverting the subject.

'Dull, but the barman was hot.'

I rolled my eyes.

'Do you want to come in or shall we hit the road?' I asked, knowing Ikea was around forty minutes away.

'Let's get going, sweet cheeks,' he said, nudging my behind with his knee. I opened the front door and gave Teddy a quick cuddle and a treat, sending him off to his basket, before locking up.

'Are we still on for later?' Remy stepped out from behind the hedge, taking the measure of Josh with an eyebrow raised.

'Oh hi,' I said, blowing my fringe out of my eyes and hoping I wouldn't, for once, go bright red.

'Remy, this is Josh. Josh – Remy,' I said, making introductions.

Remy gave a little nod but remained where he was. I was sure I saw him puff his chest out slightly, which made me chuckle inwardly. Josh was all muscle, perma-tanned and extremely good-looking. Even straight guys were intimidated by him, but he was used to it.

'Hi,' Josh said, a smile playing on his lips for my benefit. Drinking in Remy in his sharp navy suit.

'This afternoon? That would be great, thank you. I can make sure we're back by three. Does that work for you?' I asked.

'Sure, I'll see you then. Catch you later.' His voice gravelly.

As soon as he'd gone, Josh shot me a look, eyebrows arched and mouth open. He knew me too well. 'Get in the car, madam,' he instructed, opening the door.

I filled Josh in about Remy on the way to Ikea. Telling him what else had happened with Valerie since we'd last spoken and how it had thrown Remy and I together. I couldn't deny there was a spark between us, and Josh's eyes glinted with delight.

'He's not interested, not really,' I admitted. The words spoken out loud were like a punch to the gut.

'Oh, honey, he's interested. Did you see the look on his face?'

I shrugged. 'Well, it's never going to go anywhere, he doesn't like kids, and he's not interested in settling down.'

'Haven't I been telling you for ages to get out there and have fun? Enjoy his company, have an open mind. Let him wine and dine you, bang his brains out and you can hibernate for another ten years,' Josh teased.

I punched his thigh, pulling a chewing gum out of my bag and feeding him one before myself.

'Also, that girl, Danielle, who lived in the house before me. She's missing!'

Josh's back straightened and he glanced at me, his smile fading. 'Really?'

'Yes really. It's all over Facebook,' I said.

'Shit,' Josh replied, his knuckles white on the steering wheel. 'Do you think she left that stuff behind in your loft... or someone failed to get rid of it?'

I shuddered, understanding straight away what Josh was hinting at. 'God, what if she was abducted or something?'

'Maybe,' he replied, coming to a stop at some traffic lights and turning off the radio. 'That's eerie, Shelly. What if she's been murdered?'

'Unlikely,' I replied, my voice faltering. Anything could have happened to her and until I met with Mark, it was anyone's guess.

26

At Ikea, we slowly pushed our trollies around. Josh manoeuvred the big one, especially for furniture, and I had the smaller one which I knew would get filled with candles, photo frames and pot plants. I loved wandering around the rooms they'd set up, absorbing the designs for inspiration.

I was always drawn to loud, colourful things and by the time we'd returned to the restaurant, I'd bought a multicoloured rug, loud Aztec-style cushions, three pairs of curtains I hoped would fit and various other bits. They had an abundance of Easter decorations, bunny bunting, woven baskets with painted eggs and plush toys. I picked out a giant stuffed chick for Lauren, I could give her with her egg once I'd bought it, and some bunting to decorate the house. On Josh's trolley, I had balanced flat-pack boxes consisting of a new TV stand, bookcase, bedside table, desk and chair.

Flopping down at the table, I took my purse to the counter to get Josh the meatballs I'd promised him and two large cappuccinos.

'My feet are killing me,' Josh said as I returned, flexing his toes and stretching his long legs across the gangway, almost tripping a middle-aged woman, who tutted loudly.

'Mine too.'

'These meatballs are the best.'

'Thanks for coming with me,' I said, laughing as I watched Josh tuck in.

I wrapped my hands around my cup and listened to Josh fill me in on his date with Jamie who he'd met on Grindr. He was the impressive torso shot Josh had sent for my consideration. It sounded as though he'd been relatively restrained when he let slip they hadn't slept together and were going to see each other again at the weekend.

'Isn't that unusual? I thought Grindr was all about hook-ups?'

'Well, it is mostly, but we spent far too long chatting.' My eyebrows crept up my forehead and Josh swiped at my hand. I wasn't going to pass comment. If Josh liked someone enough *not* to sleep with them as soon as they met, I was all for it.

I checked my watch once we'd finished eating and suggested we navigated the checkouts and make our way home. Who knew how long it would take to pay and load the Volvo? Remy was expecting me back so he could help me move the chest at Mum's house. It was a trip I was dreading, but I couldn't turn down his offer. Josh had been so kind to join me on my shopping trip, but I didn't want to monopolise his whole day.

'This lot is going to make a dent in your wallet,' Josh said as he helped reposition the boxes so the lady at the till could lean over and scan them.

'Mum's money really. I've got access to her accounts now, so that makes life easier. No more scraping by for me.'

'I'm glad to hear it. So, when do you want me over for a building party?'

'Saturday maybe? I'll see what I can manage on my own

before then,' I said, bumping hips with Josh. The cashier pulled a face and calculated the amount due as Josh tried not to laugh. She'd clearly had a sense of humour bypass.

Thankfully, everything fit in the back of the Volvo and the journey home was smooth. I had three pot plants between my feet and more on my lap that Josh and I had bought between us. It was uncomfortable trying to hold them all in place, but at least we didn't get stuck in traffic.

Trying to get the boxes in the house once we got there was more of a struggle. Eventually we managed, both of us exhausted and desperate for a cup of tea once the furniture had been piled into the front room.

'Are you sure you're happy to leave it like that?' Josh said, slurping from his mug and gesturing to the flat-pack carnage in front of the sofa that Teddy was having a good sniff at.

'Yeah, I'll sort it tomorrow. No biggie.'

My phone rang. It was Anna, checking in to say the kids were having a great time and Lauren was a closet adrenaline junkie. Apparently she was the bravest of all of them and had no desire to leave the park.

'I'll text you when we leave and drop her in on the way home.'

'Are you sure, Anna? I'm happy to pick her up from yours?'

'No, don't be silly, you're not far from the motorway, are you, I've got to drive past anyway.'

'Okay, if you're sure, and thanks again,' I replied.

Josh had finished his tea and was rinsing his mug when Remy knocked at the door. I noticed a difference in Remy around Josh, his voice sounded huskier, and he looked taller, shoulders rolled back, chin tilted skyward. Was he trying to make himself more manly to convey he was straight in front of Josh? I'd witnessed men do that when we were out, as though it would ward him off, although it was never obvious Josh was gay. Not just from looking at him.

Remy waited patiently as I got my things together, his hands clasped on his hips, stretching the fabric of the coral-coloured T-shirt tight across his stomach. He'd changed from his suit earlier into casual grey jeans and trainers I knew Josh would approve of. I tried not to ogle, and his expression gave nothing away. I wanted to see it written on Remy's face, he'd been thinking of us, pressed against my front door, a few steps from where he was standing. But it wasn't a Jane Austen novel and Remy kept his cards close to his chest.

Josh had clocked the subtle change of atmosphere, his best friend trying to act cool and nonchalant when I was anything but. He could read me from a mile off and he let me know it with a smirk as we said our goodbyes. I thanked him for driving to Ikea and told him to pass on my thanks to his mum too for loan of the Volvo. We'd never have got anything in his Fiat 500 or my battered Golf.

Remy cleared his throat as Josh pulled away. 'I got a transit van from work, you never said how big the chest was.'

'That's great, thank you, we'll need it. So, what is "work"?' I asked as I locked up and we walked around to Valerie's where a dusty white transit van blocked the driveway. The sign on the side read MVS Construction. 'Ah I see, construction.'

'Well, I'm more of a project manager. I don't tend to get my hands that dirty any more,' he winked. 'I manage the building contracts that come in. Make sure we have enough staff, materials and the projects run on time and to budget.'

'I didn't think you had the hands for construction,' I teased as Remy opened the passenger door and I stepped into the cab, which I imagined would be filthy but instead was spotless.

'What's wrong with my hands exactly?' He winked and my throat constricted.

By the time he'd got into the driver's seat, I'd composed myself and Remy was already asking for directions to Mum's cottage.

'Is Valerie okay? I was kind of worried she'd woken up the whole street last night,' I said, sheepishly.

'It's my fault, I left the keys on the side. I've had to start locking her in, otherwise she just wanders. She's having a nap now.'

I nodded, Remy must be finding it hard to manage work and his mum. I remembered juggling those plates, it wasn't an easy task.

As we went, I watched him drive the van, which was strangely erotic. One minute Remy was sharp in a suit, clean-shaven, crisp, and pristine. No doubt for business meetings with clients. But I was also attracted to the laid-back, casual version, with his Adidas trainers and ruffled hair. It was like having the best of both worlds. I had to stop daydreaming about which Remy I wanted to sleep with more and focus on the task at hand. Something which became easier the closer we got to the cottage.

My chest started to feel as though it was in a vice, tightening with every turn as we neared our destination. Roads I'd driven a hundred times but now avoided like the plague. Limbs grew rigid, muscles frozen in position as the cottage came into view ahead. I lowered my gaze, shoulders clenched so tightly I feared I wouldn't be able to get out of the van when we stopped. I looked at the place where I'd had the worst night of my life, unsure if I could go back in.

27

Remy turned off the engine, his smile quickly fading when he spotted my pinched expression.

'Are you okay?'

I let out a whistle, waiting for my heart to slow. It was a few seconds before I was able to respond.

'Bad memories, I guess.' I stared at the cottage.

'We'll be in and out,' he said, taking charge and opening the door. A whoosh of air rushed in like it wanted to trap me inside the van, where I was safer. I climbed out on wobbly legs, joining Remy at the white wooden gate. The dark cottage with its paint-chipped windows seemed menacing, although I was sure to everyone else it was picturesque. A quaint cottage in an idyllic location with a cherry blossom tree in the front garden, coating everything in pretty pink petals.

Each nerve ending screamed run and I forced myself to ignore the impulse as we made our way down the path to the front door. The grass was a little overgrown either side, but I'd tried my best to make the place homely so I could get the best price for it. I would have taken the first offer, whatever it had been, to get shot of the place. But Josh had talked me around and made me see sense. I had to get as much as I could, especially with the amount I was going to lose to inheritance tax anyway.

He was right and what with Mum's savings, Lauren and I would have enough to live comfortably. I'd spent years eating beans on toast or packets of dried pasta because it was cheap, but constantly worrying it would be detrimental to Lauren's growth. We bought everything from the value range, relying on recipes from the internet to turn meagre ingredients into meals. Mum had rarely put her hand in her pocket, she'd said it was character building. No one had handed anything to her on a plate. She'd struggled and it hadn't done her any harm. I had no idea the amount of money she'd squirrelled away until I contacted the bank, seething about how much she had, and that we could have lived rather than existed.

I blinked the memories away and fumbled for the key to unlock the door, pushing it open to the tune of an ominous squeak.

'That needs oiling,' Remy said.

'It's not mine any more – well, it won't be on Saturday. Let the new owners do it.' My words came out a little harsher than intended, but the cottage put me on edge.

I stepped inside, taking in the gloom, before Remy flicked the light switch and the emptiness was illuminated. My upper back juddered of its own accord. Mum was walking over my grave. Out of hers and over mine.

'Where's this chest then?' Remy asked.

'Upstairs unfortunately,' I admitted. How on earth we were going to get it down, I had no idea.

The wooden stairs creaked as we climbed, the carpet nearly threadbare and I watched as Remy surveyed the place. Judging me, judging my mother. A lead weight formed in my stomach, getting heavier with each step.

'You can see why I wanted to move, right,' I said with a nervous laugh to break the tension.

'It would be lovely with a bit of TLC. I presume it's a listed building?' he said.

'Yep, all three of them are,' I replied, gesturing to the neighboring cottages out of the upstairs window.

'This it?' he said, as we entered Mum's old bedroom. The room was colder than the rest of the house, although it could have been my imagination. The large ornate chest sat in its usual place, the only item left in the bedroom. Imprints of Mum's bed remained in the carpet, but I turned my face away, knowing I'd see the image of her laying there, slowly shrivelling to nothing. 'What are you planning to do with it?'

'It's going to the tip,' I said flatly.

'Is there anything in it?' Remy asked.

'I don't think so.'

Remy lifted the lid. The chest was like a Tardis, it seemed huge inside, although when I'd been locked in it, it hadn't been so big. The wood was dark with lots of scratches at one end, marks I'd made as I'd whiled away the hours of my punishment. At the bottom of the chest was a blanket and a duvet cover. I'd forgotten to empty it after all.

'What's this?' Remy leaned in and picked up something from the corner, it tinkled in his hand.

My head snapped back. The sound of the bell hurt my ears and I winced, snatching it out of his hand and throwing it across the room. It smacked against the wall and dropped to the carpet, the chime echoing around the empty room.

'That fucking bell.'

Remy frowned at my outburst, a little taken aback, but he

calmly retrieved the bell, holding it in his hand. It was small, made of brass, so me launching it at the wall had made more damage to the wall than it had to the bell. He eyed me curiously, waiting for an explanation.

'I gave it to Mum when she stopped getting out of bed so much, it was meant to make life easier for the both of us. But she'd ring it at all hours, not wanting anything at all, or by the time I got there she couldn't remember what she wanted. I can't bear the sound of it, I should have thrown it away months ago.'

Remy put it on the window ledge, next to the van keys, pity in his eyes. I hoped for his sake Valerie wouldn't go the same way.

'Do you think you'll have to get a carer in for your mother?' I asked, the words out as soon as the thought entered my head.

'Maybe, we've got an appointment at the doctors tomorrow. I'll ask them what they suggest. Her episodes, as you saw, are getting worse.'

I nodded, glad he was taking her to see someone.

'Right, let's give this a go, shall we,' Remy said, bending to try to slip his fingers underneath the chest.

It took us ten minutes of lifting and pushing the chest before we managed to slide it down the stairs with Remy at the front, taking the weight. He said it wasn't overly heavy, but he was being polite, my spindly arms had little strength in them, and he was doing most of the donkey work. When we reached the bottom, Remy sat on the chest and wiped the sweat off his forehead. I moved to open the door, to let the breeze in, but Remy's voice stopped me.

'Don't.'

I turned to look at him, my forehead creasing. *Don't what?*

'Come here,' he ordered, his tone authoritative. Before I could move, he'd reached out and pulled me towards him by the belt of my jeans, until I stood in between his legs, my arms by my side.

I stared down, his face level with my chest, watching the dramatic rise and fall as my breathing kicked up a notch. Still holding my belt, Remy tugged it, steering where he wanted me. I leaned over him, my hair brushing his face until we were centimetres apart, our lips almost touching. Like a magnet powerless to stop moving towards metal. We needed each other, but I didn't want it to happen here, not in this hellhole.

I put my hands on his shoulders, to ease myself away, but Remy hadn't sensed my hesitation, yanking my belt so hard, my face slammed into his. Our teeth knocked together before his tongue was in my mouth. Remy groaned hungrily, pushing his hand up my T-shirt and squeezing my breast so hard, I yelped and tried to wriggle away.

'Remy, stop,' I tried to say before his mouth was on mine again, his grip on my wrist too tight. I fought a rising panic I wouldn't be able to escape.

28

I shoved Remy hard in the chest and stumbled backward as he let go of my wrist instantly, both palms raised towards me.

Wide-eyed, his face fell. 'I'm sorry, I'm sorry. I took it too far. I'm sorry,' he said, as if repeating his apology made it okay. His eyes imploring me to understand he'd just got lost in the moment.

'For fuck's sake, Remy,' I snapped, brushing my fringe out of my eyes.

He rubbed the back of his neck, gaze lowered to the floor.

I opened the door, freedom pouring in, along with blossom, blowing over the threshold. The amount of hours Mum used to spend sweeping it back out again, she swore she'd cut the tree down, but I begged her not to.

I turned back to Remy, wanting to say more. To say that, yes, he took it too far and ask what the hell had possessed him. Instead, I said nothing, letting the words fester in my gut as we shuffled the chest between us to the back of the transit in silence.

'Damn it, I left the keys inside,' he said, jogging back to the cottage.

I followed him along the path, loitering by the front door so I could lock up when he came back. I was eager to get away.

Remy returned in less than a minute and I double-locked the door before we lifted the chest into the back of the Transit and I took my seat at the front. My breast throbbed with the seat belt over it, likely bruised. Anger ate away at me until I could hold my tongue no longer.

'You took the piss, you know. I get you're doing me a favour and everything, but it doesn't give you the right to manhandle me.' My jaw clenched as Remy remained facing forward, concentrating on the road, or contemplating how to respond, I couldn't decide.

'I'm sorry, I got carried away.' His tone was flat, and I was about to continue my rant but got interrupted by a message alert on my phone.

Leaving now, be with you soon. xx

Anna had left Chessington and was making her way to my house. I couldn't wait to see Lauren and silently urged Remy to put his foot down. Instead, he drove carefully, prolonging the excruciating journey. I wanted to get home, away from him. I was so angry he'd overstepped the mark, ruining it, when it had been so long since I'd even kissed someone. I'd got my hopes up, our connection was exciting and even if it wasn't going to turn into anything permanent, Josh was right, I deserved to have a little fun.

'I mean, what is it, do you like it rough or something?' I blurted, still fizzing with annoyance I couldn't contain.

Remy laughed at my outburst, which turned into a coughing fit, eventually having to pull over, spluttering, his eyes streaming. It was infectious and I laughed too despite my irritation.

'No I don't *like it rough*, I just, I don't know, got caught up in the moment. I mean, the urge to rip your clothes is prevalent every time I see you.'

I rolled my eyes.

Remy gave a little shake of the head and pulled away from the kerb to carry on home.

'Anyway, some women like it,' he said, the statement floating around the cab of the transit.

I snorted, the light-hearted moment gone, the fire raging once more in my belly. 'This woman doesn't,' I snapped, folding my arms across my chest, wincing as I brushed my breast.

'Noted,' Remy replied, with a scowl.

When we got back to the house, I was already out of the Transit and on my way to the door before the handbrake had been pulled up.

'Wait, what do you want me to do with the chest?' he called.

'Whatever you like: keep it, sell it, or leave it on the driveway and I'll sort it,' I called back.

'You don't want me to bring it in?' He gestured towards my house, trying to make amends.

'Absolutely not, it's not going inside.'

Remy tilted his head, not grasping what I had against the chest with its ornate cherub carvings.

I turned to face him, hands on my hips, exasperated at the conversation I didn't want to have. 'My mum used to lock me in it, for hours at a time when I was a kid. It's not coming in the house,' I said quickly.

Remy's mouth dropped open, looking like he'd been punched in the stomach.

I put my key in the front door and pushed it open, greeting an excited Teddy.

'I'll take care of it,' Remy called.

'Thanks,' I replied, but I didn't look back, letting the door shut behind me.

Outside in the garden, I raised my head to the sun, eyes closed. Letting the warmth wash over me after the trip to the cottage. Teddy bounced around and I laid on the grass, making a fuss of him, knowing I'd hear the door when Anna knocked. Once Lauren was home everything would be perfect, but for now I was out of sorts. Cross I'd let myself get mixed up with Remy in the first place, that I'd given him the potential to hurt me. Something I rarely did. I never invited anyone in, just in case.

Was I overreacting? He'd got a bit physical, but had I been in any danger? It wasn't as if he didn't stop when I'd told him to. He had been apologetic but still made the comment *some women like it*. What a dickhead, and what was that all about anyway? Perhaps the women he was used to sleeping with liked being left bruised after a night with him, but I wasn't going to be one of them.

I rolled onto my front to check my phone, the breeze stroking my back. Teddy nuzzled into my side, both of us taking in the vitamin D on offer. I had another message from Mark, asking if it was possible to meet tomorrow. He suggested a park in town which had a fountain and a large play area where I could let Lauren run riot. I agreed to meet him at half ten in the morning, clicking send as the knocker boomed.

Before I opened the door, I lifted the box of Danielle's things and put them on the sofa. I wanted to take the photo with me to show Mark, to make sure it was Danielle. Then I remembered the poster still hidden down the side of the sofa, stuffing it into the box as the door thumped again.

'Hi, popsicle,' I said, lifting Lauren for a hug.

Anna stood at the door, looking dishevelled, with dark circles beneath her eyes. 'We've had a great time,' she said, her forehead a touch sunburnt.

'I'm glad, thanks so much for taking her with you,' I said, nudging Lauren to say thanks too, which she did without any further prompt.

'No problem, best be off, got to cook dinner now.' Anna was already striding towards the car when an idea popped into my head.

'Want me to take Holly to the park for a bit tomorrow morning? I can get them some lunch, drop her back in the afternoon?'

'That would be great, thanks,' Anna said, opening her car door.

'I'll pick her up at ten,' I said, knowing it wouldn't be too early. Ten o'clock was never early if you had kids. It would mean I'd get to talk to Mark without interruption and Lauren would be entertained. Perhaps, with Mark's help, I could uncover the mystery of Danielle's disappearance.

29

Lauren had a long bath after dinner. She too was shattered after running around a theme park for the day. She told me all about the rides she'd been on: The Vampire, The Cobra, although Dragons Fury sounded the scariest. We settled to watch television, trying to ignore the flat-pack boxes in the middle of the room. I hadn't even unpacked from Ikea; the pot plants and bits still on the kitchen table. Lauren was too tired to be overly interested in what I'd bought, although I had made sure to hide the enormous plush chick in the cupboard under the stairs before she'd got home.

She snuggled into me while we watched a programme about rehoming dogs and started to nod off. I was tired too, and I was relieved when she suggested going upstairs to bed.

Quick to fall asleep, my dreams were plagued by visions of the chest. My childhood self curled up inside it, knees rubbing against the wood, fingernails splintered from scratching.

The noise reverberated around my skull until I woke to damp sheets, the room dark. As if on autopilot, I drew back the curtains, letting the light from the street lamp in. Expecting to see Valerie wandering Beech Close in her white nightdress, but the road was quiet. As it should be at 3 a.m. The chest was nowhere to be seen, so I assumed it was still in Remy's van, which had vacated the close. Visiting the cottage had unsettled me, but hopefully on Saturday contracts would be exchanged and I'd never have to go back there again.

* * *

At quarter to eleven the following morning, I positioned myself on a bench outside an enormous play park, already heaving with kids. Teddy moved around, sniffing and chasing fallen blossom, excited to be somewhere new. Lauren and Holly were already tackling the rope bridge, both dressed in bright yellow T-shirts accidentally, although it made keeping an eye on them easy. Anna looked like she'd needed a break when I arrived to collect Holly, but said she was going to take Oliver to laser tag with one of his friends. We'd rolled our eyes at the relentless schedule of entertainment, already craving wine o'clock later.

I carried on watching the girls, shielding my eyes from the sun. Shifting in my seat, unsettled about meeting someone I'd only briefly spoken to online. Mark Fearn could be anyone, he could even be responsible for Danielle's disappearance for all I knew. I reminded myself I was safe, I had Teddy the rubbish guard dog to protect me in a busy park filled with people. I slurped the coffee I'd purchased from the stall in the car park on the way in. Holly and Lauren wanted a drink and an ice cream, so I relented figuring the caffeine boost would do me good.

Lauren stood on top of the large blue tunnel slide, ready to disappear, waving to catch my attention before she dropped. I waved back.

'Hi, Shelly?' I turned to find Mark standing awkwardly to my left.

'Yes, hi, you must be Mark,' I said, shimmying along the bench so he could sit.

He looked similar to his profile picture on Facebook, although his hair was now closely shaved all over, and he'd grown a short beard. He wore rolled-up beige chinos and boat shoes, with a navy cheesecloth shirt as though he was dressing for another continent entirely. A khaki canvas satchel was slung over his shoulder, dirtied at the bottom.

'Thanks for meeting with me,' he said, shuffling back on the bench and crossing one leg over the other, his ankle by his knee.

'Have you known Danielle long?'

'Yes, for three years, since she's worked at Green Fields Junior School. I teach the year threes and we're a pretty tight-knit group. All of the teachers are devastated by her disappearance.' Mark stroked at his beard.

'I'm just trying to work some things out in my head,' I admitted. 'When did she disappear?' I twisted around in my seat and wrapped the lead around my hand so Teddy couldn't roam too far, he was digging behind the bench, searching for treasure.

'When did she disappear exactly? Well, that's the mystery. We broke up from school on Friday the seventeenth of December. She was desperate for a holiday, said she was going to spend Christmas in Egypt.'

'Has she no family?' I asked, knowing Christmas was usually spent with family, whether they were close or not.

'No, her parents passed away before she joined the school, a car accident, and she's estranged from her older sister, who lives in Scotland. I'd offered her to come to ours, but she said she wanted to get some sun.'

I couldn't blame her, winters in England were depressing, mainly because they were grey, wet and rarely snowy.

'So you didn't know she was missing until term started in January?' I asked. Was my meeting with Mark going to be a waste of time?

'That's right, but when I went round to the house, there was no one there, the place was empty, and her neighbors said she'd moved out on the twenty-first of December. She never handed her notice in or said she'd wanted to leave.'

'Was it you who contacted the police?'

'Yes, they told me they'd look into it, but Danielle wasn't classed as high risk. When I pestered them, they told me she'd purchased a plane ticket for the twenty-second of December to Egypt.' He grimaced, clicking his knuckles one by one.

'But you don't believe she got on the plane?' I said, reading between the lines.

Mark shook his head. 'The passenger list isn't available to the public, I've tried that angle. The police don't seem bothered, I keep calling, but there's no pressure on them to find her. It's weird she hasn't used any of her social media.'

'What about credit cards?'

'No idea, they won't tell me if she's made any transactions.'

'Perhaps she has if they aren't worried?' I said, playing devil's advocate, but Mark was on a roll.

'She's got no close relatives, so the police are assuming she moved out to Egypt without telling anyone! Without giving notice to the job she loved. It's ludicrous.'

'What about all the stuff that was moved out of the house?' I asked, surely the removal firm would have an address for her.

'I've called every removal company in Crawley. No one had a booking for the twenty-first of December.'

I bit my lip, Remy had access to vans. Did he move her stuff? I took a second to locate the girls, waving at Holly who was on the swing, but I couldn't see Lauren straight away.

Mark followed my gaze. 'You've got kids?'

'My daughter is over there with her friend. I thought it would give us time to talk while they played.'

'How old is she?' Mark's face seemed to light up and I knew instantly he'd be a great teacher.

'She's ten going on twenty-one,' I chuckled.

'I know, they're all like that.' Mark smiled, shaking his head as though it was inevitable. 'So you're living there now, in Danielle's old house?' he continued, steering the conversation back.

'Yes, and I found some things in the loft.' I rummaged in my bag, pulling out the photo and handing it to Mark.

He shook his head as he looked at it. 'It's her and that muppet Steve. She dated him for a bit, but he treated her like dirt,' Mark said bitterly, and I knew he was sweet on her, although I guessed it was unrequited. His keeping the search alive was admirable though. 'They went out for a bit but he broke it off, she was devastated.'

'What about her neighbors? Did she ever say anything about them, were there any problems?' I probed.

'She never said if there was, but she didn't tell me everything.' Mark frowned.

I handed Mark the poster I'd taken from the park. 'Danielle put up these posters, her dog went missing on the eighteenth of December, which is what makes no sense to me. Why would she move three days later, if her dog had gone missing?'

'Exactly,' Mark replied, folding his arms across his chest. 'She loved that dog, she would never leave knowing he was missing.'

'Unless it was the final straw, or she had plans she couldn't change?' I mused, staring at Teddy, who was laying on his stomach, licking his paws. Could I leave him behind? No. It wouldn't happen. I would have stayed put until I found him if he was missing.

Danielle's disappearance made little sense, although I could see why it wasn't a high priority for the police, but they weren't asking the right questions. Perhaps if they wouldn't, I would.

30

I swapped numbers with Mark and promised him I'd keep in touch with any new findings before we left the park. Holly and Lauren were shattered, complaining they were hungry and thirsty, so I decided to take them home for lunch. Once they were fed and watered, they disappeared upstairs to play on Lauren's iPad.

It was time for me to tackle some of the furniture I'd bought home from Ikea I hadn't touched yet. By mid-afternoon, I'd built the 1950s-style TV stand and Lauren helped me lift the television onto it. At least now we wouldn't crick our necks watching a television sat on the floor. I'd laid the rug, distributed the pot plants and taken the tags off the cushions. The lounge looked vibrant and welcoming, despite the magnolia walls, Teddy already claiming the rug as his own the second it was on the floor.

I was clearing away the box for the TV stand when Anna text asking if she could pick up Holly, as her mum wanted to take them all out for dinner. When she arrived, she handed Lauren a Maltesers Easter egg.

'God, I'm so disorganised, I haven't bought any yet,' I said at the door, shamefaced I hadn't got anything to give Holly in return.

'Oh, don't worry about it, she gets spoilt, my mum always goes mad,' Anna replied, draping an arm over Holly's shoulder. I couldn't help the twinge of jealousy, I wished Lauren had a nanny to spoil her. I had to get my shit together and get some Easter supplies, otherwise there'd be no egg hunt on Sunday.

As we waved Anna off, promising to see her soon, Becky rounded the drive and I remembered I hadn't checked my email to see if she'd responded to the proposal. Was she going to offer me a job?

'Hi, how's it going?' She beamed at me.

'Good thanks, Lauren's just had a play date,' I replied, explaining the car reversing off the driveway.

'Oh great, you're free then. We're going over to Amber's, I'm sloping off work early as Niamh's back and she's desperate for a catch-up.' My face fell before I could catch it.

'Oh, Becky, I'm not sure, I have Lauren...' I began.

'Don't look like that. Amber asked me to invite you along. Lauren can come too,' she smiled directly at Lauren. 'I'm sure Amber will love to have her over – they've not been able to have kids,' Becky leaned towards me and whispered conspiratorially.

'That's a shame,' I replied, my resolve wavering, although I didn't want to go. Niamh's drinks party was excruciating enough. As friendly as they were, I didn't fit in.

'Please, Mum, can we go?' Lauren looked up at me, desperate to be included in some adult time.

'Okay, let me nip to the loo and I'll be out.'

'I'll meet you on the green. I'm going to get Niamh.' I watched Becky go in her yellow capri trousers and espadrilles, looking like she was about to board a private yacht for an afternoon of cocktails.

I closed the door and ran upstairs, throwing open the wardrobe. What could I put on in five seconds which looked good but also wouldn't make me stand out? I'd feel inferior next to them in my stonewash jeans and T-shirt.

'What about this?' Lauren picked out some white linen trousers, which I put on with my Converse and a floral vest top I rarely wore, previously deeming it a bit girly for me.

'Change your trousers and brush your hair,' I laughed at Lauren, who was still covered in dust from the park.

'Why are we getting dressed up?' She wrinkled her nose.

'You'll see,' I replied with a wink.

Five minutes later, we were out on the green, walking towards Becky and a sun-kissed Niamh who wore a cream off-the-shoulder top and dangly earrings.

'I understand,' Lauren said simply as we got closer, and I squeezed her hand as she giggled. We were like two peas in a pod.

Once they'd all said hello in a cacophony of high-pitched squeals and air-kissing, we began the walk to Amber and Leo's at number one. I felt like a fraud.

'I didn't realise you'd be back so soon, Niamh?' I said.

'Oh just four nights. Would you believe Finn has had to go back to work. It's Easter, for goodness' sake, but he's got a presentation to do today before the long bank holiday weekend. I've been left with all the unpacking and washing. I'm bloody run ragged,' she complained, looking like the least harassed person I'd ever seen.

Amber opened the door and there was more squealing. Lauren winced, and I tried not to laugh. We were so out of place. All I could hear was Josh's voice, calling them the Housewives of Beech Close – he wasn't far wrong.

'Come in, come in. Oh, Shelly, it's so lovely for you to bring your daughter,' Amber said, her beautiful dark eyes lighting up at the sight of Lauren.

She placed her hands on Lauren's shoulder and steered her

into the kitchen; we all followed. Amber sashayed forward, her hips swivelling in a black maxi dress. I stared at her curves enviously, she had a confidence in her body I would never have.

'I have some biscuits for you,' Amber purred, dipping into a large glass jar of chocolate chip cookies.

Lauren held out her hand, accepting graciously before thanking her.

'And for you, ladies, we have this...' she brandished a jug of Pimm's and Niamh whistled.

A few minutes later, we were outside in Amber's garden, which was mostly grey slate patio, with large decorative pots planted with red acers. We perched on rattan seats, enjoying the afternoon sun and sipping from large glasses of Pimm's stuffed to the brim with mint. Amber raked her fingers through Lauren's hair, who was sitting on a low Moroccan-style pouffe, and offered to plait it. I was surprised at how comfortable my daughter was, her big eyes staring back at Amber as though she was a goddess. It made me smile, how carefree she seemed. A million miles away from the little girl frightened of a wind chime.

'Tell us about your trip, Niamh,' Becky said, and Niamh launched into a blow-by-blow account of her four days away, although it didn't sound like she'd done much more than rest and relaxation. I'd kill for a few days on a sunlounger, laying blissfully in the rays and sipping on cocktails.

'Well, I'm hoping Shelly is going to come and help out with my admin,' Becky said, changing the subject once we'd drawn out Niamh's holiday long enough. I almost choked on my drink and she winked at me.

'You do need sorting out,' Amber laughed.

'I know, I'm useless at admin. I can't believe I've managed to hide it so well.'

'I'm sorry, Becky, I haven't checked my emails,' I offered.

'Oh, no worries, I'm pleased the company went for it. I'm drowning and why they can't get me someone permanent, I don't know.' Becky went on to moan about the hierarchy and how the male managers had support, but there was little for the females, who had to share one lady who was a step away from retirement.

I leaned back in my chair, soaking up the conversation. Could I work for Becky? Would she be a nightmare? Too demanding? There would have to be clear boundaries because I ran contracts simultaneously, splitting my time between each. Perhaps I shouldn't have said anything at all and not volunteered my services.

'So, Shelly, what about you, all settled in now? You've been here nearly a week,' Niamh said, interrupting my chain of thought.

'Gosh, it feels like longer,' I admitted, and everyone laughed. The conversation paused and I took the opportunity to change the subject. 'Actually, I wanted to let you know something. I found out Danielle, who lived at number three before me, is missing. I'm not sure if any of you were friendly with her?' I looked at first from Becky to Niamh, whose expressions were unreadable, before I settled on Amber. In contrast, her lip was curled, practically in a snarl. She was the first to speak.

'I'm glad she's gone. That girl was trouble.'

'Amber, you can't say that!' Niamh said, resting a hand on her shoulder.

Amber carried on plaiting Lauren's hair, who had noticed the developing tension and was eyeing us curiously.

'Why not, she was after my husband. It was obvious, the way she used to fawn all over him.' Amber gritted her teeth, her hands quickening, Lauren's head jerking back as she pulled tighter on her scalp.

Becky rolled her eyes at Niamh, something unspoken between

them. Was Amber overtly jealous of Leo around other women? I was glad I hadn't spoken to him much at Niamh's drinks if it would have incurred her wrath. He was handsome, his blond goatee made him look suave but still rugged if that was possible, but attached men were of no interest to me. In fact, most men were of no interest to me any more, until Remy and that was a non-starter. I'd given up trying to find a partner, perhaps I was unlovable.

31

'I thought she had a boyfriend,' I blurted, coming back to the conversation as I remembered Mark mentioning Steve, the man from the photo.

'No idea,' Becky chipped in, pouring herself another glass of Pimm's before topping up Niamh's. Mine was still half full, as was Amber's, who had finished Lauren's French plait and was feeding her another cookie, her face now a picture of contentment. 'Didn't Remy take her out once?' Becky added, looking towards Niamh.

I nearly choked on my drink but managed to style it out.

'I don't know!' she replied, in a tone that suggested she wouldn't have had a clue. My ears pricked. Remy had taken her out. Like he'd taken me out?

An awkward silence followed, and I was concerned I'd ruined the afternoon by mentioning Danielle.

'I think that old woman scared her off,' Lauren blurted, her mouth full of cookie crumbs. I froze as everyone stared at her, my throat closing, but a couple of seconds later, initiated by Niamh, the three of them laughed, Becky sounding like a hyena.

'Valerie?' she spluttered.

'That woman is the bane of my life,' Niamh said, the posh lilt slipping ever so slightly, before taking a long swig from her Pimm's. Eyebrows raised I opened my mouth to speak but no words came.

'Would you like to see my paintings?' Amber asked Lauren, cutting through the silence, standing to take her by the hand. Niamh's comment about Valerie glossed over.

'I'd love to see them too, actually,' I lied, feeling ridiculous about wanting to keep Lauren close to me. I was sure she'd be perfectly safe with Amber who'd treated her like the guest of honour since we'd arrived, but however irrational, I wanted to make sure she was in sight.

All of us headed upstairs admiring the artwork that filled the stark white walls. Everywhere was a canvas for Amber to colour and she did so spectacularly. Her studio, converted from the middle bedroom, had a view over the back garden and beyond to the adjoining street. It was messy, floors and walls covered in paint-splattered sheets. A large easel with a partly painted canvas was by the window. Primary colours dominated the piece and I stared, trying to understand it. I didn't, although I appreciated how pretty it was.

'Wow, could you do one for my bedroom?' Lauren asked, her eyes wide with glee.

'Oh I'd love to,' Amber said. 'What's your favourite colour?'

'Yellow,' she replied, matching Amber's grin. I had a feeling I'd hear Amber's name on loop for the next few days.

'Only if you're sure,' I said, tapping Amber on her arm. I had no idea how much she'd charge me.

'Absolutely.' Amber awarded me a genuine smile which tugged at my heart strings. I'd been quick to judge the housewives of Beech Close and I regretted being so harsh. They'd been nothing but nice to us since we'd arrived.

Lauren and I managed to escape after I'd agreed to a second glass of Pimm's, although I knew the women would remain in the garden until the shade fell or their husbands came home. Whichever was sooner. Much to Lauren's annoyance, I said I had to get back to take Teddy out. Which we did as soon as we got home, and I listened to Lauren chat incessantly about how beautiful Amber was all the way to the park.

It wasn't until she was on the swing, having bumped into a girl she knew from school, that I had time to digest the day. My quest for knowledge on the missing Danielle hadn't been particularly successful. Mark had no idea where she was, although he was adamant she was not in Egypt, living her best life. To be fair, it didn't make a lot of sense. Why would someone move country alone, with no prior warning? We all could do with a holiday, but there was a big difference between a few days' escape and a complete relocation.

Danielle's boyfriend had dumped her, so she could have been reeling from that, also the loss of her four-legged companion, but it was still extreme. She might have been having issues at work Mark wasn't privy to and hadn't mentioned, but why would she move house? She hadn't even given notice at work, no resignation, just didn't return at the start of term. Something told me Valerie was part of the reason Danielle had left. I'd only been at Beech Close for a week, and she'd been quick to let me know I wasn't welcome. Maybe Danielle wasn't as thick-skinned as I was, perhaps she'd struggled to cope with her hostility and thought sod it, I'm off. And why had Niamh said Valerie was the bane of her life? Did she torment the other neighbors as she did me, and potentially Danielle too?

Whatever Danielle was going through, Amber clearly didn't like her, perhaps in competition for Leo, who I knew to be flirty, but I sensed from Becky and Niamh's exchanged glance, it wasn't something to be taken seriously. I got the impression Amber being a little green-eyed where her husband was concerned wasn't anything new.

Becky believed Derek knew Danielle the best, although he'd declared he hadn't known her well at all, which was odd. Becky also said Remy had taken her out. Were her observations unreliable? I hoped so, as the idea made my stomach clench. Jealousy wasn't an emotion I was used to, and I had no reason for it. Remy wasn't mine, I had no claim on him and this had happened before we'd even met. Was Remy a womaniser? A player, preying on pretty women easily accessible to him? If that was the case, perhaps it was better it was over before it began.

I tossed the ball for Teddy, not realising I'd stopped in the middle of the field, having veered off course. Looking back, I could see Lauren and her friend swinging in time, throwing their heads back and laughing. Teddy chased after the ball and I followed on, rounding the bend to come back on myself so I could keep the play area in my vision as I continued to structure my thoughts.

I was getting involved in something which was none of my business, overthinking everything. I'd just wanted to return Danielle's items to her, bits she'd left behind in the move. But my intrigue for a mystery had led me to ask questions I'd never know the answers to. If the police didn't believe she was truly missing, I guessed Mark would have to accept it. Maybe she was trying to get away from him, for all I knew he could have been stalking her and her disappearance was on purpose.

Until I had a chance to take the box to the letting agent I'd put it back in the loft where its presence wouldn't draw me into playing detective. I had no right to snoop into the private life of the previous tenant. Perhaps she wanted to stay hidden. If there had been a crime, the police would have followed it up.

32

Back at the house, once we'd both eaten and Lauren was in the shower, I called Josh. Despite only having seen him for our Ikea trip yesterday, I was desperate for a few beers and a natter. He told me he was meeting Jamie and heading into Brighton but not until later.

'Pre-drinks round mine then and I'll order you a cab to the train station?' I offered.

'Definitely, I'll hop in the shower and be round in a bit. Mind if I leave the car at yours?'

'Not at all.' I couldn't wait to hear more about Jamie. It was rare Josh hooked up with anyone more than once, so I was looking forward to him spilling the beans.

Lauren wanted to wait and see Josh but agreed to go to bed once he arrived. I promised to take her shopping in the morning so she could pick her own Easter egg, guilty I'd not been more organised, but it was difficult trying to juggle the move and sale of Mum's cottage on top of half-term. The week at Beech Close had run away with me, which was another reason why I wasn't going to get distracted by Danielle. I had one more week off work, exchanging the contracts on the cottage and I wanted to make the most of time with Lauren.

When Josh arrived, he walked in smelling gorgeous, wearing a fitted azure polo shirt. His face was clean-shaven with not a hair out of place.

'You smell yummy,' Lauren said as Josh lifted her for a cuddle.

'Thank you, although I do believe it's nearly your bedtime, young lady.'

'We've negotiated, she can stay up a bit later and read in her room while we party on down here,' I teased.

'Mum, that's not fair,' Lauren whined, although she'd had enough adult company for one day at Amber's.

'Your mum and I need to have a chat about boring work, and I promise you, you won't be missing anything,' Josh lied, already carrying Lauren up the stairs, her skinny legs wrapped around his waist.

'Clean your teeth, popsicle,' I called after them before going to the kitchen to get two bottles of beer out of the fridge.

Ten minutes later, we were on the sofa, Josh telling me about his awful day at work, where he'd had to give a member of his team a final warning.

'That is why I could never be a manager,' I admitted, knowing I was too soft. 'Anyway, stop putting it off, tell me about Jamie! I thought you weren't seeing him until the weekend,' I pushed, nudging Josh's thigh with my toe.

'It practically is the weekend. Good Friday tomorrow, which means I can lay in my pit, or his, all day.' He winked cheekily.

Jamie, Josh told me, was cabin crew for EasyJet. A six-foot tall, golden-skinned and sandy-haired man with gorgeous green eyes. Josh showed me a few photos, including the infamous torso shot again. I shook my head, 'I can't believe you haven't slept with him!'

'Me neither, some restraint right!' I could see through Josh's bravado there was something about Jamie. Something which set him apart from the millions of other torsos, not to mention other body parts I'd seen courtesy of Josh. 'So what's going on with the hunt for whatshername? The woman who lived here?' Josh asked, reaching for another beer, the both of us having necked the first at speed.

'Danielle? Oh I'm not going to look any more. Too much conflicting information. Her colleague thinks something sinister has happened to her, but the police aren't looking, so they must know more than we do.'

'It's odd though, no one just vanishes.'

'It looks as though she had a flight booked to Egypt right before Christmas, whether she boarded the flight or not I don't know. Obviously that's something they'll only tell the next of kin.'

'And who's that?'

'Apparently she's got an estranged sister in Scotland, but I don't think anyone other than this Mark, who worked with her, is looking.'

'Jamie's twin sister is police, perhaps she could help?'

'Nah, it occurred to me today, maybe she doesn't want to be found.'

'It might put your mind at rest,' Josh countered. 'What's her last name?'

'It's Stobart, but I don't think there's much point,' I shrugged, standing to stretch my muscles. 'Fancy a Jack Daniel's chaser?' I asked, despite not having finished my beer.

'Stop, I'm going to be hammered. Anyway, why are you all dressed up? I never see you in anything floral!' He smirked; teasing me was one of his favourite pastimes.

'Oh, I was one of the gorgeous housewives of Beech Close earlier. We were all invited around to Amber's for Pimm's.'

'Get you, worming your way into the IT crowd,' he guffawed as

I rolled my eyes and disappeared into the kitchen to grab the Jack Daniel's and some ice. 'And what's happened with that guy, your neighbor?' Josh called from the sofa.

'Remy? Oh, not a lot, he got a bit... overzealous, you might say,' I replied, carrying in two tumblers of bourbon.

'Shame. I thought he was quite fit, he had a whiff of that bloke from *Mad Men* about him, John something,' Josh mused as I knocked back the Jack Daniel's.

The alcohol coursed through my bloodstream, loosening everything, making the worries and stresses of the week ebb away. I should never have drank the Pimm's, because once I got a taste for it, it was hard to stop.

'Are you sure you're okay?' Josh asked, looking pointedly at my empty glass.

'I think I need to exchange contracts on Mum's cottage. It's hanging over me, you know.'

Josh reached out for my hand, giving my fingers a squeeze. My chest swelled. Josh had been the one constant in my life since we'd met, never judging and always there when I needed him. There was no such thing as a better friend.

'Love you,' I said, letting his hand drop as I heard a tap at the door. 'Have you called a taxi already?'

'No, but I better,' Josh replied, tapping his phone to find the app.

Maybe Valerie was at the door, wandering around the close in her nightgown again. I wasn't in the mood to deal with her antics tonight.

'Answer it then,' Josh nagged, and I scowled, heading towards the door. Was there no peace?

'Hi.' Remy stood in the glow of the hallway light. He looked tired, shadows collecting under his eyes, his jaw unshaven. A visceral pull in my gut, as he stepped closer, opening his mouth to speak but interrupted by Josh's voice.

'My taxi is here, see you later, gorgeous,' Josh said, kissing the top of my head as he squeezed past me. I knew it wasn't, Josh had only just requested it, but it was his way of telling me to go for it.

'Have fun,' I called after him as he headed down the driveway, my eyes not leaving Remy's. Dutch courage combined with a desire for something dangerous impaired my judgement and I momentarily forgot about the altercation at the cottage. Stepping back, I pulled open the door and waited for Remy to come inside.

33

I could say it was the bourbon which had gone to my head, but as soon as the front door was closed, I pulled Remy's face to mine. I didn't want to talk. I didn't want to hear about Valerie or listen to any apologies. I only heard my body and not my head, so when I pressed my finger to my lips and took Remy by the hand to lead him upstairs, he didn't object, following me into the bedroom and letting me undress him.

I woke around four draped across Remy's chest. Our bodies entangled in the duvet, and I tried to extricate myself without waking him to use the bathroom. The house was quiet, the lamp downstairs had been left on, light creeping through the crack beneath the door, but it didn't matter. Remy snored, an arm behind his head, the duvet sat low across his hips, covering his modesty. I admired him, the man asleep in my bed. I could count on one hand the number of men I'd had sex with and although I knew it wasn't going to go anywhere, I didn't regret a single thing about last night.

The sex had been good, but I could tell Remy was holding back. Perhaps he'd have been different if I hadn't called him out for being rough with me on Wednesday. Last night he'd been overtly gentle, careful about how he touched me, as though I was made of glass. I'd been the opposite, clawing at him, hungry to feel him inside me.

'Are you okay?' Remy asked, rubbing his eyes as I ventured back out from the bathroom.

'Fine,' I whispered. 'Although you're going to have to go.'

Remy stared at me, brow furrowed in a fog of confusion.

'It's Lauren, I don't want her waking up and finding you here.'

'Okay,' he said, swinging his legs out of the bed to get dressed, still half asleep.

I tried not to laugh. Who was this woman who had sex with a man, after barely any prerequisite, then chucked him out at dawn?

Remy put his shirt on, fumbling with the buttons and ran his fingers through his messy hair.

'Will I see you later?' he whispered as we crept down the stairs.

'Sure. I'm going Easter egg shopping, but that's about it,' I said, not offering any commitment.

Remy nodded and raised a hand in a goodbye when he left.

I closed the door and hurried back to bed, snuggling down in the duvet, and tried to go back to sleep.

* * *

A couple of hours later, I woke in a cold sweat, believing Mum was looming over me at the end of the bed. It was a variation of a nightmare I'd had, one which had got worse since she'd passed. There was no chance of getting back to sleep after that, so I headed downstairs.

Teddy was sulking in his bed, as he'd been unable to get into the bedroom last night. I let him out into the garden, changed his water and fed him before making some coffee and switching on the laptop. I'd forgotten all about Becky's email, but it was waiting for me, along with a friendly email from Ebony, letting me know she'd call as soon as contracts were exchanged tomorrow.

Becky had forwarded an acceptance from her manager for a rolling four-week contract at the rate I'd suggested. If she was as useless at admin as she'd said, she might need some serious organising, but it would be manageable if I didn't renew the market research contract at the end of the month. I'd be able to start working for Becky at the beginning of May, the contract would be more lucrative without the agency taking their cut too. As long as Becky wasn't a diva, we'd get along fine.

Lauren slept in, so I left a note to let her know I was on the green with Teddy. Outside, it drizzled, the sky a depressing grey that did not bode well for the Easter bank holiday weekend. Beech Close was quiet as usual and my gaze fell on Valerie's house, picturing Remy sleeping inside when hours before he'd been in my bed. Teddy took an interest in the base of the tree, sniffing and pawing at the softened mud. It must have rained overnight as the grass was damp underfoot.

'Teddy, come on,' I pulled on his lead to tug him away, catching movement across the road out of the corner of my eye.

Over at number five, Derek was waving from his window. I raised a hand to say hello, but he wasn't waving in greeting, he was signalling for help. Dragging Teddy away from the tree, I strode over to the window where I saw Derek was on his knees, holding himself, clinging to the window ledge.

'Are you okay?' I asked loudly, hoping he would hear me through the double glazing.

'The key is under the mat,' he said, gesturing towards the front door.

I hurried over, finding the key and unlocking the door. Teddy shook his damp coat and I thought twice about taking him inside, wrapping his lead around the bracket for his hanging basket so he couldn't wander off.

'Stay, Teddy,' I commanded and pushed the front door open, wiping my feet on the mat. 'Derek?'

'I'm in here,' a weak voice called from the front room.

I found Derek on the floor by the window, in his dressing gown and pyjamas, silver hair sticking up like a mad professor. He was cold to touch and his skin ghostly.

'What happened?'

'I tripped on the rug last night when I got up to close the curtains. I haven't been able to put any weight on my damn ankle.'

'You've been here all night?' I said, forcing his arm over my shoulder to bear his weight and dragging him upwards, hanging onto the window ledge for support.

'I stupidly left the handset upstairs, so I've been waiting for signs of life.'

Using all my strength, I heaved Derek onto the sofa, where I could take a better look at him. His face was clammy, and I didn't like his pallor, it was grey.

'Let me take a look at your leg,' I said, dropping back to my knees and rolling up his pyjamas. His ankle was swollen and already a nasty purple colour, tiny thread veins covered the surface. I was concerned about the lack of circulation. 'I think we need to call an ambulance, Derek – it might be broken.'

'Really? I'm sure it's not. A cup of tea will sort me out, you know, I am parched.'

'I'll make you one in a minute,' I laughed, pulling my mobile from my pocket and calling an ambulance.

Should I phone Remy to help? Or one of the other neighbors? There was no need to wake them, Derek was lucid and talking, it wasn't an emergency as such. Although Lauren was home alone and I was keen to get back to her.

I was sure once the paramedics arrived, they would take him to hospital. The old and the young could deteriorate fast if they weren't treated and my pulse rocketed at the thought of anything happening between now and their arrival. I relayed the information to the call handler, letting them know the extent of Derek's injuries and emphasising his age and the colour of his foot. The lovely lady assured me they'd be as quick as they could.

When I came back to check on Derek, his leg propped on the sofa, he smiled at me, rubbing his grey beard, eyes twinkling.

'How's about that cup of tea then?'

34

It took forty-five minutes for the paramedics to arrive, rumbling into Beech Close, no need for lights or sirens. Derek was wrapped in a blanket and nursing a second cup of tea, his colour coming back to normal. We had spent the wait talking about some of the students he'd taught over the years, those who had gone on to do great things. Greatness, as Derek said, was easy to spot in a child, if only one took the time to look. I loved listening to Derek talk, pausing only to FaceTime Lauren, who had woken up and was eating Rice Krispies at the table. I asked her to come and take Teddy home, who was whimpering at Derek's front door to be let in, reminding her to leave our door open so she wouldn't lock herself out.

Patsy and Lisa, the cheerful paramedics, were fantastic and after a few checks deemed it necessary to take Derek in for an X-ray at the least. I offered to call someone for him, but he asked me not to, he didn't want to bother his son.

'I'm sure it wouldn't be a bother, Derek,' Patsy said, her eyes flitting to mine.

'No, no. Shelly, if you could just pack me a few bits. Phone, toothbrush, et cetera, I'd be most grateful.'

I nodded and disappeared upstairs, hearing Derek call after me there was a bag in his wardrobe I could use.

I moved from the bathroom to his bedroom, searching through drawers and collecting underwear, a change of clothes, his toothbrush, deodorant and comb. An old Samsung mobile was plugged in beside his bed, fully charged, so I put that in the bag too. I scanned the room for anything he'd find useful, packing a book about Jack the Ripper from his bedside table and a crossword puzzle. Before going downstairs I passed the second bedroom, poking my head in just to check there wasn't anything else I could pack for Derek. Inside was a neatly made double bed which must be where his guests stayed. I carried on down the hallway glancing inside the third bedroom, or box room, which had a pine desk in it, with an old-fashioned green reading lamp on top.

I stopped in the doorway, momentarily distracted as I admired the layout, considering whether to position my desk in the same spot, by the window, overlooking the back garden. It wasn't until I turned to leave that I saw it. Secured with Blu-Tack on the adjacent wall was a close-up photo of Danielle and a cutting from the local paper in which her disappearance had been briefly mentioned. I shrank away from it as all the heat seemed to leave my body and my veins turned to ice. Why did Derek have a photo and newspaper cutting of Danielle on his wall? Inching towards his desk, I pushed at the paperwork, but nothing seemed to be related to her. It was mainly household bills.

'Did you find everything?' Lisa called from the hallway.

By the time I got to the top of the stairs, Derek was already strapped into a wheelchair and being manoeuvred out the door. Over the clanking of the wheelchair, I could hear Niamh and

Remy's voices outside, the ambulance having drawn their attention.

'Coming,' I shouted down, popping back to shut the office door behind me.

I forced a smile when I joined the others outside, Niamh was chatting to Derek in the back of the ambulance and Remy's face was one of concern as he watched on.

'Take care, Derek,' I called into the ambulance before Lisa took the bag from my outstretched hand and closed the doors. I didn't trust myself to say goodbye properly, unable to meet his eyes, unsure what my expression would covey.

'Hey, are you okay?' Remy asked, appearing at my side and rubbing my arm.

'Yeah, I'm fine,' I said, my stomach still churning. 'I've got to head back, Lauren's been on her own for ages,' I said, smiling feebly, leaving as Niamh came to join us. I gave her a wave and jogged back across the green, agitated by my discovery.

* * *

My head was spinning, so much so I snapped at Lauren when I got back inside. She complained I'd been gone ages and I told her not to be such a baby. My eyes filled with tears as I locked myself in the bathroom upstairs, hands resting on the sink, staring into the mirror. I'd have to apologise, I didn't mean to be so sharp, but I was reeling from discovering the photo and cutting of Danielle in Derek's office. What could they have been doing there? Was he responsible for her disappearance?

Derek had to be sixty at least, he was retired after all. Danielle was twenty-seven, so what would a man in his sixties want with a woman of that age? The idea made me shudder. Should I tell someone? Mark perhaps? Although I didn't want to send him on a wild goose chase. It could be innocent, although I couldn't think why he'd have her photo there. Becky must have been right, he was closer to her than he'd admitted to me. Why would he lie?

I wanted to go through the box of Danielle's things, but I couldn't find them anywhere. Perhaps I'd thrown them out by mistake or maybe Lauren had? It was odd, they'd been on the floor by the sofa the last I'd seen them. Thankfully the photo was still in my handbag, but everything else, the necklace, watch and novel, had disappeared. Was I going mad? Had Beech Close sent me crazy in under a week?

I tried not to think about Danielle or Derek as I wandered around the supermarket with Lauren later that morning. I pretty much let her put what she wanted in the trolley, such was the guilt at seeing her bottom lip wobble when I'd snapped at her. It wasn't something I did often and when I'd come downstairs to apologise she'd been a little frosty. I'd suggested the supermarket knowing she'd take advantage of my remorse.

When we got to the seasonal aisle, it looked as though it had been ransacked, with only a few chocolate eggs remaining. I'd left it too late.

Lauren, unfazed by the lack of choice, ran straight to the white chocolate options.

'Can I have this one please?' Lauren lifted a large white chocolate KitKat egg from a shelf above, handing it to me.

I added it to the trolley, as well as the last remaining pack of hollow eggs and treats for the egg hunt I'd promised on Sunday.

'This looks cool, can I get it, Mum?' Lauren asked, waving a weave-your-own basket creative kit at the end of the aisle.

'Sure,' I relented, hoping we'd have a quiet afternoon at home. It was still raining outside, and I hadn't recovered from the drama of the morning. The last thing I wanted to do was head back out to find a source of entertainment for Lauren. Not when I still had flat-pack to build and curtains to hang.

Although when we pulled onto the driveway, Josh's car had gone and Remy was waiting on the doorstep, a bunch of yellow roses in hand.

35

'Happy Friday the thirteenth,' Remy said, holding out the bunch of flowers towards me despite me juggling bags from the supermarket.

'Oh, thank you,' I said, a tight smile on my lips. 'Lauren, can you take them please?' I couldn't hide my frustration at him turning up, the postcoital glow a distant memory now.

'Sorry, here let me,' he said, holding the flowers in one hand and taking a full bag of shopping from me so I could unlock the door. 'You said you weren't up to much,' he added, ruffled as he sensed my demeanour.

'Sorry, no, I'm not,' I replied, a wave of guilt washing over me as I beckoned him to follow us inside. 'Lauren, this is Remy. I don't think you've properly met,' I said, looking from my daughter to Remy.

He held out his hand for her to shake and her cheeks glowed at the adult introduction.

I put the shopping away and made us some tea while Lauren played tug of war with Teddy in the lounge.

'I don't want to encroach on your day, but you said you were around,' Remy said.

I turned to face him as the tea brewed. 'I was only going to build some furniture, try to get the office sorted, that's all. I can do it another day.' I smiled, folding my arms over my chest. Another reason why I'd been single for so long, I was used to being on my own, master and commander of my time.

'Hey, I'm not too bad with my hands, you know.' Remy winked at me, the lines around his eyes crinkling.

'It would appear so,' I laughed, and the tension between us evaporated.

We spent the day putting the office together, building the desk and bookcase. Lauren helped too when she wasn't weaving her Easter basket. By late afternoon, the rest of the flat-pack had been built and I had a functioning office. The curtains I'd brought with us in the move had been swapped for new ones and the place finally felt finished, like it had the Lucas stamp on it. Remy had rolled up his sleeves, ordering me around, reading instructions and taking control of the build. It was easy to see him on a construction site, wearing a hard hat, barking directions. Not only that, but for someone who admitted to not wanting children, he charmed Lauren with ease.

She was smitten with him from the outset, and he went out of his way to involve her where he could, so she didn't feel left out of our activities.

'I'm ready for beer, how about you?' I said, leaning back on my haunches to admire the office, which only needed some artwork on the walls to inject a bit of personality and it would be perfect. Maybe I'd ask Amber to paint me a small canvas once she'd done Lauren's.

'I hope Derek is all right?'

I'd managed not to think about Derek all day until Remy

mentioned him as we put our feet up and enjoyed a cold bottle of Corona which had been chilling in the fridge all day.

'I'm sure he's fine, his ankle was probably sprained rather than broken, but the poor guy had been on the floor all night, waiting for someone to pass by. I tell you, there's nothing good about getting old,' I said and Remy raised his beer.

'I'll drink to that.'

'You know what though, the whole Danielle thing...' I paused as Remy glanced to the heavens at the mention of her name.

'What?' I retorted, body stiffening, but Remy didn't even have the courtesy to look sheepish.

'I think you need to let the Danielle thing go.' He sighed as though I was an annoying child going on and on about a trip to the swings.

I chewed the inside of my cheek, staring at him. 'Oh? And why is that?' I asked, it was an effort to keep my voice level. I wasn't spoiling for a fight, but Remy dismissing me boiled my blood.

'Because I don't believe there's any conspiracy, I'm sure she's fine wherever she is, if she wasn't, the police would be searching for her, wouldn't they?'

'Did you take her out for dinner? Like you did me?' I asked, searching Remy's face.

'What has that got to do with anything?' He didn't deny it.

'You said you didn't know her.' I wanted to say more, but something in Remy's expression stopped me, but I wasn't willing to change the subject entirely. 'Derek had a photo of her on his wall, and a newspaper clipping,' I blurted.

Remy's eyebrows shot skyward. 'A photo?'

'Yes, a photo.' He pondered on it for a while, before speaking. 'That is odd.'

'It is, and every time I think that you're right, she's fine, in

Egypt or somewhere living some hedonistic existence, I discover something else that doesn't add up.'

'Oh, so Derek, a retired school headmaster, offed her then, did he?' he scoffed.

I recoiled like I'd been slapped. 'Forget it,' I shot back, shoving my chair back and getting up to use the bathroom.

In the bathroom, I splashed water over my face and neck, dabbing myself with a towel as I took in my reflection. I didn't know what was going on between Remy and me, but I knew I didn't want it to end yet and especially not over a difference of opinion. Perhaps Remy was right, playing Miss Marple was sending me in circles. There must be a good reason Derek had her photo pinned to the wall of his office. The last thing I wanted was to fall out with Remy over something so trivial, even if he had taken her out for dinner. It didn't have to mean anything. Perhaps he didn't mention it because it was so inconsequential. I didn't want to rock the boat, not when we'd had such a nice day.

'How did your mum get on at the doctors?' I asked, coming down the stairs.

Remy was tapping at his phone, but a black cloud crossed his face at the mention of his mother. 'Okay, they've upped her medication, which should level her out but might make her a bit spacey, they said, initially anyway.'

'Where is she today?'

'She's over at Niamh and Finn's. I think Niamh is doing a roast.'

'That's nice of her,' I said, trying to get my head around why Niamh would offer to have Valerie for the day. I could hear her voice crystal-clear 'that woman is the bane of my life.'

Remy chuckled at my puzzled expression. 'It certainly is,' he agreed but didn't elaborate further. It was almost as if I didn't get the joke, but before I could ask what he meant, Lauren joined us in the kitchen, pleading takeaway pizza for dinner.

Remy and I exchanged glances and I shrugged.

'Fancy a pizza?' I asked.

He smiled, nodding. Our disagreement minutes before seemingly forgotten.

'I like to keep the workmen fed, you know,' I teased as Lauren disappeared to find a menu.

'I'm sure it'll give me some energy for later,' Remy flexed his hands dramatically and I giggled, a stirring inside at the idea of what was to come.

36

Our pleasant evening was not to be as Remy got a phone call just as I was putting Lauren to bed.

'I'm going to have to go,' Remy sighed. 'Mum's had a nap and woken disorientated. Apparently Niamh is trying to kidnap her.' He rubbed at his forehead.

'Let me help,' I said.

I tucked Lauren in bed, whispering I'd be back shortly and was just taking Teddy outside. She mumbled a sleepy response and rolled over onto her side, clutching Jules for comfort. I stroked her hair – sometimes it amazed me how I'd managed to grow such a perfect human inside me

Remy was waiting on the driveway, eager to get over to Niamh's but too polite to leave without me. I told him to go on, while I got Teddy's lead. By the time we'd got to the centre of the green and Teddy had urinated at the base of the beech tree, Remy was already leading Valerie out of Niamh's house by the elbow. She appeared to be ranting and Remy was trying to calm her down. Niamh materialised in the doorway, illuminated by the security light, a shawl around her shoulders. She was gesticulating and shaking her head, clearly displeased, although she was too far away for me to hear what she was saying. Where was Finn?

When she looked over, I waved and she smiled, waving back before turning to Remy. It seemed as though they were arguing, the conversation obviously heated. A cold unease crept down my back when they both looked over at me in unison. Teddy had taken the opportunity to empty his bowels, so I bent down to scoop it up, glad I'd remembered to bring a bag. When I stood, the front door of number six was wide open, but Remy and Niamh were nowhere to be seen. Valerie had disappeared too. The scene looked eerie from afar, the door wide open and not a soul around.

I shuddered in the damp air, the chill taking hold, wishing I'd thrown on a sweatshirt. Drizzle coated everything in a blanket of tiny droplets, my bare arms had a sheen to them. It was the kind of weather that caught you out, where you ended up unexpectedly soggy. Rather than standing still, I circled the green, debating whether to wait or go back inside. It seemed Remy had things under control, and I didn't want to leave Lauren alone too long.

My attention was drawn to Derek's house, which was lit up like a Christmas tree. He must have been discharged and a slow smile reached my lips that he wasn't as badly injured as he could have been. I hated to think of him lying on the floor all night, unable to call for help and I was glad he was back home. The light streaming through the window turned my pupils to pinpricks. Derek hadn't closed his curtains, allowing a view straight into his lounge. The memories of the morning came flooding back and I still didn't know what to think about the photo of Danielle in his office, despite what Remy had said. On the outside, Derek seemed like a lovely old man, but didn't they all? First impressions weren't always the right ones. My thirty-three years had taught me that.

Teddy pulled on the lead as he sniffed at a spot towards the edge of the green. Movement caught my eye from Derek's window.

Through the net curtains, I saw him sat in the armchair staring out into the darkness. Could he see me? The street lights were on, but surely the light was too bright inside to make it clear out here. He was still now, like a statue, sat rigid, looking out, directly at me.

I pulled Teddy's leash, a sudden urgency to get back to the house. The atmosphere in Beech Close was off, as if something was bubbling under the surface.

'Come on, Teddy,' I said before cold fingers dug into my shoulder. I whirled around, dropping the lead, and letting out a yelp. Valerie squinted at me, jabbing her bony finger at my chest.

'You're dead,' she whispered.

Fear lodged in my throat, and I was unable to speak, managing only to stumble back a couple of steps. Teddy bounded off towards the house, making his getaway as I searched past Valerie for Remy. Relief hit like a brick when he came out of Niamh's and jogged towards us.

'You're dead,' Valerie repeated, this time her finger prodding into my breast. She recoiled with a gasp, clicking her tongue on the roof of her mouth repeatedly and shaking her head.

'Come on, Mother, home now, it's been a long day,' Remy said, a touch of forced frivolity in his tone. He rolled his eyes at me, but I could only look on in horror, Valerie's words ringing in my ears. *You're dead*. Was it another threat? 'Are you okay, Shelly?' Remy frowned at me, taking in my ghostly pallor. 'What did she say to you?'

'Nothing, no, I'm fine. I've got to go,' I replied, backing away as fast as I could, to where Teddy was waiting, scratching at the door to get away from the scary woman.

Inside, I locked the door, pressing my head against the wall. What was wrong with everyone here? Was it me or were the people of Beech Close unsettling?

Teddy was already in his bed, curled up, head bowed, glad to be back inside. I went upstairs, checked on Lauren, who was already snoring, and then went to my bedroom at the front of the house. I peered out between a crack in the new curtains, but Remy must have taken Valerie home as they were both gone. Niamh had to be safely tucked inside, even her security light had gone out. Derek's house too was now in darkness, but still I was unsettled.

What did Valerie mean? Her habit of creeping up on me was terrifying, the stealth-like way she moved, but I didn't believe she meant me harm. When she touched me, the revulsion on her face was bizarre. Dementia had got its claws into Remy's mother and it would only be a downward spiral from here on out. There were going to be some bumpy roads ahead for him.

I ran a bath, trying to be quiet so as not to disturb Lauren, wincing at sound of the pipes as it filled. I opened the window wide to let out the steam, the sky outside now pitch black. When I slid beneath the water, the heat washed away my tension and I closed my eyes, listening to Valerie's wind chime tinkle. The sound was similar to my mother's bell, and I understood why it frightened Lauren so much. Nanny frightened her, she frightened us all.

Tomorrow, the cottage would no longer be mine. The sale would be complete. Memories would stay, of course, no matter how hard Lauren and I tried to lock them away, but at least the property would be gone. Finally she'd gifted me some peace, knowing Lauren and I would no longer have to struggle was a weight off my mind. I'd be able to give Lauren all the things I didn't have as a child, but, most importantly, all the love I possibly could.

Closing my eyes, I sank deeper into the water, my muscles relaxing in the warmth, feet planted at the end of the tub to anchor me. I didn't want to think about Remy, or Valerie or Derek.

I had no desire to relive Danielle moving through this house or question if she was the one who scratched LEAVE NOW into the wall of the airing cupboard. Yet my mind had other plans.

I ran the hot tap, hoping the heat would purge my thoughts before sinking back down, the water to my chin. Lethargy enveloped me and I closed my eyes, allowing myself to doze for a second. I drifted off, listening to sounds of the house, pipes settling and floorboards expanding, that was until long fingers crept around my throat, and I began to choke.

37

'Mum!' Lauren screamed as I shot upwards, bending my knees and coughing. Tepid water sloshed over the side of the bath, drenching the bathmat on the floor. Lauren stepped back as a puddle edged towards her, her yellow nightie had slipped off one shoulder in her haste to get out of bed. To get to me.

I coughed, gripping the sides of the bath to haul myself onto my feet.

'Are you okay?' Lauren asked, grabbing me a towel. 'I heard you screaming.'

I wrapped it around me, clutching it with one hand and touching my throat with the other. There was nothing there, no fingers gripping me tight, and my neck in the mirror bore no marks.

'I think I was dreaming,' I said, stifling another cough.

'Nanny?' Lauren asked, knowing all nightmares stemmed back to her.

It was so real, being strangled, having the air squeezed out of me as I gasped for breath. I must have fallen asleep in the bath and slid under the water, swallowing a mouthful as I woke up. I reached into the few remaining bubbles and pulled the plug out, goosebumps peppering my skin, before lowering myself onto the toilet, knees weak. What an idiot. I couldn't believe I'd been so stupid to doze off. I could have died.

'Go to bed, honey, I'm fine. I'm sorry to wake you.' I held Lauren's hand for a second, until she squeezed my fingers and let it drop, rubbing her eyes and yawning.

'Okay, if you're sure?'

I nodded.

'Good night then,' she said sleepily and padded back down the hallway to her bedroom, closing the door with a click.

I wrapped my hair in the hand towel and listened to the wind chime tinkle, sounding more ominous than ever.

'I'm losing it,' I muttered to myself, pulling on my pyjamas.

Downstairs, I microwaved some milk to make hot chocolate, waiting for my hair to dry a little before going to bed. Sleep wouldn't come for a while, I knew that. As I waited for the microwave to ping, I hunted around for the box of Danielle's things, still frustrated at their disappearance. Had Lauren moved them? She'd have no reason to. I checked behind the sofa and the hallway again, but they were nowhere to be seen.

Could someone have taken them? Removed them from the house? The only person to come inside was Remy, although Niamh and Becky had been at the door. Valerie too. Perhaps it had been taken as a deterrent. Maybe because I was already getting too close. The stuff inside the box was evidence of Danielle's life at Beech Close and what she'd left behind.

Remy didn't want me looking into her disappearance, that much was obvious, but was he the only one? Niamh and Becky hadn't batted an eyelid when I brought Danielle up yesterday afternoon. Amber, on the other hand, clearly didn't like her. And what about Derek, who initially seemed like her only ally in the close? Had he posed a danger? Had Valerie scared Danielle off first? Had she made death threats against her too? I had an inkling all the residents in Beech Close knew more than they were letting on. Perhaps Leo and Maxwell could shed some light on it.

Fully awake now, I finished making my hot chocolate and took my phone to the kitchen table. Fingers fumbling over the screen to my messages, I clicked on Josh's name.

Happy Easter! Sorry I missed you when you got the car. I know I said not to, but (I know what you're like) did you get a chance to ask Jamie's sister about Danielle?

I knew it was a long shot but worth a try.

Despite the late hour, his message came back quickly.

Happy Easter to you too. No-go, I'm afraid, doesn't have access to search the police database as she works in the custody suite or something. How was your visit from Remy?

I quickly responded, fingers flying across the screen.

I have a lot to tell you! But it was good. How was Brighton?

Josh's text came through in less than a minute.

Good, and same, a lot to tell you too! 😭 Mum wants you to come to lunch on Sunday. X

I smiled at the text, I adored Josh's mum, Joyce.

As for Danielle, I was no further on. She had an older sister though, in Scotland, Mark had said. Would her name be Stobart too? Despite it being late, I sent a message to Mark, asking if he knew the name of Danielle's sister. If she was her next of kin, then the police must have given her updates, the reasons why they weren't progressing with the investigation into her sister's disappearance. If I could speak to her, maybe it would set my mind at rest.

Unlike Josh, who was practically nocturnal, Mark didn't respond straight away. It was likely he was in bed asleep, which was where I should be. I messaged Josh to say we'd love to come and finished my hot chocolate, heading upstairs to bed and crawling beneath the covers, reluctantly switching off the lamp and plunging the room into darkness. Telling myself I was safe; the doors were locked, and no one was out to get me. I'd become paranoid, Danielle's disappearance amplifying the feeling. We'd been living at Beech Close for a week and already so much had happened. It hadn't been a settling-in period, more of a baptism of fire.

I closed my eyes and pictured Danielle, my renewed vigour to find out what had happened to her. Someone didn't want me to know and that spurred me on. Number 3 Beech Close had already given up some secrets. Anyone could have scratched LEAVE NOW into the wall of the airing cupboard. But it was possible it might have been Danielle leaving a message for future tenants, or maybe someone had been trying to scare her. Becky had said tenants never stayed around for long, no more than a year, which posed the question, who had been at Beech Close before Danielle? The mystery buzzed around my head until the sun emerged and I eventually fell asleep.

* * *

Lauren gently shook me awake, already dressed in a pretty polka dot playsuit, her hair brushed and clipped away from her face. I tried to shrug off the fog of being woken from a deep sleep and pulled myself upright.

'I've made you breakfast and a coffee.' Lauren rolled onto her tiptoes in excitement, and I couldn't help but smile. I rubbed my eyes and looked at the clock, it was almost ten. 'I've also fed Teddy and taken him over the green.'

'You mustn't do that, Lauren. I don't want you taking Teddy out on your own, it's not safe,' I gently reprimanded.

'I'm ten,' she replied, giving me a withering look.

'I know, and I appreciate it, I do, but do your old mum a favour and don't go out on your own. Not here. I don't know the area well enough yet,' I said. I didn't want to let Lauren out of my sight, especially with Danielle's disappearance hanging over Beech Close.

38

I got out of bed and kissed the top of Lauren's forehead before pulling on my robe and going downstairs. I didn't want to fight with her or make her feel like she wasn't allowed to do anything, but Lauren was all I had in the world now. It was just me and her and I had to protect that.

As I entered the kitchen, the smell of burnt toast hung in the air and a peek in the bin revealed she'd made two attempts before the perfectly toasted slices which lay on my plate.

'Wow, thank you,' I said, making a show of slipping into the seat and opening the butter.

Halfway through my breakfast, I checked my phone. Mark had text back an hour ago, letting me know Danielle's sister was married and now called Maria Taylor. He'd been in contact with her at the time of Danielle's disappearance, but she hadn't been forthcoming.

Four months had passed since then and if anyone had any inside knowledge on the police investigation, or lack thereof, it was her. Perhaps a female touch might be what was needed? It was worth a try.

Another text followed Mark's initial one, this one with Maria's number. I responded quickly with thanks and said I'd update him as soon as I had any news.

'What are we doing today?' Lauren asked, sat at the opposite end of the table.

'I don't know, honey, what do you want to do? Have you eaten?'

'I had cereal,' Lauren replied with a faint air of superiority, which made me smile. She was growing up too fast.

'Ummm, I don't know. We could go bowling, or down to the beach?' It was sunny outside, although I hadn't checked the temperature. Perhaps a day trip was what we both needed.

My phone bleeped again, distracting me from Lauren's excitement at the proposal of a day at the beach.

Just checking in, are you okay? You seemed a little freaked out last night. Did Mum say anything to you? Anyway, had a great day. Got work this morning but might be around later. R x

'Mum!' Lauren complained.

I turned my phone over without replying to Remy. It could wait.

'Why don't you pack a couple of towels and some sunscreen. We'll jump in the car down to Widewater Lagoon, what do you say?'

Lauren beamed and rushed away to gather everything she wanted to take to the beach.

A shower could wait, I'd had a bath late last night anyway. Not the relaxing one I'd originally planned. I shuddered, recalling the fingers that felt very real at the time, around my throat. Instantly I lost my appetite and binned the rest of my breakfast, determined to push that to the back of my mind, I threw on a T-shirt dress and tied my hair into a messy topknot. Within twenty minutes, we were in the car, picnic packed, glad to be leaving Beech Close for another type of beach. One which would be much better for relaxing.

Widewater Lagoon was a huge nature reserve in Lancing, around thirty-five minutes from us. If I had any downtime and it was a warm, sunny day, I would drop Lauren off at school and hit the beach with a book for a few hours. When we got there, the car park was almost full and I snagged one of the last spaces. Hauling our bag from the car, we found a good spot near the water's edge, out of the wind, sheltered by some rocks. The tide was on its way out and had left us some sand to sit on, instead of the painful pebbles.

I laid down our towels, and Lauren, in her flip-flops, went straight in for a paddle, throwing stones for Teddy to chase into the surf. I laid on my front, watching the waves shimmer in the sun. It could have been a little warmer for a beach day, but it would do. At least the dog wouldn't get too hot.

Lauren paddled, whooping water in high arcs above her head and dashing out of the way of the falling droplets, making Teddy bark. While she was distracted, I made the call to Maria Taylor. Hoping she would answer a call from an unrecognised number. It was Saturday and nearly lunchtime, which seemed like a good time to ring. As long as the sound of squawking seagulls in the background didn't drown out my voice.

'Hello?' a wary woman answered, the same tone I had when I didn't know who was calling.

'Is that Maria?' I asked, keeping my voice light and upbeat.

'It is, who is this?'

'My name is Shelly, I'm a friend of Danielle's,' I lied, my mind scrabbling with what to say next.

Maria waited for me to continue.

'We used to do Pilates together,' I cringed, remembering my first meeting with Niamh.

'Have you seen her?' Maria asked, her voice curt.

I signalled to Lauren who was going further out, the hem of her playsuit dangerously close to the water.

'No, no, I was going to ask you the same question,' I said, keeping my voice friendly.

'We're not in touch,' Maria replied flatly.

'Do you know if the police are looking for her?' I pushed gently, it was the question I was desperate to know the answer to, but if I pressed too hard, too fast, I could tell by her short responses Maria would shut down.

'No, they aren't looking for her,' Maria sighed, and I remained quiet, hoping she would volunteer some information. It seemed I was wrong, and the silence stretched out.

Fearing I was going to lose her, I said, 'Do you think she went to Egypt?'

'The police have a record of her taking the flight as well as using her bank card out there, so yes, she's in Cairo somewhere.'

'Really?'

'Have you been in touch with Mark?' she said, sounding exasperated. 'Look, this isn't the first time she's done this, when things get too much she runs away. It's her MO, only this time she's fooled everyone into thinking she's been kidnapped or something. Always the bloody centre of attention,' Maria ranted down the phone.

'I'm sorry, I didn't mean to—' I began, but she cut me off.

'Please don't call unless she's been in touch. I'm not chasing her halfway around the poxy world. She'll come back when she's ready.' With that, Maria left the call and I gazed out to the shore, watching Lauren play.

Maria had said Danielle had upped and left before, and clearly didn't seem too concerned. If the police knew she'd got on the flight and her card had been used in Egypt, they obviously wouldn't be searching for her. I shouldn't be searching for her either as she wasn't lost. It seemed Danielle had wanted to disappear, for whatever reason. Raking through the reasons why was of no benefit to anyone.

I laid my head across my folded arms and listened to the waves lap, all the week's tension floating away from my body. Nothing had happened to Danielle, there was no conspiracy at Beech Close. No mystery to uncover. She was just a girl who'd lived in the house before me, who had left some of her things behind when she moved on.

39

Despite it not being the hottest day me and Lauren had spent at the beach, both of our shoulders and faces were glowing by the late afternoon when we loaded our things into the car and headed home, our bodies covered in a mix of sun cream and sand I couldn't wait to shower off.

On the dual carriageway, Ebony called to let me know the good news. The sale of Mum's cottage was complete, funds deposited into my account. I no longer owned the home that held so many bad memories. The sale, combined with the confirmation Danielle had been on the flight to Egypt, lifted my mood.

Instantly lighter, the future seemed bright and any reservations I had about living in Beech Close had disappeared. I could even suffer being Valerie's neighbor for the time she had left there. I was sure at some point Remy would have to get her additional help or assisted housing. Although the thought gave me a twinge of guilt. Having had first-hand experience of caring for someone with dementia, I knew how much of a battle Remy had on his hands.

I let Lauren and Teddy into the house, going back to the car to retrieve the beach bag. Outside, I hung the towels on the line as Teddy lay in the shade by the fence, waiting patiently for his chew he hadn't had at lunchtime.

'Here you go, pal,' I said, handing him the bacon-flavoured treat. As I did, there was a rumble against the fence and Becky's head popped up. 'Jesus, Becky,' I said, jumping backward with a laugh.

'Sorry, I didn't mean to intrude. Maxwell and I are about to enjoy a cider in the hot tub. Do you want to join us?'

It was an effort not to recoil in horror at her suggestion. Climb into a hot tub, half naked with relative strangers? No thank you.

'We've just been to the beach, so I've got some bits to catch up on, but thank you,' I said politely.

Becky grinned knowingly as my cheeks flushed with the lie. 'Did you receive the email I forwarded on? Are you happy to come onboard and organise me?'

'Definitely, I can start in May, gives me time to wind down the other contracts.'

Becky grimaced, she wanted me right away, but there was nothing I could do. I had other commitments and it was only two weeks.

'Okay. I'll send some bits to your email, not work,' she corrected herself quickly. 'I mean sharing my files, so you'll have everything to hand. I'll get HR to put the contract together and get it over to you for signing.'

'Brilliant.' I smiled, already backing away towards the house.

'I'll let you get back to your day. I think Niamh was on about having another party tomorrow or Bank Holiday Monday. I'll let you know.'

Terrific, another awkward social marathon I'd have to endure if I couldn't come up with a good enough excuse to get out of it. I didn't say anything but smiled willingly until Becky's head lowered behind the fence.

After a shower and a cup of tea, I text Mark to tell him what I'd found out from Danielle's sister. He responded quickly with a short '*guess that's it then*'. I imagined the frustration, hours spent searching, only to find out Danielle had deserted him without an explanation. It wasn't how friends should treat each other and I found it hard not to think of Danielle's actions as callous, but I didn't know her side of the story. Who was I to judge?

'Nanny's cottage has gone now?' Lauren asked out of the blue, twirling her hair in her fingers.

'Yes, sold today. We never have to see it again.'

I watched Lauren visibly deflate, as though she'd been holding her breath.

'Do you think she's in heaven?'

A lump formed in my throat at the innocence in her face. 'I'm sure she is. She'll be doing all the things she used to love, like gardening and...' My words drifted, as I had nothing more to add.

'Will we go to heaven?' Lauren's bottom lip wobbled slightly, and I pulled her into my arms.

'Definitely.'

Lauren extricated herself from my grip after a minute, despite me being reluctant to let her go, and resumed her position on the sofa, controller in hand. While she was content, I put some washing on and pushed the hoover around upstairs, popping my head into the office and smiling at the space I couldn't wait to use. At Mum's, I worked from the kitchen table, with barely enough light to see in the dark oak beamed room. It was any wonder I'd been able to build a successful client base, but sheer perseverance had paid off.

We had an early dinner and I promised Lauren a trip to the swings as Teddy needed a walk after sleeping in the shade all afternoon. As we left, clicking shut the front door and locking it, I glanced around Beech Close. Derek's car remained on his driveway, and I doubted he'd be going anywhere in it soon. Even with a sprain, he'd struggle. A sense of responsibility niggled at my side, and I decided to pop in on him on the way back, to check he was okay. He might need some shopping and I wanted to be neighborly. I reasoned I didn't have to go in the house, and I was sure I'd be safe, despite what his intentions might have been towards Danielle.

Amber and Leo's drive was empty, and I assumed they were out, enjoying their Saturday, probably somewhere in town perusing an art gallery and sipping espresso martinis. Becky and Maxwell were likely drunk on cider by now, shrivelled to a prune and naked in the hot tub. Over at Niamh and Finn's, the Range Rover was missing. Perhaps he was working again or frolicking with a twenty-something secretary in some secret tryst while Niamh planned another extension.

'Mum, what are you smiling at?' Lauren asked, as I chuckled to myself at my ludicrous thoughts.

'Nothing, honey, have you got Teddy's ball?' I said, heading towards the green.

'Uh-huh,' she replied, holding it out for me to see.

Remy's car was absent from Valerie's driveway and it reminded me I hadn't text him back yet. Perhaps it would be good to play a little hard to get, some distance might be an idea as I didn't want to get too attached.

The park was busier than I'd ever seen it. A family were having a late picnic, playing cricket on the flat grass and there were lots of children in the play park. Despite no swings being free, Lauren bounded in, keen for the company of people her own age. I did the usual circuit with Teddy, throwing the ball and getting him to bring it back until his tongue was hanging from his mouth.

I rang Josh as I made my way back towards the swings, he answered breathless, and I was worried I'd disturbed his time with Jamie.

'I've just got back from a run,' he said, still panting when I queried what sounded like a dirty phone call.

'Are you mad?' I knew he was where fitness was concerned, ever striving for the perfect physique.

'Gotta feel the burn, baby,' he laughed. 'Are you still coming for dinner tomorrow?'

'Yes! Will it be the four of us?' I enquired. Was it serious enough for Josh to bring Jamie home to meet his mum?

'Yes,' he replied, a playful edge to his voice because he knew what I was alluding to.

'Okay, well I can't wait. I'll let you go and get in the shower, I bet you stink.'

'Try not to dream about me lathering up too much,' he shot back.

'Don't flatter yourself,' I said with giggle. There was only one man I was dreaming about and I still needed to text him back.

40

I beckoned to Lauren, who stomped back towards the gate, protesting she didn't want to leave yet. I was already thinking about a cold bottle of lager in the garden, reading my book in the glorious sunshine. Celebrating the sale of Mum's cottage and the end to a perfect day.

'Come on, Lauren, I want to go back now.'

Lauren sulked and moved at a snail's pace to annoy me. When I said I was going to check on Derek, she held out her hand for the key and I was glad to get her out of the way.

I knocked on the door, aware of a fluttering of movement through the window. Derek pulled the door open, a welcoming smile across his face. He held on to the frame to keep his balance, his foot slightly lifted from the ground, strapped in a boot.

'Here's my saviour,' he said, running a hand through his grey hair, trying to flatten it down as though he'd been asleep on the sofa.

'How are you?' I asked. 'Was it broken?'

'No, no, just sprained, they want me off it for a few days, but it's already healing. The swelling has gone down.'

'I'm glad you didn't break it. Is there anything you need, any shopping?'

'My son has been over already today, stocked the fridge and brought me a nip of whisky too, so I can't complain.'

'Well, don't drink too much and fall over again,' I said, chuckling.

'It's the boredom. Daytime television is what's wrong with the generation today, and don't get me started on *Love Island*,' he said. A brief image of Derek's office and computer flashed into my mind, Danielle's photo on the wall. Who knew what his Google search history might contain? The warped idea made my throat tighten and I coughed, eager to make my escape.

'Well, as long as you're okay. Take care, Derek.' I considered offering my number in case of an emergency, too used to being someone's nurse, but Derek had a son who was perfectly capable of looking after him.

Remy's Mercedes pulled into Valerie's driveway as I was crossing the road. He climbed out, wearing jeans and a white T-shirt, heading towards me. Before I could say hello, he planted a kiss on my lips as Teddy jumped up to get some attention of his own.

'Well, hello,' I said, raising my eyebrows.

'I've been thinking about doing that all day,' he said, unabashed, snaking his arm around my waist and nuzzling into my neck, on full display to the neighbors. He was a heady mix of sweat and antiperspirant and my resolve weakened as he brushed his hand across my backside. My mind already straying to when Remy spent the night and how good it felt to be intimate again.

'I've got to get some dinner for Mum, but are you around later tonight, once she's safely in bed?' He gave me a wink and I had an influx of irritation. Was I just a booty call? I couldn't deny I wanted him over, but was there any more to us than lust?

'Sure,' I said, eventually, watching Remy's frown at my answer taking too long to morph into a grin at my acquiesce.

'I'll see *you* later,' he said, emphasising the 'you' so there could be no mistake as to what his intentions were.

Butterflies continued to flutter around my chest as I negotiated an early night with Lauren. Bath, book, cuddle and bed was our routine and I hoped it would still give me time to freshen up before Remy arrived. Thankfully, it did and I managed an attempt to look sexy and tousled without it seeming like I'd put much effort in. I had the same clothes on as earlier, but the underwear I'd put freshly on was one of only two matching sets I owned.

I waited by the window, staring out into the dusk, drinking first one beer, then another, feeling more pathetic as it got to ten o'clock and Remy still hadn't arrived. I hadn't been stood up by a guy since my teens and as the minutes ticked past I became more annoyed. At half past when there was a tap at the door, I left it for a few minutes before opening. He tapped again before I answered. The evening had brought rain with it and the shoulders of his T-shirt were damp.

'You managed to sneak out then,' I said, without bothering to smile.

Remy stepped over the threshold, shaking droplets out of his hair. He closed the door behind him, eyes glinting as I stepped back against the opposite wall, about to move into the lounge. The hallway was cramped, discarded shoes pushed to the side and Lauren's coat shoved in the corner.

'Wait,' he said as I made to move. 'Close your eyes.' I did as I was told and Remy took the beer bottle from my hand, the clink of it making contact with the tiles as he lowered it to the floor. I was acutely aware of his breath at my neck and the smell of bourbon that came with it. The door to the lounge behind me clicked shut, Remy making sure we were alone, sandwiched together in the small space. A finger traced along my collarbone; our faces so close his lips brushed my ear when he whispered his question, 'Do you trust me?'

I nodded, despite it being a lie. My pulse throbbed in my neck, suddenly galloping as the hand at my collarbone moved to my throat. Remy rubbed the skin with his thumb, a gentle caress before the pressure intensified. His other hand found its way between the waistband of my jeans and my stomach, zip pulling apart. Before I could slow things down, Remy pushed his fingers into me, and I gasped. A mix of fear and pleasure fought inside my head as his breathing quickened from excitement. Remy's thumb and forefinger were lodged underneath my jaw, squeezing, restricting my airway as I orgasmed, legs trembling.

I slumped against Remy, opening my eyes to find him grinning, revelling in his achievement.

'That wasn't so bad, was it?'

I pushed away from him and through the door to the lounge, holding myself upright on the arm of the sofa. My groin pulsed and for a second my head was as light as a feather.

'Look, I'm not a pervert or anything, it just intensifies it. Tell me that's not the best orgasm you've ever had.'

I scoffed at him, incredulous. One minute Remy was the perfect gentleman, the next he was an arrogant prick. It was like he had two sides, two faces. It was clear he was a man used to getting whatever he wanted.

Remy's brows knitted together, frustrated by my lack of response, but I was at a loss what to say. Yes, it had been nice, but did I like to be choked as a rule during any kind of intimacy? Absolutely not.

'It was intense, yes, but it's not something I'm into. I thought you understood that.'

'I didn't hear you saying no back there.' Remy's sullen teenager act was pissing me off.

'It's not about consent, I gave you consent, I did what you asked, but would I do it again, knowing what you intended to do? No, I wouldn't,' I snapped.

'I don't think you know what you want,' Remy sneered.

My cheeks were on fire and I pulled myself upright.

'I'd like you to leave,' I said, pointing towards the door.

'Really?' he said, surprised at the sharpness of my voice.

'Now,' I added.

Remy stared at me for a second, open-mouthed, as if he couldn't understand why his visit hadn't gone as planned. It made me second-guess myself. Was I wrong? Was I weird not to want it? He'd been late, there'd been no evening spent together, just a fumble in a hallway. And what? I was supposed to be grateful. The silence filled the room until there was no air left.

Remy let out a cold laugh, shaking his head in disbelief as he walked to the front door and opened it. 'I'll tell you who liked it... Danielle, that's who. She couldn't get enough of it,' he said, his parting shot dripping with venom.

41

It took another two beers before I was able to go to bed, the time almost midnight. I'd locked all the doors and windows. Remy's words echoed around my head as I climbed beneath the covers. At first he'd alluded to barely knowing Danielle, then I'd found out from Becky he took her to dinner, and now he was boasting how much she enjoyed his weird sex games.

He could be spiteful when he wanted to be, and I was ready to draw a line under our brief fling. It was no wonder he was unattached. Perhaps he was a narcissist and him playing nice – helping me build furniture and move the chest at Mum's cottage – was specifically to reel me in. Get me to trust him so he could draw me into his deviancy. I should never have got involved in the first place.

Perhaps I should take Lauren away for the last week of the Easter holidays, use some of the funds from the cottage for a last-minute trip? But that would mean running away, which wasn't something I ever did, and I wasn't about to start now. Remy and I could be civil I was sure, and if he couldn't, I'd ignore him. We needed this house, this address, so Lauren could get into Briarwood High School when it came time to apply in September. I couldn't lose sight of why we moved here in the first place.

* * *

Despite the awkwardness of the evening with Remy, I slept like a log for the first time in ages. I attributed it to the sale of the cottage having finally gone through, the massive weight now off my shoulders. With each week that went by since the passing of my mother, I was able to relax more. The tension in my shoulders slowly easing with the realisation life would be so much better moving forward.

I woke on Easter Sunday before Lauren and headed down-stairs to put out her giant chick I'd bought from Ikea as well as the KitKat egg she'd chosen and the Maltesers one gifted from Anna. I added the hollow chocolate eggs we'd use for the hunt later once back from Joyce's. While I waited for her to wake, I pinned bunting to the wall and, satisfied with the display, made a cup of tea. Knowing Lauren would squeal with delight when she got up, nothing excited her more than chocolate and she was the only kid I knew who loved Easter more than Christmas.

I was determined we'd have a great day and was looking forward to visiting Joyce and spending time with Josh. If anyone could talk me out of my funk, it would be him. He'd tell me to kick Remy to the kerb, forget about him and move on. Team Lucas all the way. It's what Lauren and I had always been, and I would be content going back to that. A relationship, or even a brief fling as it turned out, was sometimes more hassle than it was worth, and I wanted to pour my energy and focus into Lauren. We needed to heal after the nightmare with Mum, and we would, in time.

My concentration was broken by Lauren's shriek as she

rounded the bottom of the stairs, causing Teddy to bark, tail wagging ready to play.

'Happy Easter, honey. We're going to go to Joyce's for a lovely roast dinner.'

'What about the egg hunt?' Lauren was already cuddling her chick, tweaking the beak.

'We can do it when we get back.'

'I'm going to call her Chica,' Lauren said, opening the egg and digging into a Maltesers bunny. I didn't argue, it was one of the rules. Chocolate for breakfast was only allowed two days a year: Christmas and Easter.

I fetched Lauren a glass of water and opened the back door so Teddy could chase a pigeon who'd dared to land on his turf. He barked and I winced, hurrying out after him.

'Teddy, shush!' I snapped, waiting for him to urinate and pointing for him to go back inside. As I turned, I could hear muttering, words carried on the breeze I couldn't make out. Stepping down the path, they grew slightly louder, coming from Valerie's side. I edged onto the grass, covered in dew, trying to be as quiet as I could.

'She's gone, she's gone, she's gone,' Valerie's voice came through the fence. Who was gone?

'Valerie, are you okay?' I asked. Was she talking to herself or was Remy there?

As soon as I spoke, the whispering stopped abruptly. I looked at the fence, searching for a tiny divot I could peek through. I found one, around chest height, and bent down to look through into Valerie's garden. All I could see was an expanse of grass and the opposite fence. I placed my palms either side of the hole, pushing my face against the scratchy wood, straining my eye to see as much as I could into Valerie's garden.

A second later, a muddy grey eye stared back, blinking at me.

I screamed, jumping backwards, hands trembling.

'Valerie?' I said, looking back through the hole and taking in the slate mix of her iris.

'Danielle,' she gasped, and the eye was suddenly gone, replaced with white fabric. I recognised it as her nightgown. She had straightened her legs, face no longer level with the hole in the fence, and now clawed against the wooden panel, raspy breaths that unnerved me.

'Valerie, where's Remy?' I asked, keeping my voice calm and non-threatening.

'Mum?' Lauren called from the kitchen. Perhaps she thought I was going mad, talking to the fence.

I shooed her away with my hand, mouthing the words 'go back inside'.

'Why are you here? What do you want with my son?' Valerie snapped, sounding more like the woman I'd met on my first day at Beech Close.

'Nothing. Is Remy there, with you?'

'He's mine! You can't have him,' she spat, banging on the fence so violently I jolted back. I had half a mind to tell her I didn't want anything to do with her son, not now, but before I could reply, she began hollering at the top of her voice. 'You shouldn't be here.' Repeating the words again and again as Teddy barked from the kitchen.

Trying to communicate with her had been a mistake. Did she think I was Danielle? Had she hated her too? If Remy had taken her out, it was likely Valerie would have known about it, and no doubt loathed the idea.

Trust me to land myself with a nightmare neighbor, I thought to myself as I went back inside and double locked the back door. Leaving her yelling in the garden.

'She's mental,' Lauren said, her mouth full of chocolate, teeth covered in brown slime. I grabbed my phone, typing a short message to Remy to tell him his mother was yelling in the garden. I waited for the two blue ticks to show me it was read before setting it down again.

'No, Lauren, she's sick. Enough egg now, go upstairs and get dressed and don't forget to clean your teeth please,' I said, annoyed I'd let Valerie sour my mood. I turned on the radio, loud enough to drown her out when I heard Maxwell shouting from his back garden. Valerie must have woken him up. I sniggered to myself, imagining a harassed Remy having to come out in his boxer shorts to fetch her inside. It would serve him right.

42

We got to Joyce's around midday. Lauren had picked out a bunch of flowers from Marks and Spencer's on the way, as well as a lemon pavlova with lashings of whipped cream. Joyce knew I wasn't the best cook, but I was sure she would appreciate my token offer of dessert. In stark contrast, Joyce was excellent in the kitchen and had cooked me many a roast dinner over the years, exclaiming I needed feeding up whenever Josh brought me home. I adored her, even more so when she made it clear I was always welcome at her house.

At the time, I hadn't realised it, but looking back she'd sensed my mother's lack of maternal instincts – my skinny physique, occasional unwashed clothes and hair I'd cut myself with household scissors. I would have happily moved in, but my mother made it known she didn't like Joyce, whom she believed was only too happy to poke her nose into someone else's business, when in reality she was only concerned about my neglect. She referred to her as an 'interfering old cow' whenever she was mentioned, and I quickly stopped telling her I went round there. She knew where I was, as a teenager I spent as much time out of the house as I could and Joyce's door was always open.

When Joyce greeted us and beckoned my daughter into her arms for a hug, I got a pang of sadness that hit me like a bolt in the chest. Joyce should have been the nan Lauren got, the one she deserved. She still wore her large round glasses, the same style she'd had for years, her once brunette bob now a silvery grey.

'Hello, my lovelies, come in. Josh is laying the table...'

'Hello, Joyce, these are for you,' I said, handing her the flowers and pavlova.

'Thank you, darling, you really shouldn't have.' Joyce kissed me on the cheek.

'Now, you, my precious,' she said, turning to Lauren, 'I have a job for you.' She led Lauren through to the kitchen, where she was decorating Easter meringue nests with cream and chocolate mini eggs, Teddy following the smell of lunch cooking.

Josh's childhood home was a stone's throw from Mum's cottage, where I'd grown up. However, her mid-terrace was large in comparison. We'd not known each other as kids, having not attended the same school. Josh had gone to an all-boys school across town, somewhere he'd told me his young sexually confused self had suffered. I'd gone to an all-girls school, where I'd been the class mouse. We'd changed a lot since those years, but not much had altered in Joyce's house other than a refresh of paint and soft furnishings.

The place still held wonderful memories which warmed my heart. In the kitchen we'd eat freshly made bacon sandwiches Joyce would prepare when Josh and I would roll home after clubbing all night. At the table, she'd helped me write my first CV so I could get a proper job when I left school, constantly assuring me I was going to do more with my future than tend a bar.

'Hello, gorgeous,' I said, finding Josh in the daffodil-yellow dining room and wrapping my arms around him. He returned the hug, still clutching a fist full of knives and forks.

'How are you, my lovely? All okay?'

'Yeah fine, it's been a mad few days. I've got loads to tell you,' I said, finding the placemats in the drawer of the Welsh dresser and helping lay the table.

'Spill the tea,' he said with a raised eyebrow.

I used the opportunity without Lauren's listening ears to tell Josh all about Remy, how his little sexual quirks had been a step too far for my vanilla world.

Josh listened, his head tilted to one side, looking at me woefully. 'Best off out of, at least you got a little bit. It still works then?' Josh asked cheekily, trying to make me laugh.

'Yes it still works!' I smacked him on the arm, knowing my abstinence was a subject he loved to tease me about.

'It'll tide you over for another five years at least.' Josh rolled his eyes and cringed away as I raised my hand to wallop him again.

'Anyway, how's Jamie?' I asked, changing the subject.

'Lush.' Josh gave a theatrical sigh.

'Well, fill me in,' I said. It wasn't normally like getting blood from a stone.

'Later,' he replied as footsteps padded down the hallway and Joyce and Lauren entered the room laden with condiments and napkins.

Joyce had cooked a gorgeous leg of lamb with all the trimmings, and we tucked in until we were laid back in our chairs patting our full to bursting stomachs. Josh spoke a little about Jamie and Joyce winked at me, her glee at him seeming to be smitten obvious. He was the apple of her eye, an only child, like me – something we'd bonded over as teenagers.

When the conversation turned to how I was getting on at

Beech Close, Lauren asked if she could get down from the table, bored of the adult talk. Joyce sent her into the garden to play with Teddy, which she was thrilled about as Josh's old wooden swing still stood in the corner, the frame green with algae. She jumped straight on it, swinging in the sunshine as we watched through the patio doors. With her now occupied, I recounted my run-ins with Valerie.

'So Danielle isn't missing?' Josh asked as I brought him up to speed, Joyce listening intently.

'Apparently not. I mean, it's odd, don't get me wrong. There's no record of a removal company in Crawley coming in, and I'm not sure why she'd leave so soon after her dog had disappeared, but if the police are satisfied, I guess there's no mystery to solve.' I got up to help Joyce with the plates and Josh scratched his chin thoughtfully.

'Maybe it was Mark she was trying to get away from?'

'Maybe, or Steve, the ex-boyfriend. Apparently Remy took her out too,' I added, grimacing, omitting the part about her enjoying being choked, if that was even true and not Remy being vindictive.

'Hmmm, and Valerie called you Danielle? Do you think she believes you are Danielle?'

'Potentially. Me living in the same house has obviously baffled her,' I replied, balancing the plates and carrying them out to the kitchen.

Josh followed me in, the table cleared.

'What if when she said "you're dead", it's because she thought you were Danielle? You should ask her what she knows, maybe she saw something,' Joyce suggested, her brow furrowed with concern.

'She's not always lucid, Joyce, so I'm not sure how helpful she'll be.'

'Do I need to be worried?' Josh said, picking up on the tension in his mother's stance.

'No, I'm sure it's just a misunderstanding with Valerie. You remember how my mum would get,' I said, trying to appease them. I was sure I wasn't in any real danger, not from Valerie.

Joyce relented and gave my shoulder a squeeze at the mention of my mother. I took the rubber gloves out of her hands and shooed her into the garden while Josh and I washed up. I wanted her to enjoy Lauren while she was here and vice versa, plus it gave Josh time to give me the low-down on his most recent date with Jamie, who he'd been clubbing with in London last night.

'He's funny, you know, and he, like, gets me. Gets all my weird quirks and stuff.'

'I'm pleased for you. I can't wait to meet him,' I added hopefully.

'You will soon, I promise. I don't want him to freak out if I get too serious too soon, I mean, we've only met a few times.'

'Well, he seems keen,' I said reassuringly, watching Lauren through the window play catch with Joyce.

'How's she doing now?' Josh gestured towards Lauren, who was flailing her arms and laughing as she ran for the ball.

'She's fine, I think. We don't talk about it,' I said, knowing Josh was alluding to the final day with my mother.

'Do you think she remembers what happened?'

'No,' I replied, 'I think she's blocked it out.'

43

We didn't leave Joyce's until late in the afternoon, savouring our desserts, which Joyce served around three, once our dinner had finally gone down. Josh would have to roll Lauren and I out of the house and into the car, we'd eaten so much.

On the way back, we stopped off at local woods to walk Teddy somewhere different. It was a place all the teenagers used to hang out in high school to drink cider and smoke weed, but I was never invited. I wasn't one of the cool kids, although I knew it went on, I'd overhear the whispers on a Monday morning of what happened at the weekend. Who hooked up with who? They used to call it Tramps Paradise. Even now, there were condom wrappers and discarded vodka bottles littering the earth.

'Come on, this way.' I grimaced, steering Lauren in the opposite direction, where the path was a bit easier to navigate and with a lot less debris. 'Did you have a nice day?' I asked, and Lauren grinned.

'Joyce's cooking is banging,' she said, making me laugh.

'It is,' I agreed, and thinking of my conversation with Josh, I added, 'Do you remember the day Nan died?'

She considered the question for a second and nodded slowly. 'I won't tell anybody, Mummy.'

My body tensed as the words spilled from her lips, but I kept moving, one foot in front of the other. I didn't need to find a change of subject because Lauren launched into a list of her suggested hiding places for the egg hunt she still wanted to have when we got home. Despite still being full from lunch, she hadn't forgotten the promise of chocolate eggs and I was grateful she was so easily distracted.

At home, I dutifully hid the eggs around the house, noting where I'd put each one, and let Lauren loose while I took Teddy into the garden to play tug of war. Valerie wasn't out, but I could hear the motor of the hot tub humming over on Becky's side, I imagined she was taking advantage of the remnants of afternoon sun.

Within ten minutes, Lauren had found all the chocolate treats bar one, which I sneakily saved for myself to have with a cup of tea later. Stuffed to the brim, she took herself upstairs to Face-Time Holly. Taking the opportunity to use my new office for the first time, I logged on to my laptop. I'd had nothing through from Becky, no contract, but it was Bank Holiday weekend after all. She hadn't sent any files or links to shared access either, but I guessed HR had advised her not to do anything before contracts were signed, which was sensible. If Niamh was having another hideous drinks soirée tomorrow, I could check in with Becky about it then.

I rolled my eyes and prayed for rain. I wasn't much of a joiner and having to smile and feign interest in the activities of the housewives of Beech Close wasn't my thing. Guilt nudged at my side, they'd been nothing but welcoming, but we were so different and the more time we spent together, the more obvious it was.

Also it might mean bumping into Remy, which was something

else I was avoiding. He hadn't been in touch, not that I wanted him to. But I was waiting for the first awkward exchange. I could hardly ignore him, we were practically neighbors with Remy spending so much time at Valerie's. It crossed my mind that I had no idea where he lived. Did he have another house somewhere? A flat maybe? I could hardly ask him now, not when he'd behaved like such a dick. As far as I was concerned we were done.

* * *

Niamh's get-together on Bank Holiday Monday turned out to be a full-on afternoon barbecue and despite my silent prayer for rain, the spring weather let me down and it was sunny with barely a cloud in the sky. Reluctantly, I got ready, putting on one of the only summer dresses I owned, a long flowing mint-green number with a shirred waist.

Lauren couldn't wait to go, hardly able to keep still as I plaited her hair and tied it with a yellow ribbon. She was excited to see Amber again, although I'd warned her she might be busy. The party was for grown-ups and we wouldn't be staying long, only showing our faces to be polite. I didn't bother to ask Niamh whether Lauren could come with me. I had a child, I wasn't about to leave her home.

'Turn that frown upside down,' Lauren said, mocking me.

I scowled at her as we walked across the green laden with our morning's purchases. After a trip to the park to throw the ball for Teddy, we had been to Tesco and filled our basket with flowers and a bottle of Prosecco, which I'd put in the fridge as soon as we got home. At least this time, I wouldn't be a pauper arriving with a warm bottle of cheap wine.

When we arrived, Niamh opened the door wearing a long

colourful kaftan, making a good impression of the leader of a
sixties hippy cult. I watched closely for her face to change when
she realised I'd brought Lauren with me, but it didn't and she
invited us in warmly.

'Ah bubbles!' she exclaimed when I handed her the bottle,
condensation running off it. It seemed bubbles were the drink of
choice, but in the kitchen was a large bowl of fruit punch, a ladle
by the side for serving. Probably why everyone looked so happy,
they were all half-cut already.

All of the residents of Beech Close were there, except for
Derek, Remy and Valerie, and I sighed silently with relief. There
would be no daggers across the decking. I lost Lauren to Amber as
soon as I arrived, who looked thrilled to see her.

'Ooohhh I love your dress,' Becky said, waving a glass of
punch in my direction, which I took gratefully.

'Thank you,' I replied, trying not to blush as Amber, Niamh
and Becky's eyes fell upon me momentarily.

'I'm just glad he's got it sorted. I mean, the other day she was
out there howling at the sky,' Becky said to the others, going back
to the conversation I'd walked in halfway through.

'Who?' I asked, taking a sip of the punch, which was more
vodka with a dash of cranberry juice and an orange segment.

'Oh, we're talking about Valerie. Remy has finally got some
help, a live-in carer is coming apparently. It's too much for him to
manage, poor sod,' Becky continued.

Niamh scoffed, clearing her throat.

'How is he going to afford it?' Amber asked, frowning.

'Don't worry about that, the construction firm does extremely
well,' Niamh cut in, her tone razor-sharp. Was she jealous?

'Well, he did your extension beautifully, I'd love him to do
mine at some point,' Becky said wistfully.

'And it's not just her extension she's talking about,' Amber said, rolling her eyes.

'Amber, there's children present!' Becky snapped, but her cheeks went pink all the same.

44

The women stood in one corner of the kitchen, talking. The men smoking cigars on the decking outside. Lauren soon got bored and went to put on the television. Amber, Becky and Niamh talked about their Easter weekends, which had been reasonably quiet. Becky moaned about going back to work tomorrow, groaning loudly when I told her I had another week off before Lauren went back to school. It was obvious she wished she was in the position of Amber and Niamh who could come and go as they pleased. Perhaps Maxwell didn't have the earning power of Leo and Finn?

After around half an hour, I excused myself to use the bathroom, disappearing upstairs despite knowing there was a toilet on the ground floor. I couldn't help being nosy, wanting to see the scope of Niamh's designer skills and whether they continued upstairs. The layout of all the houses were the same, with the exception of any additional building work. I hadn't known Remy's company had done Niamh's extension. I'm sure he was incredibly busy if the workmanship of the build was anything to go by.

I poked my nose into the blush-pink master bedroom, the

bed perfectly made with bolster cushions on top and a throw draped across the bottom. Everything was feminine. Even in the bathroom, there were small injections of pink in the fixtures and fittings. I bet Finn let her get on with it, anything for an easy life.

I locked the door and used the toilet, washing my hands with Molten Brown soap before drying them on fluffy Egyptian cotton towels and applying a layer of hand cream. It smelt divine but wasn't something I could afford. We had Carex, courtesy of Tesco, in our house. I imagined Niamh wrinkling her nose at the offering and it made me giggle.

I opened the door, having satisfied my curiosity, and collided with Finn coming out of the master bedroom.

'Oh God, sorry,' I said as we bumped into each other. I bounced off him; he was such a unit, his chest was solid.

'My fault, wasn't looking where I was going,' he said, smiling and gesturing for me to go ahead. He didn't ask why I'd come upstairs instead of using the downstairs toilet and I was compelled to say something.

'The downstairs toilet was occupied,' I lied.

'No problem, *mi casa es su casa*,' he replied, and I wasn't able to stop my face creasing. 'Too much?' He laughed at my expression, running a hand through his sandy hair sheepishly.

'No not at all,' I giggled. 'I'm not used to having such friendly neighbors.'

'Hmmm, yes so I hear. Valerie has been difficult recently, but now Remy is getting help in, things should get better.'

'Oh no, I meant where I lived before,' I said, skin burning at the base of my neck, a flush ready to creep upwards.

Finn smiled awkwardly. 'Ah I see, I shouldn't have jumped to conclusions.'

I lingered on the landing, debating whether to bring up

Danielle but figured I had nothing to lose. 'I believe the lady before me, Danielle, might have had some issues with Valerie?'

Finn shifted from foot to foot, but I held fast, pretending not to notice I was blocking the stairwell. He could have flicked me down the stairs with his finger, but he had the aura of a friendly giant. Although I hadn't forgot the black eye Niamh had last week, the bruising now gone or well hidden under her concealer.

'I believe she accused Valerie of hurting her dog, ridiculous notion. Shall we?' he replied, gesturing for me to move.

I smiled and made my way downstairs. Danielle seemed to make everyone nervous. Perhaps she was someone Beech Close would rather forget. A blip in their perfect tight-knit community.

I was hardly surprised by Finn's admission though. Valerie had tried to hurt Teddy by dropping chocolate over the fence, she must have known it was poisonous to dogs. It wasn't so outlandish to think she might have done the same thing to Barney.

I checked on Lauren in the front room, who was listening to Amber talk animatedly again about the canvas she was painting for her. In the kitchen, Niamh was setting out canapés, her kaftan sleeves swishing as Becky lingered behind her.

'Can I help?' I asked politely, noticing a red ring of bruises at the base of her wrist as the kaftan inched up her arm. Marks left from being gripped too tightly? Perhaps Finn wasn't such a gentle giant after all.

'No, no, grab another drink, Finn will be firing up the barbecue soon.'

I ignored her suggestion, my drink still half full on the counter, and stepped out onto the decking into a cloud of smoke.

Josh and I used to smoke cigars back in the day, when we were blotto and walking home from the pub. Not wanting to buy a packet of cigarettes, we'd get the thin Hamlet cigars. The smell evoked so many memories.

'What are you grinning about?' Leo asked, an eyebrow raised. Maxwell shuffled to the left and I was welcomed into the circle.

'I used to smoke cigars after a night out as a teenager. I still love the smell.'

'Want one, for old times' sake?' Leo winked. He was flirtatious, and I tried to ignore the butterflies in my stomach. There was no denying his good looks, but the fact he was aware of it made its appeal lacklustre.

'No, thank you though. I better not.'

'Suit yourself. Maybe some other time,' he replied, slipping the packet back into the pocket of his navy shorts. The question hung in the air, was it an offer? Had he been the same with Danielle and she'd misread the signals, assuming Leo was coming onto her? With a wife like Amber, I doubted Leo seriously looked too far from home. She was simply stunning, but again you never knew what went on behind closed doors and perhaps Leo was the type of man who liked to have his cake and eat it too. Either way, I had to tread carefully, not wanting to give Amber the idea I may be after her man.

'Seen Remy lately?' Finn asked, all eyes upon me.

'Umm, I did on Saturday briefly,' I said, trying to maintain an innocent expression, but Maxwell raised an eyebrow, the corner of his mouth turning upwards.

'All the ladies love him, don't they.' Maxwell sniggered, nudging Finn's arm, who looked increasingly uncomfortable.

I cringed, inwardly wishing I could make my escape.

'He went out with that other lass from number three, didn't he, Danielle or something?'

'I don't think it was serious, Maxwell,' Leo chipped in diplomatically, his eyes drinking in my expression, which I was trying to keep neutral. It didn't take a genius to realise they all knew something had gone on between us.

'Where's Derek?' I asked, desperate to change the subject.

'Oh he might be over later, his son is taking him to get his ankle checked over as it's still a little swollen,' Finn replied, finishing his bottle of lager and placing it on the table as Niamh appeared with the canapés. 'Right, I'll get the barbecue going.' He clapped his hands together and I moved away, leaving Leo and Maxwell to debate what was better, a gas barbecue or a *real* one.

Becky came out onto the decking and handed me my glass, filled to the top with fruit punch. I winced as I took a sip, it was so strong.

She chuckled at my face, adjusting the straps on her sundress. It looked as though she was wasting away, her collarbones were so pronounced, spaghetti straps drawing attention to her slight frame.

'These look delicious,' I said, purposefully picking a bruschetta and biting into it. Becky watched me, smiling politely but didn't follow suit. I looked longingly at the door, counting down the minutes until I could get away. Finn had only just started cooking and I'd arrived barely forty minutes ago; I sensed I was in for a long afternoon.

45

Lauren came to find me when I was on my second drink, already feeling the effects of the fruit punch. I'd been cornered by Maxwell, who had a sweaty top lip, complaining about the quality of the broadband we received in Beech Close. Becky came to rescue me, swatting Maxwell across the stomach affectionately for talking too much. They were polar opposites. I couldn't understand the attraction for Becky at all. Maxwell had no idea how lucky he was.

Niamh took it upon herself to serve the food instead of us helping ourselves, and Lauren and I queued for a hot dog and pasta salad. I needed something stodgy to soak up the fruit punch. Everyone seemed to be able to tolerate a lot more alcohol than I was used to. Although with no children to look after, it was easy to have an afternoon nap if you'd had too much at lunch. I'd never had that luxury. Lauren whined she was bored as soon as we'd finished eating and I gave her my phone to entertain herself with. I wanted to leave as much as she did, but didn't want was to come across rude.

As it happened, Finn pulled a free-standing hammock on a frame out from his shed and Lauren seemed content to lay swinging on it. The afternoon stretched out and I slowly relaxed, finding myself easing into conversations with Niamh and Amber, the dialogue free-flowing, the alcohol making us all loose-lipped. Amber revealed her and Leo were trying for a baby again, after a number of devastating early miscarriages, her eyes misting as she spoke.

Niamh reached over and squeezed her hand. 'It'll happen for you, I just know it will.'

Amber smiled gratefully at Niamh before turning to me. 'How old were you when you had Lauren?'

'I was only twenty-two, young really. She wasn't planned,' I admitted.

'Where's her father?' Amber asked, her face carrying no judgement, only empathy. Had I formed an opinion on these women too quickly? Was I so worried about being judged I'd deliberately closed myself off to their offer of friendship despite our differences? Or was the alcohol making me warm and fuzzy.

'Sebastian left us when Lauren was a few months old. Parenting wasn't for him apparently.'

Niamh and Amber collectively gasped.

'Did you have any support at all?' Niamh held her hand to her chest as though she couldn't imagine anything worse.

'I had my mother, we lived with her for years, but she wasn't the most maternal.' It was an understatement, but the politest way to describe her.

'Wasn't?' Amber picked up on my use of past tense.

'She passed away a couple of months ago; she had dementia.'

'I'm so sorry,' Amber said, Niamh nodding in agreement. I couldn't bear their looks of pity, as though I was poor orphan Annie, struggling to raise a child alone without any help.

Thankfully, Becky came over to ask if there was any dessert on Maxwell's behalf, ending the conversation as Niamh left for the kitchen to fetch some.

'We'd better go, I should get back for Teddy,' I announced, following Niamh in, realising I'd been there for almost four hours. Unsteady on my legs, I'd drank far too much punch. No sooner than I'd got inside, the sky clouded over and rain spat onto the skylights.

'Rain,' Niamh called out the door, watching the men launch into action, closing the lid of the barbecue and putting away the hammock and garden furniture. Everyone dashed inside before the downpour.

'Bloody English weather,' Becky griped as a flash of lightning streaked across the sky and rain hammered against the windows with no warning.

A crack of thunder right above our heads shook the house and Becky squealed.

'This wasn't forecast, was it?' Maxwell grumbled, checking his phone.

Just as another bolt of lightning lit the sky, there was a thud at the front door. We all looked at each other before Finn went to see who it was.

'It's Mum, she's gone wandering again.' Remy stood in the doorway, the material of his dark T-shirt sticking to his skin. He was drenched, rain trickled off his forehead and down his nose. Before I knew it, I was beside Finn, who was retrieving his coat, stepping past him out into the rain.

'I'll help look,' I said, the icy water down the back of my dress instantly sobering.

Remy looked at me eyes wide, his lips curving into a smile. 'Thank you,' he whispered, and I felt a pull towards him I couldn't control.

'Lauren, stay with Amber,' I called back into the house.

Leo and Maxwell joined the search and we split up, each going in a different direction. Trying to avoid puddles in my sandals, I was soon as drenched as Remy. I headed towards the entrance to Beech Close, sure I'd seen a glimpse of white in the gloom. As I got closer to grass verge at the top of the close, I found Valerie crouched by the road sign, clinging to it as though it was a raft in choppy waters.

'Valerie, are you okay?'

'You shouldn't be here, why are you haunting me?' Valerie squealed, pushing her face into her knees. Her nightdress was sopping and her papery arms cold to the touch.

'Come on, let's get you inside,' I said, gently, trying to get purchase around her small frame to pull her up.

'Get away from me. You're not here, you're in my head. I'm not leaving. I'm not leaving,' she rambled, making little sense. Her hands gripped the road sign, knuckles white, and I stood little chance of removing her myself.

'She's here,' I shouted back towards the street, barely able to see the figures of the others in the downpour.

Thunder cracked again and Valerie screamed, putting one hand over her ear.

It struck me I had a chance to ask her before the others got to us. 'Valerie, what happened to Danielle?'

'You're dead, you're dead, you're dead!' she shrieked into the wind, shaking her head violently.

I could hear footsteps approaching, soles slapping on the wet tarmac.

'What did you do?' I cried, grabbing Valerie roughly by the shoulders, but before she could answer, Remy was upon us.

'What the hell do you think you're doing?' he shouted in my

face, assuming I was hurting her and pushing me aside so I fell onto the sodden grass.

'Nothing, I was trying to get her to snap out of it,' I lied, wiping my slick fringe from my eyes.

Remy didn't respond, he just eased his mother up onto her feet and led her away, leaving me sitting in a puddle of mud.

46

I returned to Niamh's, waiting on the doorstep for Lauren to be
sent out, thanking her and Finn for their hospitality before going
home. Remy had taken Valerie straight home. I didn't believe he'd
told the others what he'd seen me do. How rough I'd grabbed
Valerie out of desperation to find the truth. I was starting to
believe Danielle was a massive secret everyone knew about but
me. For whatever reason, I was being deliberately kept in the
dark. It rattled me, because if Danielle leaving wasn't sinister,
what was there to hide? Yet everyone I spoke to seemed to with-
draw at the mention of her name.

I stripped off in the hallway, leaving my dripping dress in the
sink of the downstairs toilet to deal with later. Teeth chattering, I
instructed Lauren to open the back door for Teddy in case he
needed to relieve himself, while I rushed upstairs for a shower.
Hot water pummelled my skin, chasing away the goosebumps,
and I scrubbed at the shame which lingered. I'd manhandled an
old woman, an infirm woman with an illness. What kind of
monster was I? She knew what happened to Danielle though, I
had no doubt about it. She wasn't out in Egypt living her best life,

I was certain. Something had happened to her here, in this house. In my house. Harm had come to her and what if I was next? What if Lauren was next?

My head reeled with accusations and hypothesis. Remy had dated Danielle, she'd liked it rough, if his words were true? Did something happen between them? Was it a sex act gone wrong and covered up? Someone had taken the box of Danielle's things and four of my neighbors had been at my door in the past week: Valerie, Niamh, Remy and Becky. Perhaps it wasn't any of them, maybe Derek was involved? He had Danielle's photo and news clipping on his wall after all.

No matter how hot I turned the thermostat, I still felt chilled to the bone. Giving in, I got out of the shower, put on my pyjamas and bathrobe and went downstairs to find Lauren drying Teddy with his towel.

'I fed him and he reluctantly went outside for a wee.'

Through the kitchen window I could see the rain was still coming down heavily outside. Was the party continuing in Niamh's kitchen, or had Valerie dampened spirits yet again?

'Thanks for sorting him out. Do you want a drink or anything?'

Lauren shook her head and yawned, flopping onto the sofa, and switching the television on. I sat the other end, Teddy nestling between us, and tried to concentrate on the movie she'd chosen for our evening's viewing, but my mind kept drifting. Likely down to the vodka I'd been drinking all afternoon. Now I'd stopped I knew I'd be in for a headache in an hour or so, but I couldn't bring myself to drink any more.

What had turned out to be a pleasant afternoon had ended in drama once again. Why couldn't Remy lock Valerie in? I used to lock us in the house and hide the keys when Mum began wandering. Ignoring her objections to not being allowed out. Why wasn't he more on the ball? At least he was getting Valerie some help, her erratic behaviour was happening almost every other day, and that was just what I'd seen. Who knew what I hadn't seen? There had to be a reason why Niamh said she was the bane of her life. Even friendly neighbors who helped out were finding her problematic.

By the time the comedy about two undercover cops trying to infiltrate a sorority house finished, it was almost nine o'clock and I was ready to sleep. Lauren could barely keep her eyes open too and didn't put up a fight when I suggested we went to bed. We cleaned our teeth and I crawled under the covers after I'd tucked Lauren in, checking my phone before switching it off. Josh had posted a photo of him and Jamie outside Piccadilly Circus, the lights bright in the background. He looked so happy, it made me smile. I commented with a fire emoji and turned off the phone, plumping my pillow and rolling over as a dull ache crept across my temple. Hopefully I'd be asleep before the headache hit.

* * *

It took a long time for my eyes to adjust to the dark when I woke. They were glued together, the lids heavy and unwilling to open. The clock on the bedside table read 2 a.m. I'd been asleep for over four hours, but it seemed like less. There was no air in the room, it was humid and claustrophobic. Mouth dry, I rolled out of bed, intending to go to the en suite to get a drink when I heard the noise.

Freezing mid-step at the end of the bed, the only sound now was my heart pumping furiously in my chest. Had I imagined it? The third stair creak I was so used to avoiding. It gave an eerie, drawn-out sound when trod on, low in pitch but rising almost to a squeak when weight was lifted. Was that what woke me? Could Lauren have gone downstairs in the middle of the night? She wouldn't, not in the dark and not without waking me first. I tried to swallow, perhaps it wasn't someone going down the stairs, what if it was someone coming up?

Straining my ear towards the hallway, I tried to make sense of the shapes in the shadows. My bedroom door was open a few inches and I always closed it, unable to relax entirely until I was safely cocooned in my room. I felt my bladder loosen. Had someone been in the house, in my room? Or had I simply forgotten to shut the door, too exhausted to remember before I fell into bed last night. It didn't sound like me, but under the haze of alcohol, anything was possible.

My throat was thick and syrupy, the pulse in my neck throbbing as I tried not to hyperventilate. I needed the toilet but was too terrified to move, to create any sound that might alert an intruder. From somewhere below, I heard a click, it sounded further away. Teddy's low growl sounded as he scratched at the double doors in the kitchen. Eager to get to whatever was on the other side. Rooted to the spot I waited a full five minutes, listening for any sign someone was still here. When I couldn't hold my pee any longer, I turned on the bedroom light, eyes blinded, and hurried into the en suite, racing to pull down my pyjamas and sit on the toilet, all the time fearing someone was going to bowl through the bedroom door from the darkness of the hallway.

My lungs were tight, as if I'd been chain-smoking. Wide awake now, I was on high alert, wishing I had something to use as a weapon upstairs. Other than a hairdryer, I was pretty limited. Armed with a can of hairspray, I edged open the bedroom door and skirted first along the hallway to check on Lauren. She was sound asleep, omitting tiny snores from her open mouth. Closing her door gently, I crept down the stairs, feet pressed to the edge near the wall. I managed to avoid any creaking floorboards, relieved when I got to the bottom and switched the light on, illuminating the lounge, which was just as I'd left it.

Checking all the doors and windows, nothing looked like it had been disturbed. Had I imagined the noise or had an intruder been and gone? If so, what did they take? My handbag was still on the kitchen table, Lauren's iPad outside of her room on the hallway carpet because I didn't trust her not to play on it all night. The house looked untouched.

Teddy was pleased to be let out of the kitchen early and I took him outside for a wee. Looking up at Valerie's house, the light of the back bedroom was on, but I couldn't see any movement.

I was sure I hadn't imagined it; someone had been inside my house, the air felt different, like it had shifted. Goosebumps peppered my skin as I checked the front door again, it was still locked. Did someone have a key? It was a rental after all. The estate agent obviously had one, and what about the owner? Had a stranger let themselves into my home in the middle of the night? The idea made my stomach clench, the urge to throw up difficult to overcome.

I pushed my key into the door, knowing that even if someone had a key, they wouldn't be able to use it with mine in the other side. It was a quick-fix security measure before I could sort something better.

Why would someone break in and not steal anything? It didn't bear thinking about and my imagination ran away with me on what the intentions of a masked man would be. I'd die before I let anyone touch Lauren.

47

The sound of Maxwell dragging his bin down the driveway woke me at seven. I hadn't gone back to bed, instead curling up on the sofa with Teddy underneath a blanket. Before settling down, I'd grabbed a wrench from under the sink, placing it on the floor. Teddy rarely growled, he had to have heard something too, which meant I hadn't imagined it.

'Did you get up last night?' I asked Lauren when she came downstairs a little after eight.

'Nope,' she said, fetching herself a bowl of cereal, splashing milk on the counter as she poured it. I nursed a coffee, hung-over despite not having drunk anything since yesterday afternoon. I'd prayed Lauren was going to tell me it was her, she'd gone downstairs for a drink or something, but I knew deep down she hadn't.

'What are we doing today?' she asked, raising her eyebrows hopefully, her dark hair wild like it had been backcombed.

'No idea, popsicle,' I replied. I wasn't motivated to do much other than purchase a security chain for the door and attach it.

'Can I do some painting?' Lauren asked hopefully.

I let out a low whistle, pretending she'd asked a lot before winking.

'Absolutely, we'll walk Teddy and I'll set you up in the garden later.' That way, I could relax on the grass, as long as it was dry enough, and read my book. 'I do need to pop to B&Q first though,' I added.

Lauren shrugged but didn't complain, it was somewhere she liked to go and roam around the kitchen models.

My legs were like lead on Teddy's walk, and I couldn't wait to turn around and go home.

Lauren chattered beside me, telling me about the house she was building in her game. 'I need 500 Robux to finish it. If I tidy my room can I have it, Mum, please?'

I was barely listening, my mind wandering to last night and whether the vodka compiled with an overactive imagination had conjured what I'd heard. No it was real, I was sure it was.

'Mum!' Lauren tugged on my arm, her voice whiney.

'Yes, yes, of course, honey,' I replied, happy to give her money for her game if it meant I got some peace.

On the way to the park, I noticed the missing poster for Danielle's dog had been removed from the lamp post. I stared at the concrete space. Who had taken it down and why? When Lauren dashed into the play area for her usual morning swing, I took my phone out and text Mark.

I don't think Danielle got on the plane.

I had no proof, but something in my gut told me she wasn't in Egypt, the police were wrong. Everyone was wrong. What if Danielle had never left Beech Close? The thought made me shudder as I remembered Valerie's words. Why was she convinced Danielle was dead? She knew something and I couldn't let it lie.

Mark responded quickly.

Me neither, but I'm out of ideas. The police don't want to know.

I chewed on my lip, not realising Teddy was waiting patiently at my feet for me to throw the ball I'd left at home. I found a stick nearby and tossed that instead. There was no way to convince the police without evidence and I couldn't prove Danielle wasn't in Egypt. Feeling torn, I called Josh, who would be at work. He answered after one ring.

'Early for you, isn't it?' he said, his voice laced with sarcasm.

'Piss off, I'm out with Teddy,' I said, stifling a laugh.

'What's up?' Josh was able to tell something was on my mind before I even had a chance to tell him. I rarely called him at work, knowing his job was full on.

'So much weird stuff is going on,' I began before reeling off what I'd learned at the barbecue and what Valerie said.

Before I had a chance to mention the intruder last night, Josh interrupted me. 'Do you think you're getting a bit obsessed with this, Shel? I'm worried you're blinkered and not seeing the obvious.' I could tell he was trying not to let his frustration show as he continued in a measured tone. 'Her sister said her card had been used, that she got on the flight. To me, that's case closed.'

The problem was it felt wrong. I wanted to tell Josh about last night, to get some reassurance from my best friend, but I could tell he was busy at work, it would have to wait.

'Go and have a nice day out with Lauren, take her to the zoo or something. Before you know it, you'll be back at work.' I could hear Josh smiling, but sensed he was eager to get off the phone.

'I will. Love you.'

'Love you too.'

Ending the call, my mind wasn't eased, in fact it was the opposite. Everyone seemed to want me to forget Danielle, to pretend she'd never been at Beech Close, or that was how it appeared. But I'd never been able to take instructions particularly well. My mother used to say, when I was younger, as soon as someone told me not to do something, you could guarantee I'd do the opposite, just to spite them. I wasn't immature now, but the stubbornness was deeply ingrained.

* * *

We were in and out of B&Q in ten minutes. I bought a simple but sturdy brass chain which attached to the wall and hooked around the door handle, having watched one being fitted on YouTube. I had a small drill already, one I'd purchased when I had to attach locks to mine and Lauren's bedroom doors back at the cottage.

'What's it for, Mum?' Lauren enquired at the self-checkout.

'It's just a precaution, poppet, that's all.' I wasn't going to tell Lauren I suspected someone had been inside while we were sleeping. She'd have nightmares.

On the drive back, Lauren told me about Amber's painting, how she'd told her all about the nearly finished piece of art and couldn't wait for me to put it on her wall. I was happy for the change of subject. Lauren said she wanted to try the same method Amber described, flicking paint at paper, so I was glad we had the patio for her to experiment on.

Once home, I got her stuff out in the garden, all of the paints, paintbrushes and paper, before leaving her to it and busying myself attaching the chain by the front door. I yanked at it, numerous times, pleased how it ensured no entry, opening less than a few inches when in place.

Despite moving on to chores, no matter how hard I tried to think about something else other than Danielle, I couldn't. Not even the mundane tasks of hoovering or washing made any difference. What if Danielle's disappearance was connected to my night-time visitor? Was someone trying to scare me into silence?

It was no good, I was going to try Maria again. If anyone could appeal to the police to look harder for Danielle, it was going to be her next of kin.

With it being nearly lunchtime, Lauren had finished her painting and I went outside to peg the soggy paper onto the washing line to dry whilst I made the call.

'Hello, Maria, it's Shelly, Danielle's friend,' I said when she answered the phone, surveying the mess Lauren had left all over the table.

'Is there news?' She sounded hopeful, as though despite their differences, Maria still wanted to know someone had heard from her sister.

'No, I'm afraid not. I'm sorry to get in touch, I can't stop thinking about her. Do you really think she's in Egypt?'

'The police believe so. Shelly, I don't know if Danielle ever told you, but she was bi-polar, and she took medication, but sometimes if she didn't take it, she'd... change.'

'She never said,' I replied, swallowing the lie in my throat. I felt like I'd met Danielle, although I never had.

'Yeah, well, she'd be erratic – one day manic, the next week she'd not get out of bed. In fact, I'm surprised she held down the teaching job as long as she did.'

'So you're saying you think she just wanted to get away?' I asked, deflated. If I couldn't get Maria on side, there was no moving forward.

'I'm saying it's likely.' She sighed, exhausted by the conversation.

Perhaps I needed a different tactic. 'I have some things

Danielle left behind, in the house she was living in before. A silver necklace with an infinity symbol on it.'

I heard her sniff down the phone and guilt swept through me. The last thing I wanted was to open any old wounds.

'We both had one. I bought them when we were teenagers, two identical.'

'There was a watch too, a leather strap—' I began but she interrupted me.

'With blood on it?'

My heart leapt into my mouth. 'Yes, yes, well it looked like blood.'

'And she never told you whose it was?' I noted the suspicion in Maria's voice.

'No,' I lied, trying to sound innocent.

'It was Dad's. Our parents died in a car accident. The watch was one of the things they recovered from the wreckage.'

I gasped, closing my eyes to absorb the information.

'She would have taken it with her,' Maria's voice was as soft as a mouse, and I could hear her subdued sobs. 'I'll call the police, see if I can get them to run another check. I'll let you know how I get on. Keep the watch safe for me, okay, it means a lot to us.' With that, she hung up and I stood in the garden, hand on my hip, stomach somersaulting. How on earth was I going to tell her the watch had gone?

48

My belly churned as I cleared the paints away. The watch was no longer in my possession. I'd look again, but I was sure it wasn't in the house. Someone had taken it, although who, I had no idea.

'Mum, I'm hungry, can I have some cheese and crackers?' Lauren stood at the back door.

'Sure, but you could have cleaned some of this yourself.' I frowned, juggling all the paints as I carried them inside. 'Give Teddy his chew, would you?' I asked as I put everything back in the cupboard out of the way.

Lauren and I both had crackers outside in the garden. I could hear Becky talking next door and the hot tub whirring. Unable to relax, I headed up to the office and logged on to my laptop for a distraction. I'd had an influx of emails and Becky's contract from her HR department was at the top. Opening it, I saw it was a rolling four-week contract as Becky and I had discussed, which potentially wouldn't be long-term, but would be lucrative, especially as no agency fees would be taken.

I printed it out to sign and scanned it back to the HR advisor's email address, filing my copy in one of the fuchsia-pink ring binders. Now I needed to advise the agency I wouldn't be continuing on with the market research company when my contract ran out in two weeks. They wouldn't be happy, but that was life, I had to go with the best offer, and right now, that was Becky. I was still unsure how successful we'd be working together, whether we were a good fit. I couldn't stand being micromanaged, but I believed Becky would leave me to it to get the job done.

Next was an email from Ebony confirming the exchange of contracts and completion of Mum's cottage. The funds were in my account, and she was going to provide a total figure of inheritance tax I would have to pay from the proceeds of the property, as well as the money in Mum's bank account. She'd already told me it was forty per cent, but what was left was going to be enough to buy somewhere small outright or something bigger with a mortgage. I'd think about that when the time came to move out of Beech Close for somewhere more permanent.

Amidst lots of junk mail was an email from Becky giving me access to her shared drive. Unable to curb my curiosity as to what I would be doing for her, I clicked into a folder and looked at the files inside. Becky had various letters, press releases, website content and spreadsheets of journalist contacts and print magazines, but it appeared everything was lumped together and not in any obvious order. Hopefully once we'd spent a bit of time together, I could at least organise her online filing system so things could be easily located.

One of the files I opened was from a corporate travel agent AMEX and detailed a list of flights booked, which I imagined would be staff travel. Every month, a statement was sent as to what had been booked, I doubted by Becky, but I wasn't sure. Her role was in public relations, unlikely she would have booked any flights herself, but perhaps she was able to get concessions for friends and family. I opened a few, scanning through the names and destinations until I paused, a familiar sight stopping me in my tracks.

MORGAN/NIAMH/24DEC21/0825LCA/1124LGW

The name jumped out at me first. I knew LGW was Gatwick, the airport up the road from us, but googled the airport code LCA, which I learned was Larnaca Airport in Cyprus. Late December seemed an odd time for a holiday. Scanning back through the PDF, I searched the month looking for the flight out from Gatwick, or for Finn's name. Surely Niamh hadn't gone alone to Cyprus right before Christmas, and even if she had, why was there no outbound flight booked? How did she get to Cyprus in the first place?

It was possible her parents or close relatives lived out there, I didn't know anything about her family after all, but if Becky had booked her the return flight, where was her flight out? It could be on the November list maybe, but when I scanned the files, I couldn't find the AMEX statement from November. Becky must not have moved it from her emails. I checked what I had access to, but there was no link to Outlook, so I couldn't see her inbox.

It struck me, if she'd booked Niamh's flight, maybe she'd booked Danielle's too, but on searching through the December list again, there was no passenger by the name of Stobart. Maybe Becky and Danielle weren't friendly enough for Becky to offer her cheap flights?

Moving on, I spent half an hour perusing various documents trying to guess what might be asked of me. None of the documents looked overly complicated. It seemed Becky was right and just needed some organising, which would be easy enough.

I shut down my laptop and listened to laughter drifting in through the open window of the office. In her garden, Becky had visitors, hooting at something one of them had said. As I went outside to unhook the back door from the latch so I could close it, I kicked over an empty ceramic plant pot.

'Shit,' I winced, hopping on one foot and clutching my toe.

'Shelly?' Becky's face popped above the fence, making me jump.

'Shit, Becky,' I repeated. Seeing her head appear had nearly given me a heart attack.

Becky laughed, her fingers snaking over the top of the fence. 'Sorry, I'm standing on our bench. I didn't mean to scare you.'

'It's okay, I was miles away,' I said, waving a hand, 'before I tripped over.'

'Come and join us, we're all bunking off work early. It's Maxwell's birthday.'

'Oh, happy birthday,' I said before Lauren appeared at my side, intrigued to find out who I was talking to.

'Go get your swimsuit on, Lauren, come in the hot tub,' Becky said with a wink. Inwardly, I groaned, knowing there was no avoiding it now.

'Can we, Mum, please?' Lauren tugged at my arm, and I relented, smiling through gritted teeth at Becky, who clapped her hands, oblivious.

'We'll be right there,' I said, wishing I had managed to close the back door without being overheard. I could be relaxing on the sofa binging a Netflix series, knee-deep in chocolate digestives.

Ten minutes later, Lauren was in the hot tub, looking like the cat that got the cream. Becky was showing her the controls and well on her way to being drunk, her coral lipstick slightly smudged.

'We're having mojitos,' she said, pouring me one from a large jug. 'They're Maxwell's favourite.'

I felt awkward I'd come empty-handed but relieved Lauren

and I weren't the only guests. Niamh and Finn were there too. Maxwell's shirt hung open, his belly round and smooth poking out, droplets of water still on his skin.

'Happy Birthday, Maxwell,' I said, and before I knew it he'd pulled me in for a kiss.

'Forty! I remember when I used to be young and slim,' he reminisced.

Finn raised his glass to that. 'Happens to us all, mate.' Although it hadn't looked like it had happened to Finn in the slightest.

'You should have brought your bikini,' Becky said.

'I don't own a bikini,' I admitted, 'and there's no way you'll ever get me in one,' I laughed. I hated showing too much skin and I couldn't think of anything worse than hanging around in a hot tub with your nearly naked neighbors. Especially ones you'd only known for just over a week.

'Ah that's a shame, you could have borrowed one of mine?' she said, twirling around to model the one she had on.

'Very nice,' I said as she posed in her orange halter-neck bikini, a long sheer kaftan over the top which dwarfed her tiny frame.

'How are you feeling, Shelly?' Niamh appeared behind me, a giant in wedge sandals. She hadn't been in the hot tub yet, her hair twisted back off her face was dry, unlike Becky's. But she had come ready, neon pink bikini straps stood out underneath a simple black cotton broderie dress. It irked me how she always looked effortlessly chic.

'I was a little worse for wear this morning,' I admitted. 'How's Valerie?'

'She's fine,' Niamh said with a roll of the eyes. 'Remy said you manhandled her?' Her lip curled into a suggestive smile. Was she playing with me?

'I didn't manhandle her, I was trying to get her up off the grass. She was practically sitting in a puddle in the pissing rain,' I said, letting my annoyance slip through, unable to believe Remy would have told Niamh about it.

'Mum!' Lauren scolded from the hot tub at my language and Niamh laughed.

'He does like to overreact. Such a mummy's boy,' she said scornfully. Becky sniggered. It was the first time I'd heard her speak of Remy with any distaste. Had he upset her or was I only just understanding the dynamics of Beech Close?

49

I sipped slowly at my mojito, not really wanting any more alcohol after yesterday. It had too much rum and my head still felt fuzzy, but I didn't want to be the party pooper. I had no idea what time Becky and Maxwell started drinking, but I assumed it was some time ago. The closer it got to dinner, the louder and more raucous they became. Niamh was restrained, perhaps, like me, a little hung-over from her barbecue yesterday. She didn't mention Remy or Valerie again and I didn't either.

The conversation had moved on to Finn's golfing trip, he was leaving tomorrow and wouldn't be around until the end of the week. Niamh's expression was pinched, and I sensed it may have been a sore subject. Perhaps she didn't like being left alone?

'Your tickets came through all right?' Becky asked, slurring slightly. The jug now empty, only the remnants of mint leaves left behind.

'Yep, all on the app.' Finn patted his pocket where his phone was.

'Where are you off to?' I asked, having no idea where someone would go to play golf.

'Seville, only for a couple of days with my brother. Becky gets good concessions,' Finn said, raising his glass in her direction.

'Sssshh, Finn, don't tell everyone.' Becky giggled, holding her finger to her lips before giving me a wink. 'You let me know if you want to go anywhere,' she whispered, 'I'll hook you up.'

'You went to Cyprus at Christmas, didn't you?' I said, turning to Niamh, watching her eye twitch. She frowned, I imagined she was questioning how I would have known such an intimate detail. 'It's on Becky's statement, she gave me access to her files, I was just looking through some of them, getting an idea of the company,' I explained, the tips of my ears pink as Niamh regarded me curiously.

'Then you've seen what a mess I'm in, no organisation, I can't bloody find anything when I want it,' Becky jumped in.

I waited for Niamh to elaborate on her trip to Cyprus, or why there had been no ticket out, only a return, but instead she turned to Maxwell and asked him about the mpg on his Mazda MX5 because she was thinking of getting one.

It wasn't any of my business, Niamh's comings and goings, but she seemed a little out of sorts. Perhaps she was pissed off Finn was going off golfing and leaving her to fend for herself. Although it wasn't as though she had anyone to look after, she didn't even have a cat. Finn would come back to find her having redecorated the upstairs or had an annexe built in the garden. I chuckled to myself and went to find Lauren. She was sitting on a love seat in the corner of the garden, swinging it gently.

'Can we go home, Mum, I'm cold and I want to play Roblox with Holly?' she asked, her hair still damp from the hot tub, a dark patch seeping down the back of her T-shirt. The sun had disappeared behind a stream of clouds, making the cool breeze no longer welcome.

'Sure, let's go and say goodbye to the others.'

We said our goodbyes and wished Maxwell a happy birthday again. They were discussing ordering pizza and I was worried Lauren might catch on and want to stay, but she was keen to get home and into her warm pyjamas. The idea of vegetating on the sofa even more inviting than a couple of hours before.

'I know, after dinner let's look at holidays on the laptop. We can get some ideas for the May half-term perhaps,' I suggested to Lauren.

'I want to go to Spain,' Lauren said, excitedly before she ran upstairs to change out of her clothes.

'Then that's where we'll go,' I replied, although the dog posed a problem.

I chucked a couple of jacket potatoes in the oven and opened a bottle of beer. Teddy stared at me with my feet up on the sofa until I couldn't bear it any longer.

'Okay, come on.' I sighed, retrieving his lead.

'Lauren, I'm going out with Teddy, are you coming?' I shouted up the stairs. A resounding no coming back at me.

We walked out of Beech Close to the lamp post where Barney's poster had been tied. It was still missing, so we carried on a bit further before venturing back towards the house to do a couple of laps of the green.

Becky had ordered a pizza van which drove to your house and cooked pizzas to order from the road. The group were gathered outside, chatting animatedly with the chef. Finn waved when he saw us, patting his flat stomach.

'Shelly,' Derek's voice called from his doorway, beckoning me over.

'Hi, Derek, how's the ankle?' I asked, holding tight on to Teddy's lead as I approached the door.

'Not too bad, almost healed. It's a delightful colour though,' he smiled, scratching his beard. 'I'm sorry to ask but would you help me lift something? Finn isn't in and neither is Remy. I saw you passing and thought I'd grab you,' he chuckled.

'Sure. Finn is over at Becky's, it's Maxwell's birthday,' I said, hoping it wasn't a secret as Derek obviously hadn't been invited.

'Oh, I see. It's a mattress, not heavy per se, but it's awkward and I can't get it upstairs by myself.'

I smiled, tying Teddy to the hanging basket bracket.

'Stay here, Teddy,' I said, ruffling the fur on top of his head.

Derek moved back gingerly, and I could see the new double mattress, still in its plastic film leaning against the wall.

'Treated yourself?'

'It's for the spare room, the old one was, well, old,' he chuckled, going to the far end of the mattress and pushing it forwards.

I grabbed the other end and we manoeuvred it towards the stairs, me pulling and Derek pushing.

My hands damp, I struggled to hold on to the plastic as I tried to pull it upwards and around the corner at the top of the stairs. Derek had his shoulder pressed into the bottom, using his weight for leverage. When I reached the top, I looked around to see how far we had to bend the mattress to get it into the spare room. The office door was open, but I couldn't see the wall Danielle's photo had been stuck on.

'Almost there,' Derek said, sliding the mattress along the carpet. My forehead was slick with sweat as I heaved the mattress into the spare room. Before I knew it, I was wedged between the wall and the mattress.

'Derek, stop pushing,' I said, as my leg was crushed against the bedside table. I looked over the top of the mattress but could only see the back of Derek's head, bent low, shoulder still pushing forward. He had a hearing aid slotted behind his ear, was it working? 'Derek!'

'Oh sorry.' His head popped up, chuckling. 'I didn't hear you.'

'Perhaps pull it back towards you and we can lift it onto the bed together,' I suggested. I wanted out of here. Teddy was outside and Lauren was at home. My skin was peppered with perspiration, and I needed the toilet, the cocktail having gone straight through me.

'I could, but I have you trapped now, don't I,' he chuckled, a glint in his bright blue eyes.

'Derek, stop messing around,' I said, summoning a nervous laugh. Wedged into the corner of the room by the mattress, I was trapped unless I tried to scramble over it.

'Who says I'm messing around?'

I glared at him over the mattress, my stomach constricting. Is this what happened to Danielle? Had he lured her inside to help him? It was the same method Ted Bundy used with his victims. I refused to cower despite my knees threatening to buckle. Staring him down until his smile shrank.

'Okay, okay, I'm kidding,' he said, raising his palms to me.

I shoved the mattress away and he pulled at his end, it toppling half onto the bed, half onto the floor.

I gritted my teeth, anger bubbling beneath the surface, replacing the fear which had gripped me moments before.

'That wasn't funny, Derek,' I snapped, but yet he still blocked the door.

'It was only a joke,' Derek replied, bemused at my annoyance.

'Please move out of the way. I want to go home now.' What was it with the residents of Beech Close?

'Shelly, please,' he said, putting his hands together in a praying motion, seeming to find the whole thing comical. The implication I was overreacting boiled my blood.

Curling my hands into fists, I stepped towards him, but instead of holding fast and blocking my exit, Derek stepped back out of the door into the hallway to let me pass.

'You can get Finn to help you with the rest,' I spat, moving down the stairs and out of the front door as fast as I could.

Was Derek a harmless ex-headmaster, or did he have a penchant for hurting women? Could he be hiding in plain sight, having convinced his neighbors he was an ordinary guy? All I knew was I didn't want to be trapped in a room with him again, he gave me the jitters.

I took Teddy back home, trying but failing not to look over my shoulder as I walked across the green. Was I expecting Derek to come chasing after me? Glancing up at Valerie's house, I saw her at the window, smiling manically, tapping away on it like a bird as she watched me hurry past. I looked away, remembering the last time I'd seen her standing there, before the headbanging.

Beech Close was like the twilight zone at times, its own self-contained atmosphere, but no one else could see how strange it was.

Safely inside the house with Teddy, I called out to Lauren who was in her room to say I was back. Checking my phone, I saw I had a missed call and a text from Maria.

Police have checked, there's been no activity on Danielle's bank account since December. I've urged them to keep looking for her.

I knew it. Something about the whole thing felt off.

Surely if Danielle had looked at Facebook, or contacted any of her friends or colleagues, she would have known people were looking for her. She would have been in touch with someone, if only a text to say she was okay but wanted to be left alone. There was the possibility she was purposely hiding from the police, but I had no idea why that would be, and it wasn't a theory Mark was pursuing.

I responded to Maria, letting her know I would be in touch if I heard anything my end. Then I texted Mark to tell him the police were going to look again at Danielle's disappearance. It was progress and that was something.

Later on, after Lauren had gone to bed, I was upstairs getting changed into my pyjamas when the police car arrived, the neon signage reflecting the street lamp and catching my eye. I'd turned the light off before undressing as I hadn't closed my curtains yet. The car crawled along past the houses, slowing as it got to mine but eventually passing and coming to a stop outside Valerie's. What had she been up to?

I watched a pair of uniformed officers get out of the car and descend down the driveway until my view was blocked by the hedge. Perhaps they were here for Danielle.

Creeping forwards, I opened the window, straining to hear the conversation, but all I heard was the tinkle of the wind chime. Perhaps I should go over there, give them my suspicions about Derek. Suggest he may be worth looking into. What was he doing in December around the time Danielle was last seen? Who was the last person to see her anyway? Was it someone here in Beech Close? One of my neighbors, or the removal men? It seemed like I was missing an important piece of the puzzle.

Didn't the police want to always speak to the last person to see someone alive? Was that Remy? Or Valerie? The police had turned up at their door, it couldn't be a coincidence. Perhaps they knew more than they were letting on. Remy had been coy when it came to talking about Danielle. Was he keeping secrets for someone else or was he the one to hurt her? My mind bounced around, flitting from one scenario to the next and I found myself standing by the window for around half an hour, until the police emerged from next door. They got into their patrol car and drove away, leaving me frustrated and wishing I could hear through walls.

Sleep didn't come for hours. I laid awake listening for noises, the security chain not giving me as much comfort as I'd hoped. When my brain eventually gave in, Lauren woke me because she'd had a nightmare about Nanny. She crawled into bed beside me, passing out within minutes as I stroked her hair. When the morning came, I was groggy and reluctant to get out of bed despite Lauren tugging on my arm demanding breakfast. I was on go-slow, moving at a glacial pace and already looking forward to the afternoon nap I'd planned to have later that day.

I'd only just got dressed when Niamh knocked on the door around quarter to ten. I was trying to muster the enthusiasm to take Teddy out and was glad for the distraction. Niamh brandish two takeaway Starbucks coffees at me as I opened the door.

'Sorry, it's so early, I feel like I've been awake forever,' she sighed, looking like she too had a sleepless night.

'No worries,' I said, taking the cup she handed to me, 'thank you.'

'I was hoping you had ten minutes. I wanted to chat to you about Derek.' Niamh leaned in, coffee on her breath, whispering as if she was sharing a secret. Dark circles under her eyes apparent as she got closer.

'Sure, come in,' I said, stepping back to let Niamh inside, hoping I was about to get the answers I was looking for. Or, if not, someone who might share my theory of what happened to Danielle.

50

'Hi, Niamh,' Lauren said, skipping towards us.

'Hey, Lauren, how are you?' Niamh bent down, a smile spreading across her face. I watched on bemused.

'Good, thank you,' Lauren replied, delighted to be the centre of attention.

'You know what, I've just seen Amber and she told me your painting for your room is all finished.'

'Really?' Lauren stood on her tiptoes, clapping her hands together.

'Yep, and she's baked some blueberry muffins, why don't you go and see her while your mum and I have a chat.'

I opened my mouth to object, but Lauren's eyes widened, turning to me.

'Please, Mum, can I?'

'Oh let her go, she won't come to any harm,' Niamh chimed. 'Make sure you bring us back some muffins or you can tell Amber we won't be friends any more.'

Lauren shoved her feet into her trainers and practically ran out of the door. I grabbed Teddy by the collar as he tried to make his escape.

'Stay on the pavement,' I called after her, my anxiety rocketing as she dashed around the hedge and out of view.

'She'll be fine,' Niamh said, making her way through to the kitchen so we could sit at the table. Teddy slinked back to his bed to sulk when I closed the door and followed her.

I tried not to wince at the coffee, which, although still warm, tasted bitter. Of course Niamh wouldn't have put any sugar in it, not when her body was a temple. Unfortunately I wasn't so disciplined.

'Do you want any sweetener?' I asked, getting up to retrieve the packet and drop a couple into the cup before giving it a stir. She watched me intently, narrowing her eyes before realising I'd asked her a question.

'No thanks, I weaned myself off sugar in my coffee and have never looked back,' she said, smiling widely and showing those pearly white teeth.

'You wanted to talk about Derek?' I prompted, trying the coffee again and finding it much more agreeable with an added hit of sweetness. I still felt sluggish so any caffeine was a welcome treat and hopefully would wake me up a bit.

'Well, yes, I wanted your opinion. I know you've seen him a few times, probably more than I have recently,' she said, stopping to take another drink, avoiding getting to the point.

I waited patiently for her to continue, already counting the minutes when Lauren would return. Keeping an ear out for the sound of her knocking at the door.

'I'm starting to think something isn't quite right with him, you know. I feel mean, he's been our neighbor for a few years now, but lately, I don't know.' Niamh looked at me from beneath her lashes, pausing for a response.

I wasn't sure what to say, so I drank from my cup to bide my time. I had my doubts about Derek, suspicions even, but I wasn't sure who I could trust to share them with. What did I know about Niamh anyway? What did I know about any of them? I'd barely been here five minutes.

'Remy told me he has a photo of Danielle in his office upstairs, pinned to the wall,' she grimaced. 'I mean, what if he's the reason she disappeared?' Niamh's eyes were wide, enjoying being the one to deliver the gossip, staring at me, waiting for my outrage.

I didn't share I'd been the one to tell Remy about the photograph in the first place. It was something I'd assumed Remy would keep to himself, not spread around the close. The way Niamh was talking, she was ready with her pitchfork.

'The reason? In what way?' I asked. 'In that he harassed her, you mean?' I wasn't about to show her my hand right away.

She rolled her eyes theatrically, draining what was left in her coffee cup. I drank more of mine, then ran my tongue over my teeth, cringing at the furry sensation. The aftertaste from the coffee was weird.

'I mean, the police are still looking for her, right?' Niamh continued. 'They turned up to talk to Remy last night.'

My head snapped up at the mention of the police.

'Something weird happened yesterday,' I said, watching as Niamh leant forward in her seat, ready to consume every word. 'I helped Derek with a mattress, up the stairs, and he kind of cornered me, blocked me from going. It was...' I couldn't find the word, my brain seemed to slow, the neurons not firing correctly.

'Odd?' Niamh helped me out.

'Hmmm,' I replied, gripping onto the table for support. My thoughts were floating away and I couldn't catch them. Words rolled around my mouth, refusing to form as acid rose from my gullet.

'Shelly. Are you all right?' Niamh's voice sounded far away as my limbs tingled pleasantly, like they no longer belonged to me.

I swallowed down the influx of saliva, suddenly nauseous.

'Yeah?' I whispered, giggling as my voice didn't sound like mine.

'Shelly?'

'I think I need a lie-down,' I said, using every ounce of energy I had to push myself up from the chair.

It seemed to take an age and my legs wobbled like a toddler, but I stood, blinking rapidly to concentrate on Niamh's face, which kept drifting in and out of focus. Her smile reminded me of the Cheshire Cat from *Alice in Wonderland*. I laughed, picturing Niamh with a tail.

'What's so funny?' Niamh asked, getting to her feet and taking our coffee cups over to the sink.

'Cat,' I mumbled, as she took off the lid and poured the brown liquid left in mine down the sink, rinsing it under the tap before putting both cups in her oversized handbag. 'What's going on?' I slurred, apprehension slithering up my back and latching on to my spine. Something wasn't right, but I couldn't put my finger on what. I wanted to lay down, my head was heavy, tongue thick and too big for my mouth.

'I don't think you're very well, Shelly. Here, let me help you.' Niamh snaked an arm around my shoulders as I attempted to step towards the sofa. It was a million miles away. An unachievable distance and every part of my body was like lead. I could barely drag one foot in front of the other. 'It's okay, I've got you,' Niamh said, her voice warm and comforting like a hot bath on a cold night.

'Lauren?' I muttered, my eyelids fluttering.

'She's fine, she's at Amber's, remember. She'll be back soon.' Niamh carried me along a few more steps, closer to the sofa.

I reached out a hand, but it was still too far away.

'Gosh, you're heavy, Shelly.' Niamh laughed, pausing to reposition her hip against my waist, to hoist me upwards. It was rude, you never commented on a lady's weight, everyone knew that, but I struggled to vocalise my indignance.

The blue leather sofa was so close I could almost touch it, but before I could lurch towards it, Niamh steered me away. I reached out a hand, whimpering, vaguely aware I had drool on my chin. Teddy barked, quickly silenced by Niamh hissing at him.

'No time to sit down, Shelly, we've got places to go.' Niamh's cheery tone did nothing to allay the danger my brain realised I was in. A notion so fleeting, it was there one second and gone the next.

Everything was fine, wasn't it? I was with Niamh. It was the last lucid thought I had before the front door opened and the sun streamed in, blinding me. I raised my hand to shield my eyes and everything went black.

51

At first I was sure I was still in bed when my eyelids peeled apart. It was dark but not pitch black, a crack of daylight coming through the curtains. Like a spring morning which fools you into thinking it's later than it is. A fog danced around my head, thoughts slow and incoherent. My muscles were stiff and unyielding, I yearned to stretch out and flex my limbs, but they were wholly disconnected. It took me back to days where I'd slept, wedged onto Josh's tiny sofa, waking with numb legs, a banging headache and a mouth like the bottom of a parrot's cage. Throat sore and scratchy, I licked my lips, a thirst like no other raging through me.

Where was Lauren? Was she still in bed? I had no sense of time, perhaps it was early and she was still asleep. I'd get up in a minute and make her breakfast, I needed to come to properly before I moved my sluggish body. It was a good few seconds until I was able to get my brain to tell my legs to move. My bare foot hit something hard, toes meeting resistance, something not allowing the extension of my limbs. Bewildered, I reached out and touched the sliver of light to see where it was coming from, my fingertips connecting with an unmistakeable surface.

Blood thundered in my ears as realisation set in. I knew exactly where I was as dread suffocated me, pouring into my lungs and filling me up until I could bear it no longer. Screaming to be let out, I thrashed my body from side to side, slamming into thick enclosed panels, a dark wooden coffin I knew every inch of. I was in my mother's chest and if I was here, where was Lauren?

Trailing my fingertips over the scratches and indentations I'd made many years ago, I howled to be released, my throat hoarse. Tears poured down my cheeks and I gasped for air, despite knowing I had enough. The chest wasn't airtight, but panic consumed every rational thought I had. Small spaces had been a problem for me, ever since the punishment was introduced. I'd hear the chest creak as my mother sat on the lid, berating me as I hammered from the inside, begging to be freed. Promising I'd be good, I'd do whatever she wanted, if she'd let me out.

Slow your breathing, Shelly, otherwise you'll pass out. I tried to listen to the logical part of my brain, grasping at what I knew. I wasn't ten years old, we weren't in Mum's cottage. Mum was dead and the chest had last been seen in Remy's van. Where was it now? I knew I wasn't at home, it didn't smell the same. Over the musty smell of the chest was a faint scent of ammonia scratching at my throat. I swallowed, imagining a cool glass of water sliding down my gullet, trying to satisfy my thirst.

I became still and quiet, listening for any sounds, aching to hear my daughter's voice or at least a clue to where I was. Had Niamh done this? I'd drank the coffee, was still tasting it at the back of my tongue. That was the last thing I remembered.

The muscles in my left thigh began to ping, cramping pains shooting down my leg and I kicked the bottom of the chest, wincing as my toes slammed into wood. I couldn't hear anyone.

'Let me out,' I shouted, banging with the palm of my hand.

The chest wasn't big enough for me to even turn over. I was stuck in a foetal position on my side, bones protesting at the now unnatural pose. I was too old, too big and the lack of space made me hyperventilate. How long had I been here? I had no concept of time, no watch to check.

Where was Lauren! My stomach lurched, bile rising in my throat. If anyone had hurt her, I'd kill them. Fear had me beating my fists on the wood, again and again, screaming and thrashing. 'Lauren! Lauren!' I had to get out, get to my daughter.

A layer of sweat settled upon my skin, the nightmarish claustrophobia making my temperature rocket. From above, I caught the faint sound of voices, hushed deep tones, someone talking fast. Their companion sharp and prickly. One of them had to be Remy. He'd had the chest, he was going to get rid of it for me. Maybe he'd kept it for himself.

'Remy, please let me out, I'm begging you,' I cried, my only thought was of Lauren. I couldn't protect her from inside the chest and the pull to get to her was visceral. A primal urge so paramount, I'd never stop fighting to reach her.

The sound of Mum's bell paralysed me. Jaw slack, my heart stopped as it tinkled, echoing around the chest. Shaken from above. Unable to move, the ringing paused and the chest creaked. A body had lowered themselves onto the lid. Their voice clearer now.

'All you had to do, Shelly, was mind your own business. We welcomed you in, you and your daughter.' Niamh's voice coming from above. I slammed my fist into the wood at the mention of Lauren. How dare she speak of her.

'Where is she? What have you done with her?' Spittle flew down my chin and I scraped the edge where the light bled through, trying to increase the gap, wincing as two of my nails split.

'She's fine, she's with Amber. I must admit you were out of it for longer than I expected. Those sleeping pills of yours are strong, eh.' Niamh shifted position and I imagined her crossing and uncrossing her legs. Poised on top of the chest like she was sitting side-saddle on a pony. 'I was going to run a nice warm bath for you to have your accident in, which is why I needed *your* sleeping pills. No one would question why you had your own prescribed medication in your stomach, but I couldn't have Lauren discover you dead in the tub. It would haunt her for life.'

'Please don't hurt her,' I begged, eyes filling with tears.

'I'm not a monster, Shelly, and I didn't want to have to go through this again, but you wouldn't keep your nose out. It was done and dusted and in just over a week you've dredged it all up again.'

My brow furrowed, what was she on about?

'Niamh, come on, you can let me out, I won't tell anyone, I can move, take Lauren and...' It struck me like a mallet around the head, the cool realisation none of this was about me at all. 'Is this about Danielle?'

More voices came from above, but I couldn't make out what they were saying, hurried whispers I was unable to decipher. How many people were there, two? Three? My back prickled with sweat, limbs screaming at me to move, if only I could. How long had I been unconscious for? Niamh had drugged me, with my own sleeping pills, the ones the doctor had given me but I barely used. When had she taken them? Niamh hadn't been upstairs in the house, unless she'd been inside when I wasn't there? Unless she'd been the intruder?

'Niamh, please, you don't have to do this. Is Remy there, with you?'

'The police are asking all sorts of questions, Shelly. I could tell you were putting the pieces together. It's only a matter of time.'

'Did Derek hurt her? Are you protecting him?' It was the only logical explanation. Beech Close was a tight-knit community. Everyone knew everyone. Had they all been a part of Danielle's disappearance? *Stupid Shelly, shouting your mouth off when they were all in on it... asking your questions, digging for answers, when they all knew.*

'Derek?' A cold laugh came from above, the lid creaking. 'I see you haven't quite figured it out yet.'

As long as I could keep her talking, keep her with me and not Lauren, she might be safe. Laying in a puddle of my own sweat and tears, clothes sticking to my skin, nails broken and bleeding, I'd stay here forever if it meant Lauren would be unharmed.

'Tell me what happened to Danielle.'

52

DANIELLE

Someone was in the house. I'd heard them before, footsteps scuttling around downstairs like rats. My doctor thought it was bollocks, a manic episode, and changed my meds for the umpteenth time. But I wasn't mad. People had been here and as I lived alone, and was OCD about my belongings, I could tell when the tiniest thing had moved or changed.

If Barney was here, he'd bark like he'd done before. Always my protector, unless he was in with a chance of a cuddle. The thought made me well up, I missed him terribly. He'd been gone for two days, lost, although I was adamant he'd been stolen. One minute he was on the driveway, the next he was gone. I'd only turned my back for a second and I assumed he'd made a break for freedom, down to the park we so often visited. I'd spent hours searching, but to no avail.

A creak from below made me shrink deeper into the corner. I pressed my lids together and put my hands over my ears, shutting out the sound. If I couldn't hear it or see it, it wasn't real. Part of me wanted to confront them, find out who had been torturing me, coming in when I wasn't here and sometimes even when I was.

They must have their own key, but the estate agents wouldn't let me change the locks. Nothing was ever taken, not that I knew of, which made it worse, I couldn't prove anyone had been in.

There was another reason I didn't want to go downstairs. What if it confirmed my worst fear, which wasn't a masked intruder, but that I *was* imagining the whole thing? That my bipolar disorder had stretched to manifesting noises. Deep down I was in denial, this had to be in my head, or someone was trying to drive me crazy, although why they'd want to, I had no idea. This time I'd been hiding in the airing cupboard for an hour, too embarrassed to call the police and waste their time, using a nail file in my pocket to scratch the word *LEAVE NOW* into the wall.

It was exactly what I was going to do. Leave Beech Close. I'd had enough. The neighbors were mental, like Stepford Wives. Valerie was a massive pain in the arse and not even the fling with Remy made it bearable. No, it was time to go. Christmas was almost here, I'd finished at Green Fields for the term, and it was the perfect opportunity for a change. Me and Barney were going to jump in the car and head north, perhaps surprise Maria. I had to find him first though.

A sound caught my attention, a faint familiar noise, coming from outside. Barking? My ears pricked, it was barking. Without hesitating, I threw open the airing cupboard door onto the gloom of the hallway. I'd left a light on downstairs which was filtering up, but outside the December evening was dark and wet. Rain tapped against the window, and I strained to listen, the intruder forgotten. It was unmistakable, I could hear Barney and my heart sang at the sound.

I took the stairs two at a time, jumping down the last three to an empty lounge, the barking slightly louder now. Racing to the front door, I threw it open, yanking my keys out of the lock and running barefoot onto the driveway. Freezing once again to listen, angling my head. Valerie's, the barking was coming from Valerie's house. That bitch!

Tearing around the hedge, feet slapping on the wet pavement, I ran towards her door, not registering it was ajar when I slammed into it. The red door bounced against the wall, springing back and knocking into me as I fell over the threshold. The hallway door was open, so I could see straight into the front room.

Valerie's eyes were wide, and she clutched her hand which looked like it was bleeding. Barney's fluffy paws could be seen poking through the wire cage he'd been locked in. The witch had stolen my dog.

She kicked at it, the cage rocking. 'Bloody mongrel.'

I hoped he'd bitten her down to the bone.

'Let him out,' I snarled, getting to my feet. I didn't wait for a response, pure hot rage burned in my stomach as I raced towards her full pelt. Shoving her with my shoulder like a rugby player, it threw us both off balance and we crashed onto the floor, winded. Taking my chance as Valerie gasped, I scrambled on top of her, my jaw clenched so tight I could hear my teeth grinding together. Valerie's arms flailed as she tried to fend me off. Sharp nails scratched at my face as she attempted to defend herself. Barney barked, louder now, growling through the cage.

'That dog won't bark for much longer,' she said, her voice raspy, still managing to grin. The old woman was crazy, but she'd gone too far this time. My hands found her throat, wrapping around her delicate swan-like neck. My fingers slowly compressed as I remembered all the taunts, the snipes, and the abusive notes left on my car. Valerie banging on the walls at all hours of the day and night, throwing her rubbish over the fence, doing anything she could to piss me off. She'd been relentless since I'd arrived, worse when she found out Remy had taken me for dinner. She was how it had come about, him sweet-talking me around after I complained about his mother's behaviour. Giving me the sob story of her diagnosis, but nothing excused her taking my dog.

I pressed down hard against her windpipe, watching her eyes bulge. Beneath me her body twisted and bucked, but I held fast, my weight pinning her to the floor.

'Mum?' a voice called from the front door, but before I had a chance to turn there was a sudden rush of footsteps, a whooshing sound through the air and the room disappeared.

53

SHELLY

My question about Danielle went unanswered, although I could briefly hear voices, a heated discussion.

'On three,' a man said, and now I was sure it was Remy's voice. If I could just get him to talk to me, I didn't think he'd hurt me.

After the countdown, the chest wobbled, then jolted upwards. Groans came from either end as it was hoisted up.

'Wait, what's happening? Where are you taking me?' I yelled, hammering on the lid as the chest swayed from side to side. How were Niamh and Remy going to carry it with me inside? Was someone else helping?

Shuffling footsteps transported me back to Remy and I trying to manoeuvre it down the garden path, struggling with the size of it. Then the chest was back on something solid, gliding, the sound of squeaking wheels beneath. Was I on a trolley?

'Lauren!' I screamed. 'Lauren,' still pummelling the wood, my knuckles stinging.

A few seconds later, the chest wobbled again, swaying before I was dropped down onto a hard surface, the chest sliding forwards.

My elbow banged against the side of the chest as doors slammed. It wasn't until the engine turned over that I worked out I was in the back of the van – Remy's van he'd used to bring the chest home? Where were they taking me?

I pushed at the lid, remembering the metal latch. With some force, I could break it from its hinges. I hadn't been able to as a child, despite the hours I'd spent trying, but I was fully grown now.

Placing my hands in the middle of the lid, towards the edge where I knew the catch to be, I pushed. Short bursts of energy, to see if I could jolt the lid and work the catch off its hinges. At first, nothing happened, but I continued, targeting the same area, slamming the heels of my hands against the wood and forcing it upwards until slowly the creak of light around the rim grew. It was working.

Sweat puddled at the base of my back, the musty tang of sour air and perspiration in the confined space, as I continued to shove the lid, encouraged by my progress. The chest bounced around in the rear of the van, lurching at one point as Remy must have taken a turn too fast. How long did I have until they reached their destination? I silently prayed they kept driving, my wrists now in agony, arms tired and aching, but the crack was almost big enough to slip my fingers through. A couple more good shoves would do it, even if my bones snapped in the process.

If only I could roll over and lift my feet to help, but the chest was too shallow. My body ached from being in the same position, but I ignored it, still rhythmically banging on the lid. I sensed the van slowing down, gravel under the wheels. It was now or never. Smashing the lid with my knuckles, I pushed upwards, keeping the tension until the light widened still and I was able to roll onto my back, using my knees as leverage against the lid. Another hard push and a blissful snapping sound, followed by metal clanking on the floor of the van. I lurched upwards, curling my body over the edge of the chest and falling out of it onto the boarded floor, narrowly missing the now folded trolley they'd used to move me.

My arms and shoulders screamed in pain as I tried not to make a sound, the van juddering to a halt with a screech of brakes.

'We can't do this,' Remy's voice came from the driver's seat, the noise carrying from the cab.

I remained still, not wanting to alert them to my escape now the van had stopped.

'We don't have a choice,' Niamh responded coldly.

A phone rang, its shrill ringtone slicing through the silence, giving me my opportunity to crawl onto my hands and knees, towards the back door.

'Who is it?' Remy snapped.

'Amber, she's texted me once already, wants to know how long she's got to have Lauren for.'

My heart lurched at the sound of my daughter's name. She was safe.

Niamh's voice changed when she answered the phone. The sing-song cheerful tone was back. 'I'm so sorry, Amber. Shelly rushed off, said something about meeting some bloke.'

A short pause came before she spoke again.

'I've tried calling her as well. As soon as I get back from the supermarket, I'll come and entertain her for you. I know you've got an appointment.' Another pause. 'Yes, I know it's irresponsible and I'm sure she wouldn't have left Lauren if it wasn't an emergency.'

I blinked back tears listening to Niamh lie through her teeth. Whatever they were going to do, they weren't banking on me coming back. Did Lauren think I'd left her? It didn't matter, she was safe. Amber wasn't in on it, that much was obvious. I had to get to her before Niamh did.

'It's not fair, is it. Listen, it's good practice for you. I'm sure this round of IVF will work, I have a feeling in my waters.' Niamh's voice was sounding more exasperated as Amber ranted.

While she was distracted, I searched the back of the van for the door release, but there was no handle. How was I going to get out?

'I'll be back shortly, and you'll have plenty of time to get to the clinic. Got to go, I'm at the checkout.' I heard Niamh sigh, and the passenger door open.

Frantically running my hands over the two doors, I searched for something, anything, but there was no latch or handle. There was no way I was getting out of the van. Looking around, I had no weapon and in seconds they would be opening the door, expecting to find the chest, lid closed, with me in it.

'Fuck!' I whispered, the vein in my neck pulsating. I was trapped and the only thing I had on my side was the element of surprise. But it didn't matter. I couldn't fight off Remy and Niamh. Maybe I stood a chance with one of them, but not both.

'Niamh, there has to be another way.' Remy's voice sounded loud, outside the van.

'There is no other way,' she hissed. 'The police are looking again, what happens when they find out she's not in Egypt.' Inwardly, I gasped. The severity of the situation dawning on me, *they* knew where Danielle was.

'*You* were the last person to see her. People saw *you* with her. Remy, *you* arranged for the removal van. What do you think is going to happen when that comes out?'

'I... I was protecting Mum, protecting you,' Remy stuttered.

Niamh's voice carried as she walked around the front of the van to Remy's side, her footsteps shifting the gravel. 'I know, come here.' Niamh's voice was softer now. Had they embraced? Kissed? Were they seeing each other on the sly? Niamh was married. What about Finn? My mind raced with questions, but I had no time to ponder them. Any minute now I'd be discovered, and I had to come up with a plan.

54

There was only one option. I crept back to the chest, my hands skimming the floor for the clasp. I found it and slipped it into my pocket. Every cell in my body told me it was a stupid idea, but, ignoring the voice in my head, I climbed back into the chest and lowered the lid. My fingers grasping at the tiny lip to keep it down. Back into the dark again. The hinges of the lid were still intact, it was only the clasp that had popped off and, if I was lucky, Niamh and Remy wouldn't notice. Once the chest was brought out of the van, I could make my escape.

I listened for their voices but couldn't hear anything but the muffled sound of gravel underfoot, then a whoosh of moving air as the back doors opened. I held my breath, waiting for someone to mention the missing clasp, but no one did.

'Do you think she's passed out?' Niamh asked.

I elbowed the side of the chest, not wanting to touch the lid in case I gave away it was no longer locked.

'What are you going to do to me?' I cried, trying to inject as much fear into my voice as I could manage. It wasn't difficult, despite knowing I was no longer trapped, I was still petrified. As much for Lauren and Teddy as for myself. It was only a matter of time before Niamh was done with me, and what if she went back for them?

'You're going to go for a swim,' Niamh said dryly.

'Niamh!' Remy snapped, his tone biting.

My skin turned to ice. They intended to drown me.

'What?' Niamh spat back, spoiling for a fight. 'She's brought it on herself. Bloody busybody.' Niamh's voice got louder, her words directed at me. 'I didn't want any of this, Shelly. Danielle's death was an accident and I'm not going to let you ruin our lives by exposing us.'

'Keep your voice down,' Remy hissed at Niamh.

'Where is she?' I asked. With my fingers barely gripping the lid, I jumped as the sound of the trolley being hauled out of the van came from my right. Seconds later the chest was hoisted onto the trolley and dragged over rough terrain. The lid moved a fraction with the motion, and I glimpsed Remy's legs, but they hadn't noticed.

'It doesn't matter, none of it matters. We protect our own, Shelly – don't we, Remy?'

I couldn't hear his response through the sound of the trolley being dragged until the transition was suddenly smooth.

I was weightless for a second before water seeped into the base of the chest, reaching my toes first. I squealed, trying to fight the urge to throw open the lid and jump out. It was too soon, I couldn't risk exposing myself, not until I was far enough away from them. The monsters who had pushed me into a lake, or wherever I was, knowing I'd drown. How long would I float for?

'Niamh, wait. I can't do this.' Remy's deep throaty voice carried. 'Danielle... she was an accident, like you said, but this... this is different.' The chest bobbed as the hostile liquid soaked through my clothes, inching higher. I shivered, chilled to the bone, my teeth chattered and the urge to escape was overwhelming. I was sinking fast, the wooden chest heavy enough on its own without me inside.

Niamh and Remy continued to argue, their voices fading away. Water rose at speed inside the chest, my head now the only part of me not yet wet. Chest tight, lungs frozen, I pushed against the lid, but the force of water kept it closed. Every time I managed to raise it a small amount, water rushed in through the gap. I'd left it too long, I wasn't strong enough, I was going to drown.

In the distance, I could hear shouting and splashing, but I no longer cared about them, if I didn't get out of the chest I was going to die. Lauren would be alone with no one to protect her. Tears leaking from closed lids, I pictured Lauren, Teddy and Josh. It was a cruel world. I knew better than most, after what my mother had done to us, after what we'd done to her.

Towards the end Lauren and I were terrified of her unpredictability. Despite her stature my mother was strong and on more than one occasion she'd lashed out. I'd hidden the bruises but when they became more frequent I forbade Lauren from being alone with her. My mother's moods would flip, born out of frustration and the cruel disease that seized control of her mind.

The night of her death, I'd checked to see if she needed anything before Lauren and I went to bed. My mother had changed out of her nightgown and into a floral dress, dancing around the room, convinced my father was coming to pick her up and take her out. She kept calling me nurse, despite my insistence that I was her daughter, Shelly, and that my father wasn't coming, it was time for bed.

She went berserk after the fifth time I'd refused to let her leave, blocking the doorway and trying to negotiate her back into bed. In a fit of rage she'd launched a book at me from her bedside table, the corner hitting me on the side of the head and nearly knocking me out cold. The blow dazed me long enough for her to crawl up my body and bash my head against the floor, hair gripped in sinewy fingers.

I'd never felt fear like it until I heard Lauren's approaching footsteps, coming to see what all the commotion was about. My mother's death was self-defence. We told the police the truth, of sorts, she'd hit her head, but not the rest of it. Was it my penance? To die in a dark watery grave, alone.

The chest tipped upwards, water flooding up my nose, consuming the last of the space as I pushed against the lid. Suddenly it gave. A bright light blinding me, a figure in shadow leaning over. A hand reached into the water and yanked my arm, then I was gulping delicious air, swallowing lungfuls of it as though it was in short supply.

Remy was up to his shoulders in water, blood trickled down his neck, diluting in the lake. Once I found my footing, I stood on the soft silt, chin just above the water. Remy was still holding on to me, his breaths raspy, face ghostly pale.

'Are you okay?'

I wanted to shake him off but was worried I might fall over if I did. I coughed and nodded, taking a second to absorb my surroundings. Remy and I stood in a small lake, not far from the tiny jetty where I'd been plunged in. Green algae floated around us, and the smell assaulted my nostrils. It wasn't somewhere I recognised, although we hadn't been driving long.

'It's private land,' Remy explained as he saw me looking around, trying to get my bearings. Did he know the owner?

Turning towards the jetty, I began to wade through the water. Oh the irony, I'd almost been drowned in a lake I could stand in.

'Where's your girlfriend?' I shouted at Remy, realising the van and Niamh had gone.

Confusion etched onto his face, forehead crinkled, it took a moment for him to realise who I was talking about. 'She's not my girlfriend, she's my sister.'

I turned back to face him, incredulous. I had to admit, I hadn't seen that one coming. Niamh called her Valerie, not mum or mother and Remy was clearly the favourite, so much so, I thought he was her only child.

'She took the van,' Remy continued, following me out.

I moved faster, wanting to make sure he couldn't reach me. I pulled myself out onto the jetty, rushing to grab a heavy stick and pointing it towards Remy.

'I'm not going to hurt you,' he said, climbing out onto the jetty after me and flopping onto his back, palms raised skyward.

'More than you have already?' I spat back, maintaining my distance.

Remy was done, there was no fight left in him. Blood oozed down his neck, a small puddle of it forming on the wooden slats. It looked as though he'd been hit on the back of his head and I guessed Niamh wasn't happy with him not being onboard with the culmination of her plan. Families, you couldn't live with them, you couldn't live without them. But all I knew was I had to get to my daughter.

'Do you have your phone?' I snapped, holding my hand out for it.

He shook his head. 'It's in the van.'

'Dammit!' I shouted towards the sky, a flock of birds erupted from a nearby tree and scattered. Turning, I limped towards the gravel drive, to where the tracks were.

'Where are you going?' Remy called, making no attempt to move. He was in too much pain and I couldn't have him slowing me down.

'I have to get to Lauren before Niamh does. I'll send someone for you.'

55

I managed a hundred yards down the road, where the gravel had given way to a dusty track, before a Ford Ranger truck pulled up beside me. A guy in his fifties wearing a baseball cap, leaned over, lowering his window. 'What the hell happened to you?' In other circumstances, it would have been funny, but every muscle protested as I moved, my shoulders and arms like lead. A puddle followed me, clothes dripping wet. I was covered in algae, looking like a monster who'd emerged from the swamp.

'Can you call the police and an ambulance. I need to get to my daughter. It's an emergency.'

Without batting an eyelid, he turned off the engine and handed me his phone. I dialled the police first, giving them Amber's address, telling them they needed to get there as fast as they could. There was a woman called Niamh Morgan who was going to hurt my ten-year-old daughter.

Hearing my distress, the man opened the passenger door and beckoned me in. I gingerly climbed onto the seat, the dispatcher still on the line, stiff from being in the chest.

'Where do you live?' he asked.

'Beech Close.'

He frowned, trying to figure out where it was. 'Can you give me directions?' Without waiting for an answer, he started the engine, heaving the truck forwards, wheels skidding in the dirt.

'I have no idea where I am,' I admitted, swallowing down a sob. It sounded absurd, ridiculous even. As though I'd gone for a walk and gotten lost.

The dispatcher on the end of the phone told me a car was on its way. Lauren would be safe, but Remy was bleeding and needed medical attention urgently. I shoved the phone back towards the driver, who flinched, trying to concentrate on the road.

'Tell them where we are and there's a man requiring immediate assistance by the lake,' I instructed.

I hung up once the address was confirmed. Remy and Niamh had driven me to Willow Lake. The driver of the Ford rented a house further up the gravel track and rarely saw anyone, let alone the owner. I shuddered, it had been a perfect spot for a murder. I may never have been found.

As we drove, I recognised landmarks and was able to direct him onwards. With the man's phone still in my lap, I called Josh, my words tumbling out.

'You have to get to Lauren, you have to get to number one Beech Close. She's in danger,' I bellowed down the line, listening as Josh said he could be there in less than ten minutes. I ended the call, praying every second that passed Lauren would be okay. 'It's left down here,' I pointed, bouncing in my seat with adrenaline when we were yards away from home. I had to get to Lauren before Niamh did.

'Shit,' the driver slammed on the brakes and swerved as he turned into Beech Close, almost colliding with Finn's Range Rover coming from the opposite direction. Niamh was in the driver's seat, Lauren next to her, sitting bolt upright. My heart lurched and I jumped out of the truck before it had fully stopped.

'Stay here,' I said to the driver. With the truck blocking the road, no one could get in or out of the close.

Niamh gripped the steering wheel, blood fading from her knuckles as she glared at me. Her blonde waves wild, like Cruella De Vil. Lauren's forehead creased as she took in the state of me, clothes clinging to my body, barefoot and shivering. Jogging around to the passenger side, squeezing past the truck's bonnet, I tried the door, but it was locked.

'Lauren, open the door.' I banged on the window, watching as her eyes widened, pupils disappearing into tiny little pinpricks. She was terrified, looking first at me, then at Niamh, her lips moving, but I couldn't hear what she was saying over the sound of the engine. Niamh remained forward facing, clutching the wheel, but there was nowhere to go. Even if she accelerated and rammed the truck, she wouldn't be able to move it. A siren wailed, growing louder with each passing second. I had to get Lauren out in case Niamh got so desperate she did something stupid.

'Niamh, please, let her go. I'm sure whatever happened with Danielle was an accident, and we can get it all straightened out,' I begged, shouting through the glass, willing to say anything to free my daughter.

A single tear dropped from Niamh's steely eyes, it was her turn to speak, but I couldn't make out the words. She was talking to Lauren, not to me, both of them crying now.

Panic knotted my intestines and I banged again on the window, looking around for something to smash it with. The engine of the Range Rover seemed to roar, and I clung onto Lauren's door handle like I was clinging onto a lifeboat. Fear tore through me like a hurricane. Niamh's eyes were vacant, her face expressionless. I had to get Lauren out of the car. Who knew what she'd do once the police arrived? Lauren would be a bargaining tool, used to get away, and I couldn't allow that. Niamh had already kidnapped one person, what difference would it make adding another to the list? I kicked the door, and again above the wheel arch, releasing my anger, reeling back as the Range Rover pitched forwards. Niamh pressed down on the accelerator enough to stop me in my tracks.

I watched through the glass as she leant over, rooted in her bag and pulled out a paring knife, the metal blade catching the light as she angled it towards Lauren's throat. I backed away two steps, palms outwards, tongue glued to the roof of my mouth.

'Niamh, please,' I begged as the bottom dropped out of my world. *Not my baby girl.* Her eyes were remote, and the knife shook in her hand. If she wasn't careful, she was going to nick Lauren's skin. It was too close. I waved my hands gently up and down, taking another step back. Lauren froze in her seat, all the blood drained from her face. Her eyes conveyed a message which broke me. *Help me, Mummy.*

Inside the car, I saw Lauren open her mouth to speak, words flowing, no doubt begging for her life. I should be the one begging. I clasped my hands in a praying motion, feet rooted to the spot, wanting to hurl myself through the windscreen but reluctant to make any sudden movements. Niamh was trapped and she knew it, it made her desperate, a wild animal backed into a corner.

My body seemed to collapse in on itself when the police pulled in behind the Ford, their blue lights flashing. The kind stranger was still in the cab, talking animatedly on his phone, looking on in horror. But it was over, there was no escape for Niamh now and she knew it. I felt no relief, only absolute terror my daughter's life was going to be cut brutally short right in front of my eyes.

It all happened so quickly. The police officer jumped out of the car and ran forward. I turned to tell him to back away when behind me I heard a faint click and whipped my head around to see Lauren climbing down from the car. I rushed to her, dropping to my knees and wrapping my arms around her tiny body.

'Mum, you're all wet,' she said, although she didn't try to wriggle away, her frame melting into mine. I held fast, squeezing her tight, silent sobs heaving my chest.

Niamh's head was on the dash, she was bawling, the knife now discarded and in plain sight.

'Miss, back away from the truck,' the officer signalled for us to move as he approached Niamh slowly with his arms stretched out.

Josh arrived, a strong pair of arms enveloping us both, guiding us to safety.

Eventually, Niamh was led away, although not in handcuffs, a hand gripping her upper arm was all that was required in the end. She didn't put up a fight and was carefully placed into the back of the patrol car, no longer an emotional wreck. Instead she used the opportunity to bark instructions at Becky to call her solicitor.

The residents of Beech Close had come out of their houses to see what the raucousness was about. Finn had flown out on his golfing trip and Leo was at work, but Becky, Derek and Amber came over to offer their assistance. Their mouths gaping as they realised what Niamh had done. Valerie loitered by the beech tree, her hand over her mouth, giggling. She'd managed to escape again without Remy to babysit her. I was too numb to speak, gripping Lauren's hand, not willing to let her out of my sight.

The kind man in the Ford Ranger was allowed to leave after a statement was taken and the ambulance blocking him in had checked us over. He waved goodbye and I mouthed 'thank you', clasping my hands together in prayer. The compassion of a

stranger had saved my daughter's life. I had no idea how far
Niamh would have gone, but if I hadn't been able to get back, to
stop her leaving, I may never have seen Lauren again.

A police officer called Henry arrived in another patrol car and
took us all inside, where we were reunited with Teddy. I was
relieved to find him safe and unharmed. Our little family together
again. I put on some dry clothes and Henry proceeded to make a
pot of tea before sitting to record what had happened. He scrib-
bled page after page in his notebook. Eyebrows practically
climbing off his forehead as I recounted the events of what
seemed like hours ago while Josh held my hand.

It all sounded so far-fetched and if I hadn't lived it, I might
have questioned if it was real. My brain was still sluggish after the
dose of sleeping pills Niamh had drugged me with, but when I
finally finished telling him what had happened, he asked if there
was anyone he could call for me. Any family? But with Josh with
us, and Lauren and Teddy safe, I had all that I needed.

56

I had so many unanswered questions which remained that way for a couple of days. Niamh wasn't talking and the police were still investigating before confirming what she'd be charged with. I was glad she'd been denied bail. I wouldn't have felt safe at Beech Close if she had been allowed out. Becky said Finn had been beside himself, rushing back from his trip, unable to grasp what Niamh had been accused of because it was so out of character.

I'd tried to keep my head down, not wanting to fuel any of the rumours around the close, but it wasn't long before she caught me in the garden with Teddy, sticking her head over the fence to see how I was. She'd not heard from Niamh since she'd been in custody and was having a hard time reconciling the friend she knew with the monster the press had painted her as. Finn had been seen leaving Beech Close with suitcases in tow, retreating from the media circus. No one knew where he was hiding and we suspected he was laying low, dazed at how his life had blown up in the space of twenty-four hours.

I spent a couple of days recovering at Josh's mum's. He'd been amazing, taking control, packing the essentials and escorting us out as soon as Henry had finished with us. Horrified he'd dismissed my concerns about Danielle's disappearance, not realising Lauren and I were in danger. There was no way any of us could have known the lengths Niamh would go to, to protect her secret.

I was still reeling from the revelation she was Remy's sister and Valerie's daughter. Becky had known and assumed I did too, although no one had ever mentioned it. There wasn't much of a family resemblance either, nothing that had stood out, but Becky had told me Remy and Niamh had different fathers, the siblings born twelve years apart. Remy was the golden boy, Valerie's favourite, she'd made that obvious and Becky told me no matter what Niamh did to try to win her affections, nothing was ever good enough. It was something she'd come to accept, referring to her mother by name, formally, like an acquaintance instead of a parent. The last straw between mother and daughter had been Niamh's black eye and bruised wrist, which hadn't come from Finn at all as I'd suspected, but Valerie lashing out in another of her tantrums.

On the fourth day, when Lauren and I were slowly getting back to normal, the police came and cordoned off number six Beech Close. It became a hive of activity. Men in white suits and diggers were brought in, machines worked through the day and night and the sound of a low rumble was constant. As was the onslaught of journalists. I stopped opening my door unless I knew who was going to be on the other side; they knocked so often, despite the police telling them not to. We all assumed they were searching for Danielle.

Valerie had moved to assisted housing, with Remy no longer around to look after her. He'd been in hospital since that day, recovering from a fractured skull after his sister had hit him with a log. He'd told the police everything, partly to relieve his

conscience, partly in the hope of a lesser sentence for his compli-
ance. He confirmed my account that Niamh had drugged me,
locked me in a chest and transported me to Willow Lake with the
intention to commit murder. He couldn't deny he was initially
complicit in the plan, changing his mind at the last minute,
unable to go through with it. I struggled to grasp how close I'd
come to dying. Despite my hatred of Remy, I was grateful to be
alive and I was, only because of him.

Niamh had panicked, backed into a corner as I'd stoked the
fire as far as Danielle's disappearance was concerned and threat-
ened to expose her relocation to Egypt for exactly what it was,
fake. According to Remy's account, Niamh had accidentally killed
Danielle in self-defence while breaking up a fight between her
and Valerie. Valerie had always been cruel, and she'd become
worse as the dementia took hold. When Danielle arrived in Beech
Close with Barney, Valerie tormented her new neighbor every
chance she got. It intensified once Valerie found out Remy was
interested in Danielle romantically. Unable to find a way to poison
Barney, as she'd tried to with Teddy, Valerie snatched him.

When discovered, it was the final provocation for Danielle
who attacked Valerie. Chanced upon by Niamh, who had
witnessed the scuffle and tried to intervene. Danielle died almost
instantly from a blow to the side of the head. Niamh had grabbed
a rake on the way into the house, trying to protect her mother.
Swinging the wooden handle and catching Danielle on her right
temple, she'd knocked her to the floor. Minutes later, Remy had
arrived and found a terrible scene waiting for him: Niamh
crouched over Danielle, attempting CPR and Valerie in hysterics.

Seeing nothing could be done to revive Danielle, Remy took
control of the situation and immediately began constructing a
cover-up. Niamh's foundations were in the process of being laid
for her extension, so with Finn away at a conference, they

wheeled Danielle across the street in a large blue rubble bag filled with enough sand to conceal her, laying her in the partly filled trench, mixing and pouring another layer of concrete on top. Remy called off the workers for a few days to allow the concrete to dry and ensure Danielle was fully concealed.

Remy owned numbers three and four Beech Close, he and his sister having had first dibs on the houses as his construction company, which I learned was more of an empire, had built all six of the picture-perfect detached houses. None of the other residents knew he owned both, all of them surprised to discover Remy was the mysterious landlord who wanted to rent out the property for income, while his mother lived next door. The intention was, once he'd decided to settle down, he would move in there to be able to look after his mother as she got older, but it had never happened.

Remy and Valerie both had keys to number three, allowing Valerie to creep in and out of the house undetected, slowly driving Danielle mad. Remy told the police that on rooting through Danielle's house, he'd found her passport and booked a one-way flight to Egypt on her credit card. Niamh had flown out on Danielle's passport, curling her hair to look as similar to Danielle as she could. Niamh reported the man at check-in barely glanced at the photo and waved her through.

In Cairo, she had made sure to use Danielle's cards, buying items to suggest her trip was going to be long term. Then she flew to Cyprus and back to Gatwick on her own passport the day before Christmas. Telling Finn and Becky, who'd unknowingly booked the flight for her, she was going on a three-day yoga retreat. Finn had no idea he was living in a house with a body beneath the extension he'd paid Remy to build.

The final part of their plan had Remy pay two of his labourers, cash in hand, to empty Danielle's house under the guise she'd planned the move. They'd delivered all her belongings to a firm who specialised in house clearances, with the instructions to dispose of everything. When Remy discovered items left behind, stashed at the back of the airing cupboard, he put them in the loft to get rid of later. He had no idea I would discover them and it would lead me to reignite the search for Danielle Stobart. Remy admitted he'd been the one to take the box of her things when he saw them sitting in the hallway, hoping I would think they'd been thrown out by mistake.

Derek, who I'd initially suspected, divulged he had the photo and newspaper clipping up because he too didn't believe Danielle had left of her own accord when I told him she was missing. He had begun digging into her disappearance too. I had a fellow sleuth two doors away and I never knew it.

Everything had worked out fine for Niamh and Remy initially, the police had followed the trail of breadcrumbs and they were happy to state they witnessed Danielle packing her belongs and leaving Beech Close. The police had no reason to suspect any difference when EasyJet confirmed Danielle Stobart had indeed boarded the flight to Cairo on the twenty-first of December, as well as her bank releasing details of transactions made in the capital. They hadn't checked any CCTV at the airport, there was no need. Maria wasn't applying any pressure as next of kin, it was case closed.

According to the police, Danielle wasn't missing at all, she'd left of her own free will. That was until I came along and Valerie began spiralling out of control, struggling to differentiate between me and Danielle, a woman she knew to be dead. I believed if Niamh hadn't drugged me that day, with the intention to shut me up permanently, Valerie would have given the game away sooner or later.

EPILOGUE

FIVE MONTHS LATER

Lauren threw the ball, Teddy chasing after it, with Barney hot on his heels. They'd become the best of friends, sleeping side by side on the sofa and constantly playing tug of war with their favourite sausage toy. I found out Remy had taken Barney to a local shelter, tying him to the fence outside in the middle of the night so he'd be discovered in the morning. Remy was a lot of things, but he wasn't the monster I thought he was.

We'd moved out of Beech Close permanently in the weeks after it all happened. Danielle's body was discovered in the foundations of number six and Maria eventually allowed to put her to rest. The police found the box of Danielle's items in Valerie's house and I was pleased to hear they'd been reunited with Maria, especially her father's watch and the necklace.

When I saw her at the funeral, Maria had two infinity symbols on her dainty silver chain, hers and her sister's. I attended the service along with Becky, Derek and Mark, who sat with another teacher from Greenfields Junior School as Adele songs played to a slideshow of photos of Danielle projected onto a large screen. We'd talked at the wake and I thanked him for his help. Without him, Danielle's body might never have been found. He'd been relentless with his search, knowing in his gut that Danielle hadn't emigrated. It was then he'd admitted what I'd guessed all along. He'd held a candle for Danielle ever since she'd arrived at the school but never managed to pluck up the courage to ask her out despite them becoming friends.

Amber and Leo had been there to see us off the day we left, wanting to wish us well. Coming over specially to deliver Lauren's yellow painting for her new bedroom, as Josh, Jamie and I packed up the last bits from the house. The canvas was beautiful, Amber's talent undeniable. The colours she'd used inspired hope, she'd told us, and it must have worked as I had a phone call a couple of days ago with fantastic news. Amber had become pregnant during the last round of IVF and all the signs were positive for a healthy pregnancy. Her and Leo would make wonderful parents, I was sure.

Derek had since put his house up for sale, opting for somewhere more peaceful for his retirement. He said he was looking forward to inviting Lauren and I over for afternoon tea once he was settled.

Josh's whirlwind romance with Jamie was still in full swing. Jamie being the one to cajole Josh into a family dinner, so he could finally be introduced to me and Joyce after hearing so much about us both. Jamie was everything I'd hoped Josh would find and he was completely smitten. I didn't think it would be long before the two of them moved in together and I'd already sown the seed about the lovely properties just around the corner from our new address.

Lauren had wanted to start afresh somewhere new and with Mum's inheritance we found the perfect house to buy, still in the catchment of the school with a big enough garden for two dogs. When I found Barney was still at the shelter, having been

renamed Buster, we had to bring him home and give him the life
Danielle would have wanted for him. Changing his name back to
Barney for a start. It seemed like a fitting tribute, and he brought
more joy into our lives than I ever would have expected.

We were now a family of four, with Lauren back at school in
her final year and me working hard trying to organise Becky's
chaos. Niamh was charged with manslaughter, concealment of a
body and kidnapping and was still in custody awaiting trial. The
newspapers were dubbing her the 'Cul-de-sac Killer' and even
when we left, there was still a media storm surrounding Beech
Close.

Remy had been warned he was going away for a stretch for his
part in Niamh's crimes. All to protect the mother who adored him
and the sister who envied him. In a cruel blow, it had been
reported in the press that Valerie was already forgetting she had
children. He'd written to me at Beech Close while still in hospital
convalescing, a letter filled with remorse and profound apologies.
I couldn't deny it moved me, I pitied the situation he'd got himself
in, but I never wrote back. It was a chapter in my life I was keen to
move on from.

Lauren had bounced back, forever the resilient one of the two
of us. We'd managed to get away for a holiday. Anna kindly
offering to have both dogs for us, which led to Holly convincing
her mum they needed a pet of their own. Shortly after we
returned from an amazing trip to Costa Del Sol, where Lauren
spent all of her time in the pool, Beau the Maltese terrier was
adopted. Consequently, weekly trips to the park followed to
ensure him and Teddy became as great friends as Holly and
Lauren continued to be.

Lauren and I didn't talk about *that* day for a long time. I was
always on hand to listen, but I never wanted to be the one who
brought it up. We'd been gifted an Indian Summer, despite it

being September, the temperature had soared, and Lauren had begged me to get a swing for the garden like Joyce's. As soon as it was built, both of us sweating, she jumped on and I pushed her high, legs outstretched reaching for the sky.

'Do you think Danielle is with Nanny?' Lauren asked. One of those childlike questions that always came out of the blue.

'I guess so,' I said, already thinking how I could steer the conversation away.

'Niamh told me it was an accident, you know, with Danielle, when we were in the car.'

I stopped pushing and Lauren swung on oblivious, her legs bending and stretching, having found her rhythm.

'Oh? What did you say?' I asked, the hair on my arms standing to attention despite the warmth of the sun. At the time I wasn't sure why Niamh had let Lauren walk away, what she had said to her to convince her to unlock the door and let her go.

'I told her Nanny was an accident too, that I was protecting you, just like she was protecting her mum.' Every muscle in my body clenched as if I'd turned to stone. 'It's okay, Mum, she said she wouldn't tell.'

ALSO BY GEMMA ROGERS

THE
Murder
LIST

**THE MURDER LIST IS A NEWSLETTER
DEDICATED TO SPINE-CHILLING FICTION
AND GRIPPING PAGE-TURNERS!**

**SIGN UP TO MAKE SURE YOU'RE ON OUR
HIT LIST FOR EXCLUSIVE DEALS, AUTHOR
CONTENT, AND COMPETITIONS.**

SIGN UP TO OUR
NEWSLETTER

BIT.LY/THEMURDERLISTNEWS

Boldwood

Boldwood Books is an award-winning fiction publishing company seeking out the best stories from around the world.

Find out more at www.boldwoodbooks.com

Join our reader community for brilliant books, competitions and offers!

Follow us
@BoldwoodBooks
@TheBoldBookClub

Sign up to our weekly
deals newsletter

https://bit.ly/BoldwoodBNewsletter